La Vie Passionnée
of Rodney Buckthorne

La Vie Passionnée of Rodney Buckthorne

A Tale of the Great American's Last Rally and Curious Death

a novel by
R. V. Cassill

Published by
BERNARD GEIS
ASSOCIATES
Distributed by Grove Press

To one of one still such and ever so
. . . my Dark Lady.

With all thy gifts America . . .
What if one gift thou lackest (the ultimate human problem
 never solving),
The gift of perfect women fit for thee—what if that gift
 of gifts thou lackest?
The towering feminine of thee? The beauty, health, com-
 pletion fit for thee?

WHITMAN, *With all Thy Gifts*

They hate us youth.

FALSTAFF

Part One

Part One

1

Who Rodney Buckthorne Was

The first stage of Buckthorne's envy made him guess that the young people showing him the apartment were married. They smiled at him and spoke to him from a shared security that shut him out. There was plenty they weren't telling him about why—with the month of June still unfinished—they were so eager to sublet this extraordinary apartment and begone.

But no, he decided, they weren't married. Just look-alikes, though they were certainly not brother and sister, either, but like the male and female paragons in advertisements on the facing pages of an expensively edited magazine, representing to the New Generation what God must have intended in his primal decision to make the race male and female.

"Miss Cumberland worried about advertising it in *The Times*. She wouldn't—she mustn't, you know—turn it over to anyone but the right person."

3

Him? Elected? From a census of the whole world? By chance arriving at this door to be—at last and for once—the *right person?* Buckthorne's ever-youthful heart thumped in silence.

"You can see it's far from the usual apartment in this area," the male paragon urged gently.

"Certainly not what *I* expected way down here on First Avenue," his lovely counterpart said.

Oh, they wanted *him.* Their enthusiasm for him as tenant warmed him nicely. But as their wooing stirred his imagination to activity, it would not stick to what his life could be in this admittedly exciting apartment, but to envy of what theirs was going to be, wherever they were so anxious to go.

They were not going away to share a married life. He guessed maybe they were not even lovers, or not yet. They were coupled only in the blind intimacy of their youth, and that was the hardest thing for him to bear. He didn't much want to rent their apartment. If he really wanted anything at all anymore, it was to go with them when they spurned it.

Yes. But in fifty-one years Rodney A. Buckthorne had never found how to clutch exactly what he wanted. So he smiled back at their offers, a smile that sufficiently hid the grinding of his molars.

"This place was meant for you," the impatient girl said, as she saw his eyes scan the wall covered with books.

Her friend said, "At seventy-five—without utilities—Miss Cumberland will be just breaking even—"

The break-even nymph was dressed for instant departure in a white and pink suit, white gloves. Her bags sat by the door, as if to declare that whether plump, gray Buckthorne rented or not, she would not tarry to the end of this present hour. Out the door and one flight down her big, dainty foot would spurn the littered sidewalk of First Avenue as she sprang into the young man's Mercury convertible, and they

4

would be gone to beaches and elms where Buckthorne could not follow.

"—and since the rent is now paid to the first of July, that will actually bring the cost to you down under seventy a month if you stay until Miss Brule's return in September," said the Ivy League faun—he who was not even Miss Cumberland's lawyer-to-be, but merely her law school friend, handling this awkward sublease for her because handling her own loveliness was really all the world required of her.

"Why," Buckthorne said breathlessly from the bookshelf wall, "look, this first edition of *The Waste Land* is dedicated." What he saw on the title page was the inscription: "For Teresa . . . Tommy."

"By Mr. Eliot himself!" he said.

"For Miss Brule, you'll notice. Teresa Brule," the knowing voice of Miss Cumberland told him.

"I see!" he said. He saw that he had taken another nibble of their bait, and they were preparing to jerk their line with confidence. Now they could prove he was the right man to inherit Miss Brule's extraordinary home.

"Miss Brule must be—" Buckthorne's voice refused to pronounce the epithet that bubbled in his mind. "Here's another inscribed 'Willy.' One never thinks of Yeats as Willy—"

"She's one of a kind," Miss Cumberland affirmed. "She's . . . great! That's why I hope *you* will take her place. *You'd* appreciate her. You seem to know . . . what would make you appreciate her."

"I'm sure I would," Buckthorne murmured, "ordinarily." He closed his eyes and heard his one-of-a-kind heart complain again that neither luck or recklessness had ever got him more than second best. A lucky ad in *The Times* had brought him to this place and let him see, once again, beauty and youth all set for departure. The possibility offered him was merely to repose here appreciating Miss Brule's books, admiring the

5

old lady's taste and talent in furnishing such an apartment in a neighborhood where one would not expect to find it.

That morning, when his forefinger first rested on the lucky ad in *The Times,* he had been in a midtown hotel, phoning his wife in Idaho. He had called her because it seemed decent to communicate once again before he dived through the open window into the traffic of Sixth Avenue.

"Well, of course," Mildred had said. "Of course Lance got home all right. Why wouldn't he, with friends at camp and their parents to bring him back when you didn't show up?"

Lance was their ten-year-old son. He had been at Cub Scout camp on the Snake River. His father had left their home near the Vistular University campus with the professed intention of bringing the boy home after his week in camp. With any other wife besides Mildred, that father and husband would have had trouble explaining why he had turned his reconstructed Cord roadster east instead of north from Vistular and detoured three thousand miles away from the camp.

Mildred Buckthorne had been so long exposed to erratic genius that she would no longer be amazed by anything except details of when, how, and where.

She said, "Lance is *fine.* He's been back four days now." (The Cord roadster had broken down in Laramie. Having come that far, having waited forty-eight hours for the garage mechanics to confirm the impossibility of repair, Buckthorne had bought clean clothes and taken to the airways.) "It was never him I was concerned about," she told him. "I mean . . . you hate New York on principle."

And she might have added that Buckthorne's passionate life had taken its crooked shape, always, on principle. He had not been born for the mundane. In fifty-one years he had not learned to savor his daily bread. Naturally his wife expected to hear new amendments, now, to the code of the scholar

6

gypsy. "I know you're waiting for the fire from heaven," she said without undue sarcasm, "but why in that unlikely place?" Then after a while she said, "You're still there. I can hear you breathing, Rod. If you don't want to explain why you're in New York, that's all right, and if it's yet another woman, I'm beyond surprise. Only—"

Because there is an open window here, he might have said, and at least some sort of pickup audience for a stylish diver. *Plaudite amici, comoedia finita est.* . . . His eyes were fastened hungrily on the window as his moist hand held the phone close to his ear. Because in New York there are more windows high enough above the street.

"Listen," Mildred said. "My darling, you listen good and I'll tell you something. You know what Epictetus said? 'If God fails to provide for you, then He is giving the signal of retreat. He has opened the door and says to you, "Come." ' "

Indeed he knew the quote. He had given it to her last spring in the midst of his woes. Given it in the spirit of stoic resignation, given it to explain why troubles and affronts no longer fired him up as they used to. She had saved it for the time he needed it back, as a good wife should.

"You know what Epictetus is, Rodney? He's full of bullshit. Rodney, the message from the home front is, 'Don't go out just because the sonsofbitches opened the door for you.' Get it?"

"Yes," he said with a grateful chuckle.

"I know your luck she is running very, very poor this year, old man. Losing your TV program and getting little old Cynthia preggie . . . and those things happening at significant times, as you saw it. But they aren't the end. You know what you always say about yourself, that you read sign all day long like an Indian scout? All right. Read some more sign, Carson. Now that you're in that lousy city why not take advantage of it? Some of your people are there. Colloden. Lowry. Regina Whatsername. Look them up. Read some sign on them."

7

"They've—"

"I know you feel they sold out long ago. So what? I mean you'd have a better perspective on your own life if you saw them now."

Women—wives particularly, of whom Mildred was his fifth and by far the most permanent—had always carried great authority with Buckthorne. Certainly now Mildred was turning the stampede of his despair with her lusty cries of affirmation. The sound of her staunchness picked him up like an injection in his tired blood.

But the remarkable thing—which would be awe-inspiring later when he put it together with what followed—was that some other authority seemed already to have joined forces now with Mildred's long-suffering common sense.

For, as he was still mulling an answer to her suggestions, he saw a hand with extended forefinger lying on a page of *The Times* beside the base of the phone. Of course it was his own hand, but to his hysterical eyes it looked like one of those schematic hands used as a typographical sign directing the eye to a matter of note. It pointed toward this line of tiny black type:

> Attractive studio apt. Sum-
> mer sublet. Call SP 6-6161.

Mildred was still suggesting. "And there's Nickie Duart and his wife. They'd be excited to hear from you."

Buckthorne shook his head in silent refusal. Nickie had been his student the year before last at Vistular. More than student, Nickie had been an apostle. More than apostle, he had been Buckthorne's promoter and the organizer of his brief, controversial career on the local television. The program had, so to speak, ruined Buckthorne's cover and spoiled his disguise as an academician. The subsequent troubles had come from

8

this exposure of a cowbird in the academic nest. In that tolerant community he had shown himself to be intolerable.

Not all that he had suffered could be laid at Nickie's door. But he whispered severely, "I don't wish to see Nickie."

A pause then. It would have been a frightened pause with any wife but Mildred. She had absolute tolerance. If he jumped it would not much change her feelings or her opinion of him.

"It's pretty bad this time?" she asked at length.

"It's . . . *ultimate*," Rodney Buckthorne said.

Nevertheless, he had postponed his dive by following the ad which had been indicated to him. (At the very least he had to feel that his hand had been used like the indicators on a Ouija board.)

Made sensitive by cudgeling, he had luckily come upon an enchanting young couple in an enchanting apartment. Was being shaken back into the world by the insistence of a golden boy and the most beautiful girl in the world that he was "the right man" to take advantage of what he had come upon.

Unarguably Miss Brule's apartment was worth very much more than they were asking for rent. Most of its area was taken by the wide studio fronting the street. This studio was high of ceiling, booklined, brightened with the really quite marvelous paintings Miss Brule had created over the years, and ornamented besides with a big fireplace of marble and wrought iron. (The black iron looked like the shield of Achilles, he thought. And he really would like more time to study its curious figures.)

Bamboo curtains filtered the harshness of outside light. A profusion of ferns and healthy avocado plants sat on Miss Brule's sculpture stands and low stools. Besides the studio room, there was a bedroom set off from the main space by a low partition, a kitchenette, and bath.

9

The superficial reasons for their renting were now clear. Miss Cumberland—Marsie—had taken the place for the summer because her mother was a college friend of Teresa Brule. Mother Cumberland still studied painting here with her old friend during the winters when Miss Brule must make her modest living in the city.

With a summer to *use well* before returning to her senior year at Wellesley, Marsie had by now spent exactly two weeks in occupancy. From the apartment she had scouted uptown in search of employment to publishers' offices, galleries, and educational philanthropies. "I hoped to find something creative to do," she said. Of course she had found no opening worthy of her nubile magnificence. The business world had nothing worthy of it to offer.

Ah . . . and maybe there had been a distressing episode down by the garbage cans inside the street door—dark little teen-agers of the neighborhood driven to devotion by the marble columns of her legs, twittering obscenities around her in ecstatic piety while she clawed for the tear-gas fountain pen in her purse.

At any rate she had fought her share of the good fight. Now she wanted to abandon the torch into the right hands. But Buckthorne said, "I haven't really made up my mind to stay in the city."

The young man posed before Buckthorne's chair, resting his hand on his hip like Donatello's "David." Without condescension he asked, "Are you, perhaps, a creative person?"

But they heard the chord of indecision in his negative reply. Was he or wasn't he?

"It doesn't matter," the young smoothie said, "though I'm sure both Marsie and Miss Brule would prefer that the place go to an artist."

Buckthorne drew breath. "I am a . . . lover—"

He had no doubt meant to say he was a lover of the arts.

No doubt in midstatement he had realized this would make him sound like a dilettante, and he had paused to recast his identification in better words.

Yet the statement had been spilled out. "I am a lover." Signed. Rodney Buckthorne. A sound like a giggle came from Miss Cumberland's throat.

"I am what the artists labored for," Buckthorne said in a hasty recovery. "That is, I am one who has been educated, sensitized by the arts. I have tried in my turn to be an educator. As a professor, yes, but in other roles as well. No need to give details. But as it were, one who strives to be the ideal reader or spectator on whom no suggestion is lost. Someone who feels the obligation of his aesthetic exp— You noted my interest when I found the book so . . . suggestively . . . inscribed to Miss Brule by Mr. Eliot. Indeed if I were to sublet the apartment it would be in no small part because my imagination has been fired by this glimpse of the personality—or I might say the person—of our absent landlady."

"Surely," the young man said with a straight face.

"That's it exactly," said Miss Cumberland.

From the corner of his eye Buckthorne watched her stretch, perhaps in impatience, perhaps just in certainty that the bargain had been struck. "Shall I make out the check to you?" he asked meekly.

"To Miss Brule," the lovely girl said. "I'll have to write her anyway, I guess, and explain I found a suitable— What *shall* I say you do? I know the artists worked for you, but— How about that you're a professor, okay? I'll give you her address in Cuernavaca. You mail checks to her there the first of July and August."

She roamed away then to scout the apartment for her belongings, opening drawers and cupboards to make sure nothing was left behind, but she expressed only one more consideration before leaving. "Oh, Mr. Thorne. Miss Brule does

11

have a *lot* of valuable things. Her paintings, I mean, and her sculpture tools, and you'll find just thousands of records besides personal photo albums. And she's very poor and devoted to art, and this apartment is just her *life*. You'll be good to . . . to everything, won't you, sir?"

Then she walked out before he could even promise to water the avocados and ferns, leaving Miss Brule's life to a perfect stranger. For all she knew, he might pawn the faucets from the sink when the books, records, tools, and picture frames had been sold. Her duty was to herself, not to spinster friends of her mother's.

Tricked, duped, and cheated once more, he sat alone at the neat little café table among Miss Brule's ferns and avocados. Since he had been duped into renting an apartment—the girl's beauty had done the trick, of course—he was cheated of an unencumbered chance to kill himself. If he went now, who would water the plants?

He had rented an apartment, and he had no life to lead in it. With the two young people he had felt himself in the presence of life as he had always wanted it, but he had come into this presence leaving *his* life outside, like a man who leaves his shoes outside when he enters a shrine. His loneliness was merely intensified for having glimpsed the incredible girl.

And yet, as in a legitimate shrine, an extraordinarily powerful sense of a lingering presence still invested the rooms. In the silence of his loneliness, the crowing truck horns from the Avenue outside began to play on his nerves like a harpist commencing a Wagnerian overture. The hiss of airbrakes was the sighing of gigantic blond heroines, the thump of gears and tires a cavalry of desire. . . .

Inspired by this music, he turned Miss Brule's café chair toward the bedroom, for all the world like a playgoer turning to face the stage. Three small pillars and a waist-high wall

12

were all that separated the dimmer room from the studio, and these gave its gloomy depths the quality of an Elizabethan theater.

Then the tousled head of Marsie, Miss Slumberland, reared above the level of the dividing partition. She set her bare feet on the bedside carpet. With the sluggish, lithe sway he *knew so well* she ambled to the bathroom opening from the corner of the bedroom. The tinkle of female ablutions, the slushing vigor of a toothbrush correctly applied, the "Darn!" with which she greeted her first coherent thought of the day. . . . For Buckthorne it was easy to restage this much of the morning before his arrival. This much was his for renting the apartment.

Such powers of creation (that required no medium of oil, or language, or fiddlestring) had been his peculiar gift from childhood. Memory was part of the gift. His mother's first contributions to his artistic and literary education had begun the process of refining and intensifying memory. (Was he not the precocious little fellow who figured out at five what Old Mother West Wind was doing to make the bushes rattle so?) For thirty-seven years—since fourteen—nude girls and wives had left imprints on his sensuous memory like the footprints of a crowd of children in a schoolyard full of snow. How few adjustments of memory were now required to make the big, bare feet of Marsie Cumberland tread in the impressions made by one hundred and seventy others.

Whether they had intended it or not, the artists who had worked for him and died had made him a superlative fantasist. He could keep Marsella Cunnybunch here with him as long as he was satisfied to do so.

In imagination he could gaze forever at the indented plane of her belly, the peach-down glow of skin around the moon-crater roughness of her nipples, the dimpling gluteus as she turned, the modeling shadow, as Veronese would paint it, from

13

hip to knee, as delicate as the smoke that rises from an un-crushed, abandoned cigarette in a closed room, altering with the will of light.

For this much—and not a damn thing more—he had answered the ad in *The Times*. Had failed his loyal Cub Scout son, had driven the heart out of his well-loved Cord roadster, had toyed with death on a window ledge. Not everyone would think this fantasy worth what it cost.

Perhaps Rodney Buckthorne didn't. Ah, there was the question. Was a Buckthorne life worth what it continued to cost? Was it worth all his failures and the derision of the honest souls who looked on?

At Vistular his envious, hostile, and finally emboldened colleagues were beginning to call him Don Juan.

Well . . . he was Don Juan. But the joke, on him more than on them, was that by defect of imagination they were simply incapable of guessing what a real Don Juan was like. They couldn't distinguish Don Juan from what they greasily called "a stud."

Neither their envy nor their sincere disapproval could give them an inkling of the high loyalty and recklessness of his vocation. Nor of how long he had followed it truly. The very circumstances they would pick out to convict him of odious infidelity were the signs of his faithfulness.

Knocked up one of the students he was boffing, hadn't he? At least a few of his colleagues had heard that story by now. But let them gossip with the crumbs they could scratch out or muddle up with the vulgar guessing that they used as a substitute for imagination.

Those tiresome vulgarians would think his present fantasy of lust for Miss Cumberland was another sign of instability. Not so. It was the opposite. It was the sign of his constancy. Some-thing that partook of eternity had been in this encounter with

14

the young beauty, though he might never see her again in the flesh.

True. . . . But to accept this truth as his own was to go on suffering the punishment of Don Juan. This was the anguish of being torn between a reality that could not be affirmed in the flesh and a reality of flesh that could not be denied.

His grand and cherished imagination might hold the female presence captive in the rented apartment. But not even the mirrors kept any hint of her sublime lips and Hyperborean eyes.

As a matter of fact, the mirrors reflected back to him the sneaky face that most men call to mind when they snicker about aging Don Juans. A gray, curled mustache, waxed to curling points, crossed a face round as a pie. There was a small pointed beard, like an imitation of Ezra Pound's (*circa* 1923). Gray, weak eyes behind steel-rimmed glasses.

It was the face of a charlatan who might worm his way, late in life, with fake credentials, into the disorganized Classics Department of a third-rate Western university. It was a face the runny little souls of Vistular were bound to despise once they got a good, square look at it.

But the real Rodney Buckthorne?

. . . was a rosy, infant cupidon, a pink little Eros, smiling among the doves of his mother . . . trying to recognize his real self once again in the bestial caricature that stared at him from Miss Brule's mirror.

2

How Buckthorne Was Known

For six years he had taught among the Idaho mountains at Vistular University. It was not his first entry into the academic life. Between the times when he had run art galleries in unlikely quarters of American cities, published little magazines of a dangerous political cast, illustrated with photos and line drawings offensive to family taste, promoted festivals and concerts for uninterested and penniless audiences, he had often taught—for a year, two years, a semester, or part of a semester —in those schools made possible by the student population explosion of the years after World War II. He had taught courses with a hundred various titles at the fringes of higher learning, and in teaching so much he had learned a great deal. He had been fired from nearly as many schools as he had taught at and from this he had learned (though at first with scorn) the rules for security in academic life.

So, in case it should be expedient to stay for the rest of his

16

life in the security of Vistular University (and his present wife had never argued that he should stay there; only that he ought to keep that option open for the sake of their growing son) he had conferred a Ph.D. upon himself before seeking employment there.

Conferred . . . in a manner of speaking. It had required of him only one forgery on a stolen letterhead, the signature of a Registrar recently deceased, and five fake photostats attested by a presently aging spinster who worked in that Registrar's office, who was loyal yet to a girlish night when young Buckthorne brought demon and beast to her lonely couch. The papers had been fixed—then razzle-dazzled through a placement agency to his employers at Vistular.

In any case, just as Napoleon had set the imperial crown on his own brows as a sign that no other mortal was worthy to confer the title and the power, Buckthorne justified his assumption of the degree by his contempt for others who held it.

In any case, his removal to Vistular was a retirement from concern about the worthiness of the educational system at large. Going there was his retreat from activism in politics, art, culture, and sex. At Vistular he meant to develop his inner life, in despair of what he could accomplish by haranguing America at large.

And until his sixth year of teaching at Vistular, he believed he might stay there while he lived. The administration at Vistular—which had the supreme merit of being too turgid to really investigate his advanced degrees—seemed to feel that, though he was not "a run-of-the-mill" academic, there was a place for him in the "Vistular scheme of things."

They had tolerated him for the better part of six years. Yet, even in the best years of their tolerance he was known as a twinkling blade, unscabbarded. The years of his intellectual outlawry had left their questionable traces.

In good weather Vistularians saw him come downhill from

17

Bayard Street to the campus on his Hercules bicycle like a swooping falcon. He scattered the mothers with strollers at the entrance to the preschool, ignored the logging trucks at the light where Spokane Street crossed Highway 91, amused the teen-agers on their way back to high school from the Frigid Queen.

He brought a gleam of speculative wonder to the eyes of Vistular sophomores ambling with their girls. They thought—poor *Playboy*-thumbing lambs—that they had set eyes on a real live fag.

When the snow was piled in nine-foot banks on either side of the streets, he drove to his seminar on Catullus and Apuleius in the red Cord roadster, which he had resurrected from a Los Angeles dump in the years when he ran the Lustrum Book Shop in that city, near the UCLA campus. A red scarf streamed back from his throat to snap in the icy air, and his usually colorless cheeks showed a fishnet pattern of gleaming capillaries.

Three times a week he and his young son Lance worked out with foils in the men's gymnasium. The sessions were conducted in Old French, to the delight of the other fencers who, at Vistular, were all aspirants in the Drama Department, for they also concluded and rumored that Buckthorne was gay—i.e., one of them.

In meetings of the Faculty Council he rose to rebuke the English Department for offering "The Classics in Translation" at the graduate level. Surely candidates for an advanced degree should be expected to read the classics in the original.

"Wull now, we have come to know your feelings on this matter, Rodney," said Dean Wallach, expressing the consensus of those who had attended these meetings during Buckthorne's years at Vistular.

Then quavery Miss Glanville, who taught a hodgepodge of

18

rental library books called "The British Novel," rose to reply—
as she had each year when Buckthorne launched his objection.
"I wonder, though . . . much as I share Dr. Buckthorne's
concern for standards, especially now that we're offering the
Pee Aitch Dih in the English Department and must look to
our levels, and as you all know I've always stood against proliferation for proliferation's sake, and certainly I concede
wouldn't it be preferable if each candidate intending to *go the
distance* . . . I wonder if, at Vistular, we have enough potentials
who are qualified as I'm sure Dr. Buckthorne, Dean Wallach,
and you ladies and gentlemen would wish them to be . . .
qualified. . . ."

Miss Glanville's rambling always ended the wrangle over
standards and made Buckthorne fearfully cower in his chair.
For her tone betrayed the inflections of a hypnotized female
bird responding to the mating call she heard behind his well-
chosen words. Others could not help noticing his effect on
Miss Glanville, and this was one of the earliest sources of
rumor that he was a "woman-chaser." (In those first years at
Vistular the rumor was doubly false. For most of his life he
had found women without the necessity of a chase—only the
wife of an admiral, a lesbian, and a British starlet whose
carnality was reserved for her career had, in his memory, fled
his advances. It was false, also, because when he withdrew to
Vistular he had foresworn adultery. Like the gunfighter who
hangs up his belt and holsters once and for all, Buckthorne
had determined to stay out of every bed but Mildred's.)

But the ill-based rumor had persisted around Vistular. He
had known of it, with unrest and resentment, long before it
became prophetically true.

Buckthorne in the campus bookstore:
"Dr. Buckthorne, I'm sorry we haven't the quality vellum
you're asking for." This from a reddish-blond lady clerk, who

19

had probably been warned of the artistic temper of this particular customer. Told of his "dabbling" in all the arts. Told of his "finicking" standards.

"Perfectly all right," he said.

"Dr. Buckthorne, if you could remember the brand name or describe it a little better, we'd try to order it for you. I don't know where we'd order it, but we'd *try*—"

"No thank you."

"The Domestic Science students have done some exquisite script lettering on *this* pad, Dr. Buckthorne. If you'd care to try it, sir?"

"Thank you, no."

Then she caught up with him again as he paid for a twenty-five-cent ball-point at the checkout counter. A dozen assorted pads were in her hands or under her arms. "Now one of these, maybe, Dr. Buckthorne, would work out nicely. It says on this one, 'For crayola, pencil, ink, watercolors, or oils,' and surely *whatever* you have in mind to do—"

"No thank you. I have no complaints. I am satisfied, Madame. Take them away! Shoo! Please do not feel I have implied a criticism of this store. Your job, of course, is not to cater to my whims, but to assemble and disseminate the shit which the student body of Vistular can afford and is satisfied with. If you follow me one step farther with that trash, I shall scream. *Thank you.*"

"Daddy has a lot of pressures on him," Mildred Buckthorne explained.

The boy Lance asked, "Why do they put pressure on him?"

"Maybe they don't mean to," his mother said. "I guess he feels things harder than you or I—or most people—do. Maybe that explains it."

"Maybe it's because of his beard," Lance said.

20

But it was not Buckthorne's destiny to crumple under any of the pressures his sensible wife could see building around him. Strictly speaking, it was television that ruined his academic career.

That is to say, the trouble rose from an utterly inexplicable synthesis produced by him in combination with that medium. The synthetic recreation transformed him into what is philosophically termed an "emergent." Whatever the right term for his TV projection, it stopped his attempt to pass as a white crow among the academic swans. The TV camera worked on him like a special sort of X-ray, exposing most of what he was so diligently trying to hide at Vistular. It showed, so to speak, not only that he was not an albino, unpigmented crow among the legal Ph.D.'s, but that he wasn't a bird at all. . . .

His involvement with the medium began as a matter of routine.

Vistular installed closed-circuit television for several basic courses offered to swarms of freshmen and sophomores. Among these courses was one of Buckthorne's called Hellatsiv (for Hellenic and Latin civilizations). As a matter of routine his twice-weekly lectures on the Mediterranean ancients were piped to outlet screens in fifteen classrooms. He was an instant success with the underclassmen who saw his transformed face and personality on these occasions.

Content of his lectures quite aside, it was as if the impressionable children of the TV age saw an electronic reincarnation of a *figure from the past*. As if—one might conjecture—some miracle in the tubes had picked up the microwaves of another century altogether.

The freshman-sophomore notion of what the past was would be impossible for anyone to articulate, so it would be reckless to say that young eyes saw a mouth and young ears quickened to a voice that seemed to be speaking to them *from* ancient Greece or Rome—or from the cinquecento or even from the

21

fin de siècle. They just sensed that Buckthorne wasn't a *now* man.

This illusion gave Buckthorne a success rating that none of his colleagues seemed to gain from their use of the closed circuit. Enrollment in Hellatsiv jumped drastically at semester break. His colleagues began to watch his appearances, sniff, and comment. (One of the sweeter ones, a man in French Literature, said, "You look rather strikingly like Honoré de Balzac, Rodney." And behind his back added, "Or a faded caricature of the great man.") This unwanted success made Buckthorne fret over the possibility that someone would begin to investigate his degree. His opposition to his colleagues began from such small disturbances of the academic balance.

What brought the opposition to a head sooner rather than later was that young Nickie Duart—underground student, professional freeloader, and campus bum—was wintering that year on the Vistular campus. He was trying to seduce a clean local sophomore girl, and one day came into the classroom where she was appreciatively watching the idiot box—the face and features of Rolando Buckthorne, Gent.

It impressed Nickie that he could not distract her from intent watching. He smelled awful. She responded sensitively to smells, but even when he crowded himself into her chair with her, her nose did not wrinkle with disgust. And he knew Vivian Spain to be inherently distractable—he counted on this quality in her for his success. It was her firm attention to the face and voice on the set that made him begin to study the screen.

It's no use to say that Nickie Duart understood what he saw any better than the freshmen or sophomores around him. Nickie merely understood that, whatever it was, it was exploitable. Whatever it was that came on the screen in an altered simulacrum of Rodney Buckthorne was taking firm hold of

22

these kids. Something undefinable shook them up. Ergo, something was there that could be sold.

Nickie sold it first to his companions in the Vistular underground. There were several of them that winter who had already made the scene and worn out their fellowship credit at Berkeley, UCLA, or the U of Washington and were wintering at Vistular. With Nickie steering them, they began to crowd the outlet classrooms for Buckthorne's televised lectures. These wild graduate students stimulated and agitated the younger students already there, those already softened and undermined by the nameless quality Buckthorne projected on the screen. Nickie Duart seduced Vivian Spain. His friends seduced a very considerable number of the other boys and girls. An atmosphere of potential riot or religious revival grew. The Buckthorne cult on the Vistular campus was already a going thing when Nickie sought out its innocent center with a temptation to branch out.

"Man, you've got it," he said to Buckthorne in Buckthorne's office. "Stuff. Bite. Charisma, and it's not the shit you're peddling I'm talking about."

Buckthorne drew back white and angry. Anger didn't save him. Nickie knew the next step.

"I don't say there's anything wrong with the way you read your notes," he said with a pleading sneer of insinuation. "I mean you dish out the cold lunch the way you get paid to do. But what about Buckthorne's message to the world?"

"I am afraid *your* message to me is in a code I cannot decipher," Buckthorne said. But he was trembling. The young viper sitting brashly on his desk seemed dismayingly familiar. His tight-curled hair, ruddy face, and searching eyes were the very uniform of anarchy. He sat there like a messenger from the Old Gang, from the times before Buckthorne gave up working on America.

23

"You may pull the wool over the eyes of these academic assholes," Nickie said. "They don't know anything outside Vistular and their field, but I—and some others—know about you."

"Mr. Duart, I am a reputable classical scholar—though without much reputation, I admit—and holder of the degree of Doctor of Philosophy. I doubt that my colleagues are concerned about my private life or past as long as—"

Nickie failed to turn a hair when the Ph.D. was mentioned. That, at least, was a relief. He was on another track.

"There are a few of us around here, not many, I admit— who know who you are," Nickie said. "I've *been* to Frisco and LA. You're still *remembered* in Frisco. You were with Horace Gordon and the Streetcorner Theater."

"I only helped with the public relations aspect. Fund-raising. Without much success."

Now Nickie had him moving. The young man asked suggestively, "And who published *Ad Majorem?*"

"Minute circulation," Buckthorne protested. "Libraries refused gift subscriptions. No newsstand sale beyond the Los Angeles city limits."

"The hottest piece of sedition that ever saw print!" Nickie said admiringly. "Look, there are still people in Frisco that even remember you from the Wallace campaign."

"I made some peripheral contributions to that."

"You fucked the richest women in the Bay Area! At least that's the way they tell it. You brought in plenty of loot for Henry A."

"Hush!" Buckthorne commanded, rolling his eyes at the ears on the walls of his office.

Nickie was hard to hush. "I've *been* to your Lustrum Book Shop in LA recently. Those pansies have ruined it since you sold out to them. Don't kid me. I know about you and what you've got to tell this sick re-fucking-public. You can't quit

24

protest. I mean, how can you? You've got to speak out again, man. If not you, who? You know about the way we've got to live, man. Art. Orgasms. Ban the Bomb—

"You know damn well the military won't throw their Bomb into the wastebasket just because we get tired of protesting about it. The Sex Revolution hasn't happened just because we can see tits in *Playboy*."

A funny, frightened smile began to cross Buckthorne's face as he listened to his animated visitor. The old gunslinger was remembering the smell of powder. "I was indeed an . . . activist," he said with a humble nod of his head.

"You've been crucified until there isn't enough hand left to take a nail," Nickie cried. "Please don't quit just because of that! You can tell us how to live! We want to live, Dad!"

"No."

"Look. Let me tell you how I see it. You never had a chance to get your message across talking on windy street corners. You should *always* have had television. You and television could blow the whole thing sky-high so they'd have to start this country over from the Stone Age. You are the right man for that funny electronic contraption. I've seen it. I'm telling you, something funny comes over those dumb kids when they see you on it. I don't know what it is. I know it exists. It's really happening. You grab their nuts."

Buckthorne said uneasily, "I have been aware for some time that the University was not perfectly satisfied with my television appearance. Perhaps if I appeared clean-shaven—"

He was being honest in his modest error. He had heard a muttering of his popularity with students. He had heard it in garbled form so that he mistook it for censure.

Well. Nickie could quickly set him straight on that point.

Nickie did set him straight.

Nickie Duart shook him out of his quiet hiding and led him by the hand to the local television station. Nickie practically

25

dictated the terms for a program to be called "Buckthorne on the Arts." Weekly at nine on Tuesdays. Something for the cultured Idahoan.

"We get you started on this hick station and then we spread out!" Nickie planned. Tomorrow the world!

"Why does Daddy look so much like somebody else on TV?" Lance Buckthorne asked.

"Like who?" his mother wondered.

"I don't know," Lance said. "But I don't like it. Makes me feel funny to watch him."

"Then perhaps you shouldn't watch him," Mildred said. "It's not obligatory. But I wish you could tell me who he looks like—"

Because she, too, felt funny when she watched her husband appear on his weekly programs. Partly because he was so acid and ironic, verging on insults to the people he must live among. She felt the beginning tension of worry for him. But there was something else at work, subterranean, spooky, mysterious. One night when he had come home after a program and wanted to make love to her she'd cried out with hysterical giggles, "Oh, but you just did—" As if watching him on the screen had brought him into the very deepest recesses of her femininity.

The common citizenry of central Idaho took to Buckthorne's television appearances in about the same way as the less sophisticated students. The camera caught for them some grotesquerie of his appearance, of curling mustache and finicking voice, that tickled them. Perhaps on the little screen Buckthorne reminded them of the smug, smart-talking rabbit who always came out with an oblique victory over the straightforward bears and hound dogs in television cartoons. Or, if he didn't look quite like the cartoon rabbit, then he

26

looked to them like the quintessential Perfessor of frontier legend—a figure composite of whorehouse pianist, snake-oil salesman, and *idiot savant*. If they took for entertainment what he was, once again, beginning to preach as enlightenment and even the salvation of the republic, that was surely a right they had acquired with their purchase of the box.

So Rodney's program thrived with entertainment seekers. But the very personality traits and opinions that made him popular infuriated his colleagues against him. If he just would not talk about music—said the Music Department of Vistular. If he would restrain his opinions on literature—said the English Department. If he would stay off politics—said the Administration. On the tiny screen they saw a Buckthorne who sneered at their liberalism ("He is a plain fascist," they said) and at their cultural pretensions ("After all, he's an Idaho boy himself," they teeheed). The medium showed Buckthorne's arrogance and superciliousness as they would never have appeared at cocktail parties or in faculty lounges. Buckthorne was stung by the response of hostility. He struck back with increasingly pointed jibes on his program.

"He is drunk with irresponsibility," they complained. They made the station ask him to tape his programs in advance. He resigned rather than submit to such censorship.

"They've shit on you, but there's plenty of us you can count on," Nickie Duart comforted Buckthorne. Among the loyals was Nickie's friend Maris Mendelsohn, recently of Berkeley. She let old Rodney Buckthorne count on her the night his program folded. And count on her often until he began to count on the even younger Miss Cynthia Trebogen.

"The whole trouble is that poor Rodney gave everyone here at Vistular the wrong impression of himself," Mildred Buckthorne said to her neighbor and friend Nixia Gordon.

Mildred was in a mood for adding things up. After Rodney

27

had called her from New York this morning she had thought, *This time he may not come home.* Her next communication from him might be from the Middle East, the Greek islands, India. . . .

On this summer evening the mountains overhanging Vistular were almost barren of snow. Above the hammock where Mildred sprawled, the sky was deepening into the velvety, pansy shades that lowlanders never see in their sky. The two ladies were drunk, but not as drunk as they intended to be before Nixia—whose husband had not deserted her but was only playing golf with the chairman of his department—returned to her happy kitchen and an evening of TV.

"Even . . . even . . . even—" Each time Mildred tried to enunciate the ridiculous truth a bubble of laughter choked her. She hung her head over the edge of the hammock to regain her composure. "Even when he got this Cynthia Trebogen pregnant this spring it was out of shyness. He's always too shy to say what he's really hurt by. It was his way of expressing himself."

"Apparently you see connections invisible to mortal eye," Nixia said. She dug at the Buckthorne sod with the heel of her shoe, then took it off and peered down into its toe.

"Do I see connections! I learned something, living with Buckthorne. He adds apples and oranges like a computer."

"I'm against them."

"Who is not? What I wish to convey is he was one. Is one. Bad luck to talk about him 'ziff he's dead when he's probably jazzing half New York this instance."

Nixia protested, "You said a while ago he was just hiding out to think things over."

"Yeah, but—" Mildred said. "Yeah, but the way Buckthorne thinks deepest is hop inna bed and have at one if it's in front of him. It's also his form of prayer, if that's what he

28

thought he needed at this time. Prayer for the sins of the people. His lustrum.

"What's the differential between Mountain Time and Eastern Daylight Saving? Well, maybe not yet. I meant he adds up one thing and gets another. Mention just one person and instantly he's got her—or even him—changed into a mythological counterpart, seven Horatian references predicting what she'll do in the foreseeable future and a medieval allegorization of the same. I mean he doesn't just live with what he sees."

"Small wonder Vistular couldn't hold him!"

"Don't be snotty."

"I like Rodney, too, but I'm prepared to talk against him if that will help."

"There may be time for that. Let me finish explanation."

"Oh, do." Ironically Nixia twirled her shoe on the tip of her finger and let it fly up into the leafy branches over her head. Was it a bird then? No, it fell right back down. "Cynthia," she prompted.

Mildred had not meant to evade. "He'd been knocking off Cynthia—as far as his reluctant confessions would add up—since soon after he resigned his TV program last fall. You never saw the girl?"

"Never laid eyes."

"I saw her once. We had a 'confrontation,' know what I mean? Eventually we got together 'cause something had to be settled. A lovely girl. Correction. Lovely as *far* as Vistular coeds go."

"They are a hairy lot," Nixia agreed. "For which us faculty distaff are supposed to be grateful, no?" In happier times she had got some inkling of the Buckthornes' code of life. It had then sounded curious and therefore, to her liberal ear, "reasonable."

29

"So go home and heat up your TV dinner," Mildred said.

"Tell me your story. I don't really make judgments. Rodney's some sort of genius and who am I?"

"She's got a terribly thin face. Brown, tragic eyes. Oh, Philomela! Big tits. Terribly slender fanny. Odd but pretty. With a boyfriend at Berkeley, who is some kind of kook mixed up in the demonstrations. So she goes to visit the boyfriend at all appropriate holidays like Yom Kippur, Christmas, and Mao Tse-tung's birthday. And of course she's lonely when she comes back here to the mountains. And here is Rodney, who cares. So the affair moves along modestly *until*."

"Am I about to hear the connections?"

"Until those Domestic Science fakers who run the so-called Art Department humiliated him. First it was quitting his TV program. So he said to hell with them, he'd withdraw unto himself—more or less, with exceptions already noted—and do manuscript illuminating and painting. He's done a little of everything one time or another in the arts. Anyway, he'd done this painting of the nymph Britomartis. It was great big and sort of in the late manner of D. H. Lawrence, if you know what I mean, though Rodney used to paint like Renoir or de-Kooning or Rubens, depending on what the *paideuma* would stand when he *felt* like painting at any given time and this one he said was like Lawrence's.

"In the background there *was* this big, shadowy thing. That has to be admitted. But anyway we hired a truck and Lance and I helped him deliver it to the Memorial Union for the faculty show. Then Rodney and I got all dressed up and went to the opening of the show and his painting wasn't there. They hadn't hung it and I said maybe because it was a nude they hadn't hung it. But no, there was this ghastly, chalky knock-kneed nude by Fulgraf and another kind of pink blob with purple hair by a new man.

"And I said maybe it was because he wasn't a member of

the Art faculty. But no, there was a nasty black leopard by Miss Conrad in Music and a couple of studies of Hopi Indians by the man who does illustrations for the Ag publications. So I said, 'Well, ask somebody.' That's Rodney for you and what people can't understand. Here he'll paint a big red, white, and blue nude nine feet high and put it right in people's faces, but he's too shy to ask about a simple thing.

"I made him ask Fulgraf, who hemmed and hawed and finally blurted out that they thought this shape in the background was a phallus! Those blurry brush-strokes! That the nymph was worshiping a phallus! Which shows what kind of minds go around in whited sepulcher. But what it meant to Rodney—of course—was that this interpretation was a comment on his reputation. Which, I suppose, of course, it was. But it hurt him to think with all these mealymouthed pretensions they still confused the art with the man."

"So he knocked up Toboggan for that?" Nixia asked, pretending more bewilderment than she actually felt.

"So he burned the painting," Mildred said. She might not understand Buckthorne. She supposed she didn't. But she knew more about the details of his career and all the odd spots in it than anyone else. She was feeling too confident with gin to mind a little more mockery of her absent master. "He made Lance and me stay inside and he dragged it out of the truck to the trash burner and threw gasoline on it. And while it was blazing—"

"Just at dusk. I remember that," Nixia said.

"—a reporter from the *Trumpet* showed up to ask if he was burning a cross because that Negro veterinary had bought the house on the corner. And actually there was a cross bracing in the canvas stretcher, so there *was* a cross burning and the reporter took a picture just in case Rod was lying to him and there was prejudice."

"So—"

31

"So the next day Johnson started bombing Vietnam and all these things coming together just put too much pressure on the man."

"He could have signed the telegram of protest we all sent."

"He went to Cynthia Trebogen and said, 'Give me a son!' "

In the deepening mountain twilight Mildred rolled to the other side of the hammock to turn her face away from Nixia.

Nixia supposed her friend was going to cry now. The spells of crying had a way of flaring right out of Mildred's charitable reminiscence.

After a moment Mildred sat up and put one foot down from the hammock to steady herself. Her voice was now that of a spectator robbed of personal interest by the sheer passion of the drama she has to report. "Poor little girl. She said his face was terrifying when he came to pick her up in the Cord. They drove up a road until the snow blocked them. All the time he kept grinding his teeth and muttering, *'Il faut changer la vie. Il faut recommencer le vie humaine.'* "

"Impressive," said Nixia. "Nevertheless, she went a little too far with it, letting herself get pregnant."

"It was her understanding that he meant to leave me and marry her."

"Did he tell her so? Before? After?"

Mildred's chuckle was a triad of cynicism, fondness, and despair. "How would I know? But when he's ecstatic he doesn't go in for banalities. I said, 'It was her understanding.' You know where the female understanding starts from and it ain't the brain. Still, Cynthia and I worked it out in a very civilized way when the time came. She dressed up and I dressed up and we met at a roadhouse and had martinis with our lunch. . . . I said to her that, sonofabitch though he be, I didn't intend to lose Buckthorne the same way I got him."

"Oh, Mildred!" Nixia said with a delighted sigh.

"Don't say 'You never told me before.' There's a multimillion

32

things in the private lives of the Buckthornes you'll never hear about, baby. At least you knew he'd been married before. Several times, actually. He's a very marrying man. And I was his student one summer in that tourist-trap college in Mexico. He was protesting the execution of the Rosenbergs that summer. Below the Moorish goddamn wall he whispered low, 'Give me a son. *Il faut changer la vie. Il faut recommencer la vie humaine.*' I knew all about Janine Buckthorne waiting for him back in KC, where they were yet again soliciting funds for his little magazine, conducting poetry readings for packinghouse workers and jazz concerts in the Episcopal church. She was a good wife for'm too, and I knew that so I got preggie on purpose for advantage on her. And then there was Lance."

"You've . . . you've accepted the former wives and all the rest?" Nixia inquired cautiously. "I do admire that, though I can't say I understand it."

"Ha! What do you know about heredity and the way it molds character? I happen to have Mormon blood'n my veins. True. From a granduncle who had more wives than Rodney all at once. It's my hereditary disposition to admire a man who's able to *meet* his marital obligations, though they be multiple. See?"

"Oh, Mildred. I knew you people had lived the Bohemian life before Vistular, and Rodney had had many cultural irons in the fire. Yes, but—" But it had never occurred to Nixia before now how much Bohemianism has in common with soap opera.

Recklessly Mildred went on. "I've only hinted the barest possible about that Buckthorne. I mean only the ending. Lance and I are. Rod was always passionately political as well as intellectual, poetic, and . . . and *horny*. And he never tried to keep these things distinct like some people compartment them. You know, the *first* time he got married—he's told me

33

this, you nut; he's got a passion for autobiography as well—was when he got convinced that the Communist Party, of which he was an unruly member, held no hope for America's future. Then he got married again when the Spanish Loyalists were crushed. He was married to a Japanese, even, in 1945—"

"Because of the bombing of Hiroshima!" Nixia breathed.

"Then again when Churchill announced at Fulton, Missouri, that an Iron Curtain existed across Europe. And to me, Mildred, while he was still passionate about McCarthy and the execution of the Rosenbergs. I checked the dates. They correlate."

Nixia now declared, "He's certainly celebrated our historic moments!"

"Ah yes," Mildred said. "I thought I'd be 'nough to live up to him, because I'm very good in bed and all that. But he wants so much more. 'N I failed'm."

"How? You lamb!"

Mildred took a gulping breath. "I had to do it, and I had to do it my way. When Cynthia'n I met I told her where to find'n abortionist. That is, she wanted to find one all right. You bet. But stubborn Rodney, who's a man of principle, felt . . . well, felt I shouldn't have messed with his destiny. He was relieved in a way—"

"I'll bet!"

"—but he took it hard. What he's largely full of is contradictions."

The two women sat in a gloom of awe. The natural world in its hush of twilight spread around them like an extension of ancient intimations and reverences. Rising from their drunkenness and the seat of female understanding, echoed by the pine-clad mountains themselves, inaudible lamentations enveloped them. The lament was for all sons born of woman, for the absconded Buckthorne, and even for Cynthia's aborted son.

"Oh, Mildred, how does he get away with it?"

"I suppose . . . because we'll always believe him. Whatever he says, however corny or pedantic. And he's usually one or the other. Even if we know he's said the same words on the same blanket to a hundred other women. Because he *cares.*"

"About?"

"About us."

Mildred's words were a cry of bereavement, a cry of such wrenching, bottomless grief as has been seldom heard since the pale Galilean triumphed over the pagan world.

"Oh, Mildred. He won't just leave you like this. After you've forgiven him and everything. And believe in him."

"Well, he's gone," Mildred said.

3

The Connubiality of Teresa Brule

What woke Buckthorne the next morning in his apartment was the roar of many engines, a roar that seemed to move against him like the sound of an amphibious invading force converging on a tiny, green-fronded tropical island where he was the only defender.

A seven-doored truck rental garage sat obliquely across the Avenue. Between 7 and 8 A.M. each weekday morning an unbelievable number of diesels, honking, blurping, and hissing their airbrakes, rolled out to join the traffic of the commercial city. Toward five in the afternoon they came back. This twice-daily commotion must have been another compelling reason why the departed nymph had turned her dwelling over to him, and why the absent Miss Brule rented it so cheaply in summer when the windows could not be closed against the din.

The unacceptable noise was the first of the signs he interpreted that day. It meant simply: Stay inside, Buckthorne!

36

He had little inclination to go out anyway. Even after the lucky reassurances of yesterday afternoon and a night of heavy sleep, "going out" was still frighteningly associated with going out of his hotel window.

Normally he was a man who woke slowly. If he had been given quiet to wake in this morning, he might have kept the imaginary presence of Miss Cumberland with him a little longer. But with the din shattering his head he felt neither inclination nor ability to make her skip divinely around, upon, into his bed.

To cover his ears with a pillow helped only a little. Earplugs. This morning he needed the earplugs he sometimes borrowed from his wife. Mildred kept them in a drawer of the night stand beside their bed in Vistular. For a moment he devoutly wished himself there, where he could reach out for such small comforts.

But—lo and behold!—there was a night stand beside this bed. It was in fact a commodious stand with four drawers, just the sort of furniture a spinster lady would set beside her bed to contain her needs of the night—Kleenex, pills, reading glasses, light novels, linens, hairpins, orange sticks, nail clippers, and . . . earplugs. No one could live permanently with the truck noise without earplugs, and no one would carry such trifles to the quiet of the tropics.

Indeed, Miss Cumberland had searched these drawers before she left yesterday—but for her possessions, not Miss Brule's. These drawers must contain the older lady's necessities still.

So the quick mind reasoned—and locked on its reasoning —before he opened the first of the four drawers beside the bed. So Buckthorne was wrong again. It was empty.

The second was empty, cavernously empty and a little darker than the top drawer. So was the third.

Only in the bottom drawer, luminous in waxy substance

against the intense darkness of the wood, extended like pure and exuberant flesh, lay a long, blunt white candle.

And at the instant Buckthorne saw it, Miss Brule became more than a name, more than the known facts that she was a spinster of artistic bent who vacationed in Mexico. The candle made—at least for our observer, with his penchant for adding apples and oranges like a short-circuited computer—a certain predication about Miss Brule's spinsterhood. This was her candle, not for burning.

From that initial—and admittedly hysterical, admittedly offensive—predication a complete woman sprang to replace the image of the girl who had vacated the premises yesterday. The sight of the candle did just this for vile Buckthorne: It set fire to his curiosity about Miss Brule the way a match lights the fuse attached to dynamite. Lewd the original spark might have been, its results had the dimension of a cataclysm.

It was just his poetic speculation about the personal uses of that candle that led him to reconsider the paintings hung in profusion about Miss Brule's studio, the work of her creative hand. He studied them, too, as if their code could be read by those daring leaps of speculation that deciphered the candle's place in the absent lady's scheme of life.

They were small abstractions mostly, modest only in their size. These caseins and oil paintings showed at least a firm and exquisite management of the media. In color and composition they were—the thought came to him with a full panoply of awe—no less than masterful. The "right man" for this apartment he might or might not be. Let it be said, at least, that in background, training, and temper, he was a fit judge for the small-scale, transcendent genius of this lady, Teresa Brule.

Why, he thought, running his finger lovingly down the glass of a dazzling little casein in violet, orange, and pink—*why she is* somebody! For the first time he wondered why he had not recognized her name from the beginning. She was surely to be ranked with the best of her time.

Teresa Brule. Her signature stood firm, discreet, and self-assured in the corners of her paintings. Its calligraphy teased his eye, seeming almost as familiar as the signatures on the covers of art books containing the works of the modern masters. Yet, he was *sure,* he had never seen her name in print. Had he come upon that greatest rarity in the art world—the genuine master who simply scorned all competition or public display?

In the excitement of discovering what, after all, had been there before his eyes when he rented the apartment yesterday, he forgot the terrible assault of noise from across the street. Or rather, even welcomed it as a kind of barrier between the world and this apartment where he could be alone with such a spirit as the paintings showed.

As he tried to take the pictures in as a group—waltzing among the profusion of ferns and avocados as he did so—the bright and strong assemblage of small paintings seemed to swirl around him like the code flags of a man-of-war, spelling out messages that would require a great cryptographer to understand in full.

And there was one single painting among so many which powerfully, almost flagrantly, compounded the mystery of the personage it revealed. It was at the same time a display and a concealment (as all serious art is, of course, in varying degrees). This glassed casein of moderate dimensions hung in a choice spot near the fireplace. In a chosen spot, our enamored critic ventured to guess.

In pigment it was utterly, totally black. Only the delicate, at first glance whimsical and accidental, whorls of brushstroke and piling of impasto caught the light of the studio enough to suggest pattern, design, and their transcendent meaning.

39

Because of its darkness, in almost any light the glass over the painting would act as mirror, as well as window. Thus it incorporated the likeness of the viewer with the statement of the paint. And Buckthorne thought that perhaps this incorporated reflection was a trick intended by the artist. It struck his mind as one of those queer and supersubtle jokes that are so central to the art of our time.

That joke—if joke it was—was underlined by the title. She had called it "Self-portrait." One automatically asked, seeing his own face, as he must when he looked at it, "Whose self-portrait? Yours? Mine?"

It took the supersubtlety (or sickness) of a mind that would toy indecently with the candle found in her drawer to respond as Buckthorne's did when he admired the jest of her self-portrait. At least Buckthorne had learned how to respond to art by his response to the less respectable purlieus of existence. (There might be more wholesome critics than he—of course, of course—but they had not proclaimed Miss Brule's genius, and he had. At least he had this to the credit of his associative method.)

But as he began to assimilate the force and beauty of her art he—like anyone else—was moved to disavow the nasty spark which originated his response to the paintings.

He was not a simple man, so he would not think simply that the candle in the drawer was a precaution kept on hand for another New York blackout. He was a very complex man.

So at midmorning he sat pensively at the café table in Miss Brule's studio, declaring to himself that the candle—with all its lewd and poetic associations—was the symbol Miss Brule had left behind to guide him through the chthonic and Apollonian realms.

How about that?

He had showered and breakfasted royally from Miss Cumberland's leavings in the icebox when the telephone rang. The

40

ringing was audible because the rental trucks were now gone for the day. Its shrill summons was ominous to his ears. He answered warily. It might be his wife calling. He had sent her a night letter, announcing his new residence.

It might be a parent or friend of Miss Cumberland's, who must not be misled by his presence here. Not for the world would he contribute to compromising that dear young person.

"Buckthorne, you mesomorphic Sybarite!"

He recognized the voice of Nickie Duart, faltered for an instant, then said, "Ace Dry Cleaning. Sorry."

He hung up the phone with exasperation. Mildred must be more alarmed about his absence than she had previously indicated. She must have called the Duarts, here in New York, and suggested that he needed company.

He wanted no such thing. With the impact of her paintings still fresh in his mind, he wanted to commune with Teresa Brule through her small, exquisite library. Her eight hundred volumes ran from Thucydides through the virile Latins and Dante to Auden's *Collected Poetry,* with an exemplary foliation among the American writers of this century. Every title was first-rate, but the collection had no smell at all of yard-goods, ready-to-wear Great Books. The mere choice of titles was another projection of Miss Brule's personality.

His curiosity moved him first to hunt for another dedicated volume among those by her contemporaries.

His shock was to find they were *all* consecrated to her.

He pulled out *Lord Weary's Castle.* On the title page a trembling hand had written, "With gratitude. Cal."

He reached for the *Pisan Cantos.* The words *"J'ayme donc je suis"* (no signature; no signature required) appeared in a huge, incontinent scrawl.

There was no dedication in the *Divine Comedy.*

Still Buckthorne suspected a witty forgery. As a matter of fact, as a graduate student he had once rampaged through the

41

Chicago U library forging autographs in books he would like to have written.

But if this was a forgery, it was on so grand and careful a scale as to be a work of art in its own right—another great jest like Miss Brule's self-portrait.

And then, it was *just* conceivable that this unknown and veiled lady might have been the spiritual stay and good friend of Wallace Stevens, Marianne Moore, William Faulkner (signed just plain "Bill"), Archibald MacLeish, John Gould Fletcher, Federico García-Lorca, Ezra Pound, and T. S. Eliot. But when and where? In Buckthorne's vast reading would he never have caught a hint of their dark lady? Never a letter with tantalizing reference to Teresa? Or Terry? Or T.? Or Brule? Or even an unidentified B.?

When he found a book of André Gide's with "votre André" on the title page, he found himself perfectly suspended between the conviction he was encountering a hoax and the conviction that Miss Brule was indeed superhuman.

Again the phone rang into the deepening delight of his solitude.

Nickie Duart chortled into his pained ear: "You are the buck hare, you are. You are the buck hare. Come to lance the boil of the New York mind. Listen, old-timer, it needs it and we need you. Speak to us, old father. Let me tell you that you came at just the right time. I've got something going that's a natural for you—"

"J'ayme donc je suis," Buckthorne answered.

There was no use pretending he wasn't there when he'd been found. But he hung up anyway. Of course Nickie, Mildred, Vistular, suicide, and the other possibilities or responsibilities he had let creep into his life would have him out of this enchanted place.

But just knowing that they were bound to get him out

42

sooner or later gave a kind of permission to go deeper into the game he was playing with Teresa Brule.

Now that the inscribed books had piled curiosity upon curiosity about the lady, Buckthorne the Immoralist had to answer himself what he might do if he came on any of her personal correspondence.

Would he stoop (or rise) to reading it? He was afraid he might. Having come (or been led) this far, he would.

But after a while it was settled in his mind that he would never *have* to snoop in Teresa Brule's domain. The apartment and its secrets had been left purposely open to him.

Oh, no doubt Marsie Cumberland had been ingenuous in saying, "This place was meant for you." Yet her careless, reckless flattery was beginning to seem eerily prophetic. (Or more than that. Recollecting her sweet voice, straining to remember its exact inflection, one might wonder if she had not been coached to say exactly those words. . . .)

Impossible. And yet it fit. It fit as everything did in the progression of events begun when his own Ouija forefinger had shown him the ad in *The Times*. Realizing this, fitting the sequence into a coherence, he felt the wild excitement of a scholar who begins to decipher the findings in an antique tomb. He knew the incredible surmise of one convinced that his coming has been foreseen and prepared for across expanses of time and estrangement not far short of eternal.

Might one not think that before her departure, this amazing Miss Brule had arranged her *things* to welcome him as some ancient priestess of Isis arranged her funeral cerements with an eye to being dug out by a whiskered Victorian archeologist . . . ?

Love across the ages . . . an astonishingly romantic thought.

After that came the sweetest thought of all. The priestess (Brule) had even arranged that he be welcomed in her absence by a nymph (Cumberland) who would suggest to the excavator's eye the charms of the true mistress.

"I'm watching you through the window! I'm right across the street!" Nickie Duart chortled when he called next. "Us chaps have admired every move you've made with that beauty! Plow! Shoot! Plow! The master's technique has deepened and broadened! But Dr. Buckthorne, please, sir, when you've run through her one more time, will you please come out and talk business?"

Nickie was not across the street, though he would probably be at the door sooner or later. It was beginning to seem likely that he did have some reason beyond his anxious sociability for wanting to see his old mentor, leader, cat's-paw—whatever Buckthorne had been for him at Vistular.

While Buckthorne hesitated, Nickie pleaded, "I know you're shacked up with a delicacy now. But New York is full of varieties. I know where Maris is. She's dying to see you." In the times at Vistular Nickie had insistently hinted that he had pimped Maris Mendelsohn as Buckthorne's reward for going along with the television program. Whatever the reality behind those hints, leather-booted Maris had been dear to him among the snowy mountains.

"I shall be delighted to see her again," Buckthorne said. But hung up without further promises.

There was afternoon left, and he had promised himself a slow perusal of Miss Brule's photograph albums while the spell of excitement lasted hot and strong.

For most men it might be no trespass to look into someone's collection of personal snapshots. But surely the violation of privacy depends on the hunger and sharpness of the intruding eye. Buckthorne opened Miss Brule's album pages with the exquisite tremor of a peasant taking the virginity of a noble's daughter.

He had taken the volume of most recent date. There were no captions under the pictures. He thought it natural that he needed none to recognize the face and figure of the woman with whom he was so intensely engaged.

She was a tall, severe yet graceful New Englander. Surely she was past sixty. She was dressed in simple black—nunlike, athletic, imposingly tall.

The background was plainly Mexican. Behind the upright Northern figure rose the pyramid of Teotihuacán. Miss Brule was holding that standard prop of tourist snapshots from Mexico—a skull. One knew that the skull was the theater prop of a bastard culture, contrived out of the rubble of all the profitless Mexican centuries since Cortez. Miss Brule made it something else by the way she held it. As if she were in coherent dialogue with it. Bone to bone.

In the near background of the picture Buckthorne dwelt on, a young Mexican leaned on the hood of a Chevy. The chap was grinning a little more foolishly than the skull in her arms. He appeared to be tall enough to reach Miss Brule's armpit— how tall was she anyhow? He was half her age at most. And of course he was her lover.

For the grinning Mexican lad appeared in twenty or twenty-five other snaps that grouped together as the souvenir of an amorous episode. The episode of a week? Of two weeks? Surely not longer, for against backgrounds ranging from the piney mountain slopes of the Desierto de los Leones to the hotel fronts of Veracruz, the fishing boats of Campeche, and in small towns as far south as Ecuador, other Latin lads in their juicy prime grinned from other recent pictures—as if grinning at the joke of their connection with this aged lady from the North.

And in picture after picture Miss Brule held her skull . . . as if it were the trophy of an unimaginably fierce struggle of love in fisherman's shack, tourist motel, or on the jungle floor itself in some somber equatorial thicket where macaws screamed from the overhanging trees.

This was how Miss Brule spent the summers of her old age then. But where, in these albums, was the pictorial record of her contact with illustrious literary friends . . . perhaps on the quays of Toulon with Gide, on a Mississippi deer stand with Bill Faulkner . . . ? Was there a special album for such priceless testimony?

If there was, Buckthorne did not find it that afternoon. By the time the trucks began to roar back into their cavern across the Avenue he had been carefully through all nine of the albums she had left to expose herself to the right man in her apartment.

His belly growled with hunger. He had eaten nothing all day. He had, as it were, fasted in service of the curiosity Miss Brule stimulated. As he closed the last album in the twilight of the artificial jungle she had created with ferns and tropical avocados in her studio, he felt this gluttonous curiosity was at the same time overfed and famished.

The photographs were the tantalizing shadow of a magnitude beyond his direct perception. Altogether the hundreds of them he had studied bore irrefutable testimony to the vastness that might be accomplished by American womanhood extended to the utmost. (Brash Maris Mendelsohn used to like to say to him, "I've got a mile-wide pussy tonight, old man." Playfully trying to crack his cool with her toughness, she had employed this hyperbole as an expression of her youthful gusto, he understood. But the attribution, with its trail of memorable poetic ambiguities, belonged, he saw now with beating heart, to one woman alone, the one whose acquaintance he was now belatedly making—Teresa Brule.)

In this day of instruction she had made him see what a woman's life might be in the past half or more of the American Century. The photos in which she held a skull amid her

46

gigolos might be thought of as a kind of parenthetical bracket for the end of such a life. And, for a beginning, she had left for his eyes the most touching picture of herself as a child.

In *that* brown-tinted, fading snapshot a seven-year-old stood in the position children believe to be soldierly attention. Her abdomen was curved rigidly forward. Her shoulders were stiffly hunched. She was saluting an invisible flag. On her childish face was an expression of heartbreaking loyalty. *Semper fidelis. Morituri te salutamus.* The front wheel and hood of a Stanley Steamer could be made out across the school playground behind her.

Between these parentheses were the Representative Ages. Chubby-faced for one year and never again, Teresa had gone on a high-school picnic to a glade by a Massachusetts waterfall. She had been back and forth across Europe with her parents in 1922 or 1923. (As Buckthorne became conscious of the dates in her life, he had felt with despairing poignance, *She is much older than I.*) There was a closeup of her wearing a cloche hat with the frivolous statuary of the Tuileries designating where she had been on her nineteenth birthday right after the First World War.

In Greenwich Village Teresa Brule had been near Edna St. Vincent Millay's house (or had just left it?) in her early twenties. The boyfriend hugging her waist in that picture might have been a Harvard dropout turned labor organizer.

Her college had been Mount Holyoke. During her college years she had been photographed in the neo-Grecian dancing costumes popularized by Isadora Duncan. Her poses were what once had been called "eurhythmic."

In the Great Depression she had known men of all races, creeds, and colors. In the Second World War, admirals and doomed PFC's embarking from this city.

A woman's life. It was offered to Buckthorne on condition

47

of his being able to receive it imaginatively. He tried to be the right man for the offer.

But what he had glimpsed was too vast yet. His imagination lacked the muscle to hold it. Questions spilled around him like the dropped plates of an overambitious juggler.

Why had Teresa Brule never married any of the scores of lawyers young and old, medical students, poets, cadets, Bohemians, politicians, and men-about-town in whose company she had so obviously delighted (photos never lied to Rodney Buckthorne, though they might lie to someone else) in the years of her nubility?

Why . . . ? That seemed precisely the question she had meant to lead him to by leaving her albums where he could get at them. With that question she had him firmly on her hook.

In her great female life there had been a myriad of fine physiques, not to mention the unpictured relationships of the spirit. How could she have come through unwed?

How? By being more loyal to life than you were, Buckthorne.

By never having married the way you married, Rodney—one woman at a time. You took the easier way than she. You misunderstood what the fine women in your life had to get from you and gave them your carcass in moldering wedlock.

Look one more time at that first photograph.

Understand this: Miss Brule is saluting life and *all* the potentialities of her womanhood. All her adventures have been her *salut au monde,* her salute to the body electric, to the real flag of these American states.

You may have *intended* the same thing, Buckthorne. But you detoured through many marriages while she went on.

Smiling in the darkness—and the trucks across the street had stopped their dragonish thunders and blurps for the eve-

ning—he went to bring her candle from the drawer. He was
going to play with it. Mentally. He would titillate his mind
with the phalloid shape, as in the analogous fleshly comedy
(predicated by the location and mere presence of the waxy
rod) the spinster might appease the hungers of the body.

When he lighted it, though, and it stood up white and erect
from the café table in the studio, he saw that whatever the
poets said, imagination had no more right to identify the shape
as a phallus than as the rib of primal myth. His vision now
identified it as bone, the stuff of skulls and skeletons.

Oh, it thrust up like a prick into the mile-wide darkness
of Miss Brule's mysterious presence with him. But that very
darkness seemed to be supported, sustained, made possible
even, by the riblike properties of its shaft. The point of flame
made sense, so to speak, of the otherwise insignificant night.

The darkness was Miss Brule's offering to him in his loneliness; but the mystery of darkness became a treasure only to
the man with enough imagination to diddle it with the pitiable,
small illumination. Then . . . did the dark consume the candle,
or the candle consume the dark?

The metaphors were equally true, and, to his mind, just
as true as the fact that the candle would, in any case, be
consumed before long. It would end up as a puddle of wax, a
stain on the top of the table was to be all that was left of the
hour of its consumption.

These speculations chafed him to restlessness and fatigued
him at the same time.

He saved a little of her candle and went to her bed chaste
as a monk; helpless, he felt, unless she woke him with more
signs tomorrow.

4

Beyond the Dreams of Avarice
with Nickie Duart

"He has come. I have spoken with him," Nickie said. "Crazy Buckthorne is in New York, the City."

He reached behind his canvas to pierce it with a darning needle. He drew the nylon cord out tight from the front of his painting, plucked it until it gave out a fuzzy G-flat, then used it to bind his toothbrush into the gluey pigment. As the toothbrush settled into the painted representation of a hand, he bared his teeth and shook his head vigorously from side to side in front of it. These days Nickie was an Action painter, searching for the new thing, beyond Action. Tonight he was at work on a self-portrait.

His pretty little wife Vivian, who was watching from a stool behind him, took the news without a gasp. She had once been enrolled in Buckthorne's Hellatsiv class. With thirty-four other Vistular sophomores she had sat in a brand-new chair in a brand-new buff-and-gray classroom watching Buckthorne's fierce little gestures and mustache-twitching grimaces on the television set above the vacant teacher's desk. She had been, in a manner of speaking, married out of this classroom. Nickie had won her there. He and his gang of oddies used to crowd in and perch where they could laugh and cheer and carry on an incomprehensible dialogue with the box up front.

Nickie had chosen the arm of her chair to perch on. She thought he smelled worse than any boy she had ever been close to. Now that they were married she hardly noticed the smell anymore, though she sometimes missed it when she was at work.

"Is he visiting? Did you see him today?" Vivian wanted to know. Vivian typed all day at the Edison Foundation. She was not able to insist that Nickie pass her eight-to-six absence at his easel or typewriter or whatever other implement might advance his career in the arts. And she was used to not being told things until he had figured out how he could take advantage of them. "Did he get in touch with you here?" She had been given the idea that Buckthorne owed lots to Nickie from the time in Vistular.

"I deduce that he has shook his wife," Nickie said. "Anyway, the good woman telephoned me this morning and roundabout implied that the old boy had took off with a troubled mind. You know, like Tolstoy split when he was about ninety and died in a railway station running from his wife."

"Did he?"

"Lady Buckthorne was the opposite of hysterical. But I got the message that someone ought to be *close* to old Leo in his adversity. I immediately—knowing his proclivities *as I know them*—thought of Maris, who gave him the fountain of youth before, though I promised I'd administer the plasma myself."

"But Maris is all tied up with Fingersmith."

Nickie snorted the special, ritual snort that labeled his young wife's naïvetés. Maris Mendelsohn had been *his* friend

51

from his San Francisco days. She had preceded him as a pioneer on the eastward trek, spotting for him the advantages of wintering in Vistular, Idaho—where the art teachers were insecure and impressionable, housing cheap, and pot available from a pusher on the lam from Seattle.

When Nickie found a wife, Maris went on plotting and preparing their moves to Iowa City, Chicago, and most recently to Houston Street, where she had given this apartment over to them three months before when she moved in with an English journalist. "Maris was a disciple," he explained. "Fingersmith or no Fingersmith, I believe she would not be chary in the time of Leo Buckthorne's need. However, he has not yet responded to my suggestion of Maris. And I can't very well slip her in through the keyhole, because I don't know where he's at. I've got his phone number, but, damn it, it's unlisted and the operator won't give me an address. I heard a lot of noise in the background the last time I called. Must be near an airport. Maybe."

"Do you think he might be . . . really dying over there? I mean, there must be some way we could get the police to help if he needs attention."

Nickie had returned to thought. He was now sewing the corner of his handkerchief to his canvas. When it was firmly attached he blew his nose into it. "He's not dying *in that sense.* You've never quite grasped that Buckthorne is a great man. The gray-flannel crowd never nutted him. He was a mustang everywhere he went until he made the mistake of settling at Vistular. They were turning him into a husk until Maris and I took him over. I gather they pulled out some more guts last winter after we left. Now he's a mastodon without a museum to live in."

"Oh. Oh, yes. Nickie? I never did quite understand what Maris saw in him. I mean, why would she sleep with him even if she admired him?"

52

"You don't understand because you are a simple young married girl. Maris is a depraved, scarlet, hard-core member of the Sexual Revolution. *You* don't even know what an anal violin is."

"What is it?"

"I'll tell you when it's time for you to know," Nickie bayed happily. He didn't know what an anal violin might be either, but the term seemed artful.

Sulkily Vivian asked, "Is that what Buckthorne . . . played with her?"

"Like Paganini." He did not know what Great Buckthorne might have done in his sport with Maris, though he had teased her to tell him. At the superstitious root of his respect for the old man was the notion that he was a wizard of techniques that Nickie could profitably acquire.

"I don't think it's right for Maris to tell you about things like that when she never told me," Vivian said firmly. "Since we've been married she's supposed to be my friend as much as yours. And I don't see why any of you were so excited about Buckthorne anyway. He wasn't all that good on TV. He was . . . He was just funny."

Nickie farted to express a degree of disagreement tinged with annoyance and stopping just short of anger. "He's come to us when we need him, and we can't let him die until we've made his impact felt."

"Whatever that means."

"It means, whether you grasp it or not, that he's telephotogenic in some powerful way. We'll build him up here in New York. Maris—or Lois, maybe, yes Lois—can wangle him onto a TV spot here. When people get to know him, we'll parade him around the Village and get him to sponsor liberal causes. Civil rights. Folk-singing in the Square. Police brutality. There are lots of eye-catchers."

"So what?"

"So *then* you will introduce him to Karmite at the Edison Foundation. I will introduce him to Mrs. Pellew. From one or the other—why not both?—we'll raise the money for a lease on our hotel. We'll start our art center."

Barston Karmite was Vivian's boss at the Foundation. Andrea Pellew was the only very rich woman Nickie had ever engaged in even a semiprivate conversation. "Look," he said fiercely, "I don't know what Buckthorne could do with Karmite, but I do happen to know for a fact that in the old days he screwed some of the richest women in the Bay Area, and thus raised so much money for the Wallace campaign that California nearly tipped for the Revolution in '48. He can do it with Andrea Pellew."

"What's the 'Wallace campaign'? All I know is we'd be better off if you gave up the idea of taking over the Monarch Hotel," Vivian said in a tone of long-tried sweetness. "If I mention it again to Karmite, I'll be fired. Foundation employees are absolutely, strictly forbidden to solicit funds for any project. That's all there is to it."

Nickie showed his unbrushed teeth—either a smile or a mimicry of agonized determination in a good cause. "But he might listen to Buckthorne where he wouldn't listen to us. Buckthorne's had experience with . . . oh Jesus, with free universities, ghetto art centers, art for the proletariat, Black Mountain, all that jazz. Our project is a natural for him. If we can just get title to the Monarch Hotel and begin to fill it with Action painters, Action musicians, Action percussionists, Action. . . . We can change the shape of art for a century!"

"You might persuade *me*—"

"It's a natural for Buckthorne. He's been looking for this one all his life. He'll supply the poetry the Big Money people want to make them let go the loot."

"When he's not playing that whatyoucallit violin," Vivian scoffed. Skeptical she must still be, but she was very susceptible to her husband when he was in his warrior mood, dreaming of big money to dole out to his friends and hangers-on. His unleashed avarice brought out the motherly in her. Throatily she said, "And you're in no position to introduce him to Mrs. Pellew. You met her *once* at a party and she didn't like you."

"But she'll remember me! That's what counts."

"You said yourself Buckthorne *used* to be active in projects like the one you're talking about. Then you say he's all worn out. So why should he help?"

Nickie's fire grew more intense, as it usually did when confronted with reasonable objections. "Consider Buckthorne's great weakness. I'll control him with women. Gash. Poontang. That's so elementary I didn't even mention it. He can't fight frogjaw. Everyone knows that about him. So that's the way we get him in the project."

In sudden alarm Vivian said, "Not *me?* You don't intend that I'm to . . . that I should—"

He had intended no such thing. But for the moment when the possibility dawned, he eyed her with wild surmise. Then, with the air of a fisherman choosing between a plug and live bait, he said shortly, "Of course not you."

Not everyone knows it yet, but the day will come when noisy, grimy, anarchic Manhattan will be one gigantic island of culture and rest.

And this will come about because a youthful, egregious, foul-smelling visionary of our time saw the possibility of revamping a flophouse called the Monarch Hotel into an art center where his volatile contemporaries could rally and prepare the revolutionary future.

In the Great Time to Come the offices of Manhattan will be social clubs; warehouses will be studios of The Dance. Construction workers will be sculptors. Executives will make no decisions except aesthetic ones. Pedestrians will be dancers. Police in Batman costume will chase a criminal element masked like witch doctors and tragedians. Stenographers will type nothing but the poetic script for this millennial production, and . . .

All this will come about because Nickie Duart discovered the Monarch Hotel while he and Vivian were merely looking for a pad to call their own.

Nickie had taken his wife "scouting" in the badlands south of the Village. He scorned ads. It seemed to be his notion that if they spotted something suitable, though occupied, he would be able to devise a way to incriminate the tenant, ruin his family while he was on his way to jail, and move into the premises thus emptied.

The consequence of such hope was that the Duarts wasted weeks without a flickering promise of housing themselves. But they found the Monarch Hotel.

It confronted them one rainy afternoon, looming majestic and absurd. Even in its present decrepitude it had some quality of mirage and mistake about it. Its grandiose gray wings rose to twice the height of adjacent tenements and lofts. In the damp gray afternoon its ornamented cornices sparkled with forlorn glamour.

At the street level a soaked line of derelicts nudged into the arch of a sculptured doorway, partly boarded over. The Monarch still displayed the gaudy sign of its better days, though it was unmistakably a flophouse.

"Stop staring," Vivian said. "You're not thinking of moving us in *there?*"

"Zelda and Scotty. A-roompah, toopah, tee-ha. Dancing at the Monarch. Plaza to the Monarch, racing a Stutz Bearcat. First one into the fountain's a— Karoom. Jazz me, baby. Glamour is all!"

That was the way Nickie talked when he wanted to per-

56

suade without being held accountable for any specific declaration, though just what he wanted to persuade her of, he could not at that moment have said. "Relic of a better age!" he said to the monstrosity.

Probably his initial response was only that of a boy who, in an abandoned dump behind a small-town church, one day spots the shape of an ancient Packard touring car under the decaying ribs of barrels, piles of bottles, and rusted wire.

But he went back to stare at his discovery without his wife and to inquire about it, out of pure awe and curiosity at first.

The Monarch Hotel had been conceived and erected in the '90's by a man of vision equal to his. The great difference between Ellison Whitechapel and Nickie was that old Whitechapel had several million dollars to squander. He had purposely chosen an unlikely neighborhood to invest in, reasoning that the example of a big, first-rate hotel would spur emulation and draw other investment capital to the area. It was supposed to siphon prosperity into what was even then a slum.

It did nothing of the kind. The Monarch Hotel had never, never made money. The area remained a pocket of permanent depression. The hotel's taxes had been paid since the '30's by running it as a flophouse.

This grisly financial picture actually encouraged Nickie, on the simple grounds that the property could be had. His audacity was flattered when an officer of the bank that managed the Monarch agreed to see him.

Mr. Stepple did not exactly fit Nickie's idea of what a New York banker would look like. Presumably Nickie did not fit Stepple's notion of an investor. Yet the Monarch was such a desperate proposition the two of them spent an hour talking about it.

Mr. Stepple wore a shiny brown suit with wide lapels. His bald head was shaped like a white beehive, polished like a

Brancusi marble. His mustache, above almost invisible lips, was a shallow, inverted W. He got absolutely the last bit of good out of every cigarette, smoking it down until the coal was as large as the sticky brown remnant of squeezed paper.

"I have connections at the Edison Foundation," Nickie told him. It was true that Vivian had gone to work there, typing letters for Barston Karmite of the Foundation's Division of Arts and Letters. "The Foundation is on the edge of sinking several million dollars into art projects. Every day you read about art spreading. Art is, you might say, the newest of the growth industries—"

"Could be."

"It's the natural by-product of automation," Nickie said fervently. "Now, my associates and I are working up a proposal for formal and immediate submission—"

That Mr. Stepple listened was all the encouragement he needed. Mr. Stepple might not believe a word he heard, but he had been in business on lower Broadway for a long time and understood the extremes of human character.

Here, he may have understood, was a young man capable of anything. A fanatic capable of those extraordinary crimes around whose fringes legitimate business may gather legitimate profits.

Perhaps the lad would burn the Monarch down some night when it was full of hapless derelicts. There might be an insurance angle.

Perhaps if the chap got some dizzy philanthropist to listen to his scheme, he would slip beyond it and blackmail or kidnap his patron. No need to calculate the exact angles yet. In the perpetration of outrage, money might move. Bankers existed to facilitate its passage.

Nickie went home from his interview with Stepple to tell Vivian that the Monarch was theirs for two hundred and twenty-five thousand dollars.

58

"That's fine," she said. She reminded him they had four dollars and twelve cents to see them through until payday.

"I'm glad it's not less," he said. "If they'd said a hundred thousand, I'd've been worried. A hundred thousand's not a figure you can *play with*. I mean when you get other investors matching our input. You see, for only twenty-five bills we can have occupancy with an option. Then we're in a prime position to draw in other investors. NYU! Foundations! A big direct-mail campaign to graduating classes everywhere. Why not offer a Junior Year in New York in association with some classy girls' school? The girls would be based in a glamorous setting in Greenwich Village. You see the appeal. Besides, we could run it as a flophouse ourselves until we'd drawn in enough funds for the next step."

"It's *not* in the Village. No female would go near it," Vivian said. "And you tell me it's losing money as a flophouse."

"That isn't the point."

"The point is that we cannot and never will be able to raise the twenty-five we would lose if—"

"Vivian, you've got to arrange me an appointment with your boss."

"I won't."

Nickie burst into tears.

"I can't," she said. "They only give money to people who already have it. Honestly, sweetie."

She was right in principle, though wrong in exceptions. The Edison Foundation, of course, disbursed its millions prudently. But it spread the smell of its money with a profligate hand, like incense in church.

It was Foundation policy to permit a courteous hearing to some of the cranks that came after it for grants. Public relations routine budgeted time for the officers to take turns in listening to the wildest schemes, and permitted a cautious

59

encouragement to the more dangerous-looking applicants. For the notion prevailed among the upper echelons that, however anarchic and individualistic the cranks might sound, they nevertheless had the potential of grouping into a single mob.

Some morning the officers of the Trust would come to work and find the Madison Avenue entrance clogged with banners denouncing their refusal to help with cancer cures, Lysenkoist agricultural programs, the reinstitution of Brook Farm, antimissile defense with disintegrating rays, the subsidization of Harlem-in-Nebraska, the transformation of the Monarch Hotel into an Action art center, and other schemes to halt the deathward drift of the twentieth century.

Thus it was partly in fulfillment of policy that Barston Karmite agreed to lunch with Nickie. It was also partly because little Vivian Duart was an office pet. She was a daughterly, rosy-cheeked girl, still fresh as the dawns of her Idaho home. As a newcomer and very junior secretary, she had the duty of preparing coffee in the morning and martinis in the afternoon for Foundation officers. This gave her a certain amount of credit when she relayed Nickie's plea for a hearing.

"I think it's a nutty idea, myself," she said to Mr. Karmite, wrinkling her nice nose and drooping her lips in a Help-me-Daddy pout. "Nickie doesn't understand how our projects are selected. If you could spend, oh, just five minutes with him some afternoon to make him understand the obstacles—"

Mr. Karmite could do handsomer than that. The three of them had a fifty-dollar lunch on his expense account. This fifty dollars, by the laws of public philanthropy, was supposed to be the exact and entire investment in Nickie's dream.

Unfortunately the rich and unaccustomed diet made a chemical determination, absolutely cementing Nickie's devotion to his goal. His wine-stimulated talk with Karmite enraptured him and sold him on his own eloquence.

60

Karmite smiled the Foundation smile at such rhapsody. He agreed with ninety-five percent of Nickie's reasoning. Yes, there was indeed a particularly acute housing problem for young artists and art students trying to get a toehold in New York. Yes, it was a very shrewd idea to utilize existing structures like the Monarch—"commercially handicapped properties"—instead of proposing to build the required housing from the ground up. Yes, a fractional investment by the Edison Foundation might pull in contributions from other philanthropists. And yes indeed it was the Foundation's everlasting commitment to be a pathfinder for more conventional or cautious givers.

He was only sorry—when dessert came—that Nickie's praiseworthy development scheme didn't coincide with the program the Foundation Board had "outlined for the coming period."

"But don't say we didn't get anything out of it," Nickie insisted to Vivian. "By following my suggestion you got snails and *homard à l'américaine*, didn't you? You never tasted wine like that before in your life."

"I see," she said. "But what next, Little Bear?"

"Trust me." If he had zeroed on all other counts, he had engaged the enemy at close range. As a beaten guerrilla force learns fire control from the constabulary that shoots it up, he had got pointers on how to grapple with the money men.

Pointers . . . but not enough to succeed instantly with Andrea Pellew, whom he met shortly thereafter. Mrs. Pellew was obviously looking for a pathfinder, else why was she goofing around at a Village party with painters and writers no better off than he?

True, though, that he had rubbed her the wrong way. It was going too far to say he had insulted her. True, she had expressed her feelings by pouring her drink on him after he

61

had been knocked to the floor. Yet he refused to consider her a lost cause.

Instead of crying over spilt milk, he would get it up with a sponge. Buckthorne, he now saw, must be that sponge. In reliving his misadventure with Andrea Pellew, Nickie had concluded that he had been simply too *vital* to coincide with her notion of The Artist. So, throw her old Buckthorne, beard, mustache, and steel-rimmed glasses, his Latin tags and classical allusions. . . .

"Buckthorne can always be controlled by his major weakness." If Maris had resolutely refused to describe Buckthorne's techniques as Don Juan, she had passed on some impressive statistics about the old beard's erotic past. It seemed the man was highly confessional in the pad. People of Buckthorne's generation generally seemed to lack the discipline of Nickie's. Pissing and moaning and hiding their eyes between a pair of tits. No wonder they had always lost to the squares.

Now he concluded his present plan—to the amusement, at least, of Vivian.

"Where," he demanded, "is the capital of young, liberated, well-dressed, art-oriented, sophisticated, and lonely pussy that his dying instinct led old Buckthorne to?"

"We live in it," Vivian agreed.

"And who controls, in the name of good causes, such a number of Village girls as will make Buckthorne spin like a bull among the capes of the matadors? I do."

"Name three you control exclusive of me."

"Maris Mendelsohn . . . Lois Capehart—" He shook his head impatiently. Listing names was useless. The streets of New York were—as the crafty eye could see—teeming with young females who fitted his description and his present purposes. Plainly their intense potential was waiting to be channeled and exploited, as the tides and great rivers of a

62

half-settled continent might wait for a network of dams. Learning to harness this vital female power was his uncompleted task, and perhaps Buckthorne would help him learn that too, even as Nickie was in process of entangling him. Spiders must learn web-construction from flies. Where else?

Vivian said, "You claimed Maris led him at Vistular, but no one else noticed she was doing anything except the usual. So that leaves only Lois. I admit you and Lois seem to have come to an understanding while I'm at work—"

"Then Lois!" Nickie shouted. Columbus had begun with only one egg as a matter of fact. Using that to illustrate and propagate a sound idea, he had gone on to discover America. Knowing one girl who was undoubtedly willing to entangle Buckthorne seemed a considerable head start over the Wop in the project of claiming it again.

Let the web spin out from Lois Capehart's undiscriminating twat!

"So," he commanded. "You ask Lois and the gang over for spaghetti Friday night. Buckthorne's got to show his head by then. I'll keep phoning him on the hour, every hour. I'll have him here."

"You ask Lois. I thought you were the one who ruled her. You'll have to tell her what you expect her to do."

Nickie shook his head. "Leave the strategy to me. I won't tell her. It won't be necessary to speak to Lois beforehand to get her to do the right thing."

"As you wish," Vivian said. She was mocking, but she spoke truer than she thought.

An unwarned, sleeping, defenseless America lay ahead of Nickie's boat. He might indeed be operating a fantasy instead of a plan . . . ah, but didn't his aberration have the seed of unimaginable power? Wasn't it fancy, like his, that once upon a time said the world was round, that paper currency

63

was powerful, that the space among and between the stars was penetrable?

The tedious *planners* came later to make these fantasies real—bending the world on the maps, borrowing sweat, muscle, and the indifferent laws of motion for the dream of money and to send rockets whistling out into a space that mathematicians no longer affirmed to be reality.

Science, art, and economics are the children of wishes. About the power of wishing, this clean-cut, curly-haired, square-jawed, pot-smoking, good-humored, vicious American Youth knew something rare.

Part Two

Part Two

5

Matchmaking

"Dr. Buckthorne?"

Sleepily he admitted his identity. He had supposed that, once again, the phone call was from Nickie Duart. Nickie had phoned more than a dozen times in the last two days, and no one else had called at all. But there was always the chance it might be Mildred calling about an emergency, especially at this ungodly hour of 3 A.M. So he had answered and found himself hooked in conversation with an unknown girl.

"I'm a friend of the person you took the apartment from."

"Miss Brule? Miss Cumberland?"

"Yes, and there's been a kind of mix-up and she needs something very badly . . . would I pick it up in the morning on the way to work and she forgot to mention which subway stop or maybe I'll have to take a taxi and if you could just tell me which stop . . . or wait, it would be simpler . . . what is the address again?"

And because it was the middle of the night and some very simple mechanism in him had responded as it always responded to feminine need or distress, Buckthorne gave her what she was supposed to get from him. But before he went back to sleep he understood that when the knock sounded on his door the next morning and he peered out through the brass peephole to see who had found him, he would behold the respectful, cheerful face topped by the curls of Nickie Duart.

"I don't appreciate your roundabout maneuvers," he shouted through the door.

"I've brought food and *vino*," Nickie said, unperturbed. He barked like a Saint Bernard. "Sorry I had to fool you, old man. Wouldn't you rather it was me than the police? Your wife called again and she's very worried about you, but I told her not to call Emergency until I'd tried again."

He was lying, of course. Mildred would not call him against Buckthorne's explicit instructions, and he had clearly explained to her that he meant to stay holed up and incommunicado in Miss Brule's apartment until he had "thought things through." He had further explained to her that he was thus far eating a splendid fare. The vacating tenant had urged him to help himself to anything left in the icebox. He had been rather dazzled to find it full of vintage wines, prime cuts of meat, and salad delicacies. (That is, he had expressed himself to Mildred as surprised. Actually, this provision for his comfort had fitted precisely with the lavishment he had come to expect from his hostess, Miss Brule.)

"Please don't ask to come in," he shouted at Nickie. And thus he was trapped again—because his refusal to admit the young man would necessarily support the crude suspicion that he was not alone there.

He unbolted the door—but was so angry at himself and

at Nickie that he immediately strode back to the bathroom until he could compose his trembling. When he returned to the studio Nickie was sitting at the café table, reading the letter that had come special delivery last night from Mildred.

"She's right about one thing. You shouldn't be alone at this critical whatchamaycallit of your life, Herr Buckthorne," Nickie said wisely. "If Mrs. Buckthorne were here, she'd urge you to go to the Duarts' for spaghetti tomorrow night."

"I haven't been alone!"

Nickie looked interested—so lewdly interested that it seemed unfair to Teresa Brule not to attempt an explanation.

It was no use. Words failed against the simplicity of Nickie's surmises. The nightingale cried "jug-jug" to dirty ears once again, and Nickie said in brusque dismissal, "So, all right, you've been living among the sound waves in a time machine." His grin said, What you mean, Dad, is you've been beating your meat to the tune of some really far-out fantasy. Which is all your well-wishers were worried about, anyway—

"Look at it this way, *Herr Doktor*. I'm the prince and you're the sleeping beauty. There's life out there." He hunched a shoulder toward the stink and noise of the Avenue.

Impossible against such obduracy to argue the rarer life within Miss Brule's enchanted apartment. Buckthorne sighed. "Nickie, I'll admit that my presence in this city and all the exordial appearances attaching thereto must be uninterpretable."

"Yay!"

"But unless they have an inner logic—unless, so to speak, I am being initiated into the secret of survival and/or salvation —I say this advisedly—then I am . . . fearful. Very fearful. Do you understand me?"

Nickie understood what he wanted from that admission. Spreading his palms in a gesture of charity, smiling tenderly, he said, "That's what I'm telling you. Pick it up again, man.

69

You came to New York to jazz, and I'm the opposite of sitting in judgment. I mean . . . welcome to the new life! I mean, us kids is all here to help you start. Since they kicked you out of Vistular—"

"I was certainly not discharged from my position!"

"Well, since they made it too hot for you—"

"No one exerted the slightest pressure. And indeed it's very likely I shall return there after a few more days."

But Nickie was shaking his head as if he knew better. And as he bent forward his appearance seemed to change. From the brash and cocksure panderer, he was transformed into the embodiment of high-mindedness and high purpose in its martyrdom. "Maybe you will. Maybe you should," he said tremulously. "You've done your bit. If New York can't make it without you, fuck'm. You've got your retreat, high in the mountains. Go on back and let the world burn itself into atomic ash. Piss on the embers."

"My enigma is merely pers—"

"Only," Nickie said. *"Only* . . . I wanted to ask you for one thing. So I have no right to ask. I come here and break up your solitude with my smart-ass crap about the sleeping beauty—" His face twisted in an anguish of mortification and even his curls seemed to wind tighter as if they were being tortured into the tension of springs. "I was presumptuous. I just have got into the habit of thinking you'd instantly see through all my disguises and know what I really was trying to say. I've got in the habit of thinking, whatever my problem is: He's been through it. Buckthorne's been there. I've followed you so long— Well, it didn't seem right— It didn't seem *easy* to come in here with a solemn face and say the one thing you know I'm trying to say. Help!"

"Help is what I need. Look at me. What I am is a strong and virtuous person. I am! I know that! But *they* know it too. *They* have me spotted. I wake up at night sweating, wondering if *they* didn't begin to notice before I did that I had some talent, that I wanted something out of it that they weren't about to give anyone, 'cause if they gave it to even one person their goddamn game would be over, and we'd have broken through! 'Make room for me!' That was the battle cry. And I wake up at night with everything good in me choking my throat.

"I crawl on my belly asking help for the most unselfish idea in the world. Do you think *they* don't spot me? My great idea is 'not outlined for the coming period.' A pig from a foundation—one of the GUH-rate foundations—said that to me. You know what he smelled on me?"

"Yes," Buckthorne said dreamily.

"You do know! Of course you know. Why wouldn't *you* know? You've been through it all in Frisco and . . . and . . . and *America*. He smelled that I'm not trying to start this art center for my own selfish purposes. He smelled *virtue*. Oh, I'm a lousy, vicious, pot-smoking sex cat and I don't bathe much. But that wasn't what his tweaky little nose tweaked about. He smelled something *new,* something *good,* and he knew I was prepared to throw all my energy and my life into getting it. Is that horseshit?"

"No."

"Now where do I turn? I've got something going. It's like a rock starting to roll downhill. Enthusiasm everywhere—on the part of the people who can't do anything about it. We can have this art center if we only have the money."

"Just that," Buckthorne agreed, "and of course I'd be no help with that."

Nickie leaped to his feet and ran among the ferns and avocados like a panther with a bone stuck in its throat. From across the studio he cried, "You can! That's exactly how you can help, if you'll come to dinner tomorrow night. You think I wasn't listening while you were telling me about the great

71

woman who owns this apartment? Ah, please! You know I'm sometimes flip when I'm touched. I know what you feel about her . . . her *presence*. Who but Rodney Buckthorne would have the sense to detect it? But *he* wouldn't miss it. No, he would understand Miss Brule. But it breaks my heart the way it does yours that in this fucking country nobody but you knows about her. Because she's poor."

"I suspect she chose—"

"But here's the point and why you've got to come to dinner with us. Got to. There's *another* grand *older woman*. I happen to know her and I don't say she's flowered like Miss Brule. But it's all incipient. It's *in her*. And! And. . . ! Here's the crucial difference—"

"She has money."

"Loaded!" Nickie said with an angelic smile. "I know her just well enough to ask her to dinner. See, she's the kind who's looking for the secret of survival and/or salvation, too, so she doesn't mind coming to a shitty pad like ours. I can get her there. But I don't have the . . . I can't . . . I don't put it to her the way you could. I want Andrea Pellew to hear it straight from you. Not me. You'll come and meet her there in this incongruous setting. Rich, shy, withdrawn dowager among the kids. Do you see it? You will come. She'll get it from you. Savvy?"

"Well—"

"A diamond in the roof, in the rug, in the rut. She won't strike you *at first* as being what you maybe visualize Miss Brule being, but— You'll see. Would Buckthorne not see it?"

"If—"

"Andrea Pellew . . . The name's suggestive, kind of dirty and sweet and mean and promising. Right?"

Rodney Buckthorne laughed. Nickie's absurdity was not without its appeal.

72

This much of Nickie's absurd projection was true: Mrs. Pellew existed. She had a great lot of money. However briefly, she had displayed to him a flicker of soul.

He had met her at a party on Greenwich Street a few weeks before. It flattered his superstitious reverence for his "eye" that he had elbowed and maneuvered through the crowd to meet her before he knew she was rich. She was frumpish, middle-aged, and apparently bored. So it could have been an instinct of politeness that urged him to strike up conversation with her.

Of course it wasn't. His eye, which didn't always make clear to him everything it saw, must have picked up some signal of weakness in her. The first exchange of words set off a ticking in his ear, like a Geiger counter registering an invisible potency. He must find out what made her shudder like a gun-shy dog when he admitted that he was "committed to art." He found clues of vulnerability and began digging like a prospector. Any human weakness might turn out to be useful.

He found he could charm responses from her by the sheer intensity of his curiosity about her. He led her beside the still waters of self-importance. He tickled the secret areas of vanity which a merely aggressive suitor would never have guessed in her.

"You were a baton twirler," he marveled. "A champion!" Forty years ago, in the infancy of that art, she had been the champion junior twirler of Louisiana. All these years since, she had been looking for confirmation that baton-twirling was an art like painting, sculpture, or the dance. And at last, at this party, she found a young man who believed it was, it really was!

"I have seen them," he said with reverence. "Spinning in the floodlights! Higher than the goalposts! Up, up, up!" He swayed before the dear woman like a tree bowing in the hurricane of her remembered glory. This was the single moment of their intimacy.

Then he had gone to the kitchen of the crowded apartment to freshen their drinks. Out there his host, Norm Raysonner, had confessed about the Pellew money. Norm and his wife Edie had a basement gallery on East 10th Street. Of course it was their hope that Mrs. Pellew would finance their move uptown.

"Looks like you've got her going," Norm said. "She's a hard bitch to loosen up. So any good word you can put in . . . and maybe we'll take you along with us. We'll get you a cage right in the middle of the gallery. When the customers get bored you can go into your painting act. Leopard man bites canvas. Whatever you want to do."

Nickie smiled and waited to hear no more. He wanted to lead his treasure out of reach of greedy Raysonners. Take me somewhere and twirl your gold baton for me, Mrs. Pellew, Andrea!

But, as the philosopher says, we live in a snowstorm of contingency. Accidents. His mistake had been to leave her even for this long. By the time he got back with the drinks Mrs. Pellew was in deep conversation with Regina Travers. Regina was art editor of a woman's fashion magazine, a surly alcoholic with a frontal stare, immobile lips, and the habit of blowing cigarette smoke in a man's eyes instead of responding to civil comments.

Regina had steered Mrs. Pellew to this gathering in the first place and had probably watched all of Nickie's effort to move in on her charge. When Nickie offered to get her a fresh drink, too, she blew smoke in his face.

He chose to ignore Regina. He was in range. Mrs. Pellew was his Moby Dick. He had to get his harpoon in while he could. The interior voice which had kept him going for twenty-seven years said: *Do something that will at least make her remember you!*

Vivian Duart drifted by them at this point, and her version of what happened was that Nickie began to dance like a savage in the presence of a divinity. "What else should I call it? All right, I won't deny you were talking to her. I admit you used *words,* too. But how could you expect her to make sense of them when you were wiggling so?"

As he pawed the floor and gesticulated his awe of the money goddess, beautiful words had come out of his mouth. Words like eagles and doves. Like firecrackers and summer rain. He pulled his forelock in a gesture of humility. He threw back his shoulders and grumbled like Churchill defying the Luftwaffe. A voice not his own seemed to be speaking through him.

What he thought he was conveying by this display was that she, Mrs. Pellew, had not only come into the presence of the most extraordinary young personality she had probably ever encountered, but that should she only lift up her heart and seize his arm, the two of them could instantly step into a new world where baton twirlers replaced dropsical senators and Action painters drove the spoilers of art into the desert.

She must recognize his strength and virtue now! He was—have you read Balzac, Andrea, Mrs.?—he was in all immodesty Balzac's Rastignac come to conquer New York with the fire of talent and dedication, as the other incarnation had meant to take Paris. " 'Now, you old bitch, it's between you and me.' " He was quoting Rastignac's address to Paris. Mrs. Pellew thought—naturally—that he was addressing her.

Regina Travers blew more smoke on him. She shuffled her feet as if preparing to kick.

Nickie did an Astaire turn, ended half-kneeling with his hand on Mrs. Pellew's arm. "Pregnant, certainly. With meaning. We meet tonight. Twenty-five bills. Twenty-five thou. The foundations? Yes. Give them the pathfinder signal! Isabella and Columbus! Over the waves! Turn back . . . who said that? Let's discover it one more time! Hell with Ferdinand!"

At this point Vivian caught the hem of his jacket and braced her feet to lead him away.

"What does he mean?" Mrs. Pellew said, trying to edge behind Regina Travers.

"The baton!" Nickie purred. "You! Twirling! Ah, zow . . . ! Spinning . . . ! ! ! ! ! ! Over the . . . goldpost and catch it . . . ! Behind! Your back! I understood that!"

"Yes, the baton!" For a fated second she seemed on the verge of smiling again. She caught herself and said, "Perhaps if you have something to discuss, you might call my secretary for an appointment. Call some morning. Not too early."

And Vivian would argue later that if he had only had the sense to draw back then, he might at least have kept a valuable contact.

Genius reasons differently. He couldn't stop. "Our moment . . . ! ! ! ! Isabella and Columbus . . . ! ! Yes or no?"

Regina Travers smiled then for the first time since she had appeared at the party. She floored Nickie with a karate chop and Mrs. Pellew poured her drink on him.

"Ha ha," he said to the amused faces peering down at him. "There's been a little accident. The lady spilled her drink. Will you chaps see that she gets another?"

On the way home that night Vivian said bitterly, "I take it you were soliciting funds for that goddamn hotel, though I didn't hear the beginning, if there was one."

"She was extremely interested before her big dyke friend intruded."

"Look, we were just beginning to get in good with the

76

Raysonners, who at least have a gallery where sometime you might at least sell a painting. They'll never ask us again."

"I'm not playing the game for peanuts."

"You keep acting like a wild man and we'll be selling them on the street corner."

"That's not the way it will work," Nickie insisted. "Tomorrow Andrea Pellew will remember me as the most interesting person at that party. I don't say she'll approve of me. But be interested. 'Everyone must be talking about that Nickie Duart.' I'll be mentioned. You don't understand what lonely lives the rich lead. Very isolated. She'll spend a couple of days trying to puzzle out my character and motives. Then it will come to her I'm *fundamentally* different from the other creeps who want her money. The rich don't want to bother with the ordinary—"

"You're different, yes."

"—and her curiosity, if nothing else to begin with, will lead her to call me. You may think I was drunk from the way I talked to her. But it was all coldly calculated. With all that shit about her baton I reached her subliminally."

Vivian sighed. "You certainly do understand human motivation."

"You'll see. When your husband whistles, the quails come."

"And if she doesn't call you?"

"I'll make it easy for her. I'll call her. You heard her invite me to call. In the mornings. Not too early."

77

6

Buckthorne Snared

In the mirroring eyes of the young people dining at the Duarts', Buckthorne saw himself as the central figure in a painting he had long admired. It was the painting of John Sloan's called "Yeats at Petitpas'." There the merry, seasoned old rogue and mystic presided over the company at table as much by the aura his presence shed as by the ripeness of his conversation.

There were nine of them eating Vivian's spaghetti, not to mention the baby brought by the young Fanchinelli couple, who seemed to prefer crawling with the roaches toward the garbage can to sitting in the improvised high chair assigned her. Again and again through the dinner Buckthorne noticed the infant's determination to follow the ripe garbage smells. Once he saw that she had retrieved an eggshell, either from the can or the floor beside it, and was cheerily licking it out while two insects climbed her arm for their share.

"Bohemianism, to give it that not improper name, had a rather different flavor in my young days," he opined. But did not add that his Bohemian fellows would have been as loath as he to let a child fallen from their carouses scavenge for its food in a garbage pail. (Thoughts of his son Lance, clean-living baby, brought a tear to his eye at this point. He repudiated it as improper.)

No, he would not fault these young people for their differences from his generation, though in his present wine-and-spaghetti mood he was impelled to speak of them.

Depression, fascism, and war had been the negative background against which his youth was shaped. "Those are white man's troubles, Dad," said the young man seated on his right. Now they had The Bomb, Vietnam, and Meaninglessness. Yet, one-up him as he might, this black-bearded youngster was not at all trying to stifle Buckthorne's reminiscences. Rather, he lapped them up, as if in hungry need. "Of course the past was ye better age," he said. "In geometric progression."

"The past is what we drop behind us like a trail of excrement." There! Buckthorne was shocked to hear himself saying so. It had been one of his thoughts in the hotel room in midtown. The idea itself had become excremental during the intervening days, and he felt a violent shame for dropping it here where genuine and figurative infants were crawling. So, to make up for the lapse, he cried with a positively old-time exuberance, "No! Nonsense. The past is, I would say—it sometimes comes to me that—the past is essentially feminine. A feminine thing on which the, so to speak, *stallion* present breeds its foals!"

"How about that?" the girl on his left breathed sardonically. Her name was Lois Capehart. She had been attentive to him from the moment he entered the apartment—and consistently putting him down when she judged his speech to be too high-flown. "Stallions. How about that?" Her sardonic little smile beneath lowered eyes reminded him of someone.

So, perhaps, they all did. His hostess, Vivian Duart—shining her clean-looking arms at him and showing her clean innocence by her awe of his aphorisms—reminded him of his second wife, Beth, though Beth had kept their loft on Clark Street in Chicago immaculate while they were there with the WPA Art Project. Vivian's step (too) was lithe. Her laugh was quick and tinkling when he reminisced with her about Vistular University. "I'm sure Nickie never even mentioned me to you, but, boy, did I know you. From your TV program. From Nickie. And from—you may remember her—Maris Mendelsohn?"

They both blushed together when he admitted a memory of that girl.

"But being feminine—as you put it—I'm more interested in the way, way past," Vivian said, quickly. "And the question I always wanted to ask you if I ever met you in the flesh—" she blushed again—"was why you weren't an expatriate like some others. I mean, with your opinions about American life and in your time it was the thing to do."

Buckthorne spread his napkin from shoulder to shoulder like Yeats at Petitpas' and began to answer in the stagey, finicking tones that always made his spoken autobiography so different from his passionate recollections.

"Vivian, the central factor was my patriotic feeling about America—"

A young man who reminded him of poor old Nazeman, the Reichian, leaned down the table as he heard the obsessive word. "You tell'm, Buckstorm. America is a bum fuck."

"I was always unwilling to concede that," Buckthorne continued. The young man went back to his spaghetti. "Vivian, I suppose that by the time I was ready to go abroad, everyone was coming back. Except Miller and such, of course. I was too young to be of the Lost Generation. In fact, it was already 1932 when I resigned from West Point and began to consider myself an adult."

"You're kidding, Pops," Lois Capehart sang in his ear with sudden excitement. "West Point, huh?" She appropriated this irony as if she had torn off a piece of his hide for a souvenir of a museum trip.

Buckthorne turned his Yeatsian smile on her. "No. Nor was I ever kidding. I entered the Academy without mental reservations. I was inflamed by a love of my country that, in youth, quite naturally inclined me toward serving it in the military part."

"That's what I mean. The way you talk," Vivian exulted. "On the TV you never sounded . . . natural."

"However," he said, "it was the very zeal that brought me into my cadet year that rather quickly determined me to go out by the other door. The imprint of military discipline, which they had begun to set on my character, determined my next step. As you know, at that time a powerful political ferment was stirring America, rising from the economic dislocations of the Depression. Impressed by military discipline and its potential, I determined to follow the disciplines of the Communist Party—and the discipline of structured meter. That is, of poetry. For their sake I resigned the Academy, not to resume my military career until I was drafted."

He was not unaware that his young friends were all on the verge of giggles. He would not, now, be offended if they had giggled aloud. The true story of his life was full of ridiculous ambiguities, and he had often noted before this that the more he reduced it to bare fact and chronology the more it tended to sound funny, or sometimes exciting as the purest lie.

"Wow-sir!" Lois Capehart said. He felt the tip of her bared foot tickle his ankle in appreciation and then slide up inside his pants leg. "And then what?" she said.

81

Reminiscence came in torrents as he turned more squarely toward her. How her type had thrilled him in the year after his first divorce! How greedy he had been for these leggy, sardonic, scatterbrained, bandit-eyed girls who seemed to have pure chaos on their tongues! The truth was that his marriage to Imogen had been confined by principle and discipline, smothered by a communistic or West Point ideology of the way love ought to be loved. *Un coeur pour un coeur.* . . . Yes, indeed. He and Imogen had loved each other one hundred percent. But their absolute accounting on the decimal system had grown very irksome. Then he had needed caprice.

"Then . . . more of the same unlikelihood," he said to her. "But I have yet to go back to Vivian's question. Not only did I never become an expatriate—as you seem to *wish* I had, my dear Vivian—but I never set foot in Europe or the Mediterranean countries I love so deeply. Why not? My folly, of course. And yet, my principle, too.

"From the beginning and always I felt that though the European and the classical might far outshine American culture in accomplishment, yet these accomplishments were, in the ultimate sense, intended for *us*. Were to be naturalized. I made up the slogan: America is what the poets labored for.

"Actio in distans. Just as sometimes we find that a remote and inaccessible woman" (Oh, you, Teresa Brule!) "may work more powerfully on our cognitive emotions than one in our arms—"

"Nothing wrong with them, either. Oh, listen at him say it!" called Nickie from his listening seat.

"—just so a culture that is of the remote stretches of time may sustain us more than the available occupations of practicing the arts. I stayed away from the Mediterranean lands because I loved them so constantly.

"And so the greater my identification with the spirit of Europe and of antiquity, the more I felt designated as their missionary here. Not *here* in New York, I mean. But out *there*. In America. Do you realize I have not only never set foot in Europe, I have resisted the temptation of New York, as well, since I sailed from its harbor aboard the S.S. *Brazil* as a private soldier in 1943?"

"I understand. I understand," Vivian said and actually clapped her hands.

Lois withdrew her toes from their manipulation of his calf and said, "You've been too busy."

"Pardon?"

"Bullshitting the citizens. You've been too busy at that to get around to New York—where, I might say, it won't go."

She rose from the table and disappeared then. He supposed that he had offended her by his manner, and he regretted that. Yet, he felt, he had not offended the others, Nickie's friends and coadjutors who were, like him, gathered here for a purpose.

They were all waiting to meet and offer their talents to the patronage of Andrea Pellew. Nickie had assured him that she would be there . . . perhaps not for the meal, but sooner or later in the jollification of the evening. He had talked to her just this morning, Nickie said.

And, while they waited, they drew some sustenance from his age as he drew something from their youth.

Yes, he felt, as Nickie said, they needed him. Perhaps he was only necessary to show them that one could live through the snares and pressures of conformity and still smile. They felt warmly toward him because he rose up in their hour of uncertainty like the Gray Champion in Hawthorne's story.

Only—as the dinner ended and Nickie broke out bottles of tequila in the other gringy room—a tremor of realization shook Buckthorne. When it came right down to it, maybe they could use him now only by cheering him on to a symbolic death. They might lead him to the bars and poison him with alcohol like Dylan Thomas. And rub the noses of the

83

bourgeois in his misfortune. Or sell it to Andrea Pellew: *See, this is what your money might have prevented.*

They certainly were not waiting for him to educate them (though Vivian, who certainly needed it, asked his advice on the preparation of spaghetti and sauce). His mistake in settling at Vistular had been to think that education could pass the secret from generation to generation. At Vistular he had only come perilously close to losing it for himself. Here, at least, if they wanted him for scapegoat or sacrifice, they were giving him back something of his own merely by reminding him how much there once had been. So, in the tenderness he felt for them all when he saw little Mrs. Fanchinelli gather her cherub from the floor and begin to clean her of bugs and offal, it seemed piteous that he might have no more to give them than the death of his flesh, dumped from a window ledge.

Leaving the table, Vivian mumbled in his ear, "You're nice man, don't have to go through't with her'f you d'want to."

"What? What? I don't know what influence I could possibly wield with Mrs. Pellew, but I will indeed stay to meet her, as I promised Nickie."

Vivian frowned. "Not *her*. Oh well."

And explained nothing more.

From then until one o'clock new faces kept coming into the long, narrow apartment that had only one tiny window at the back of the bedroom, none in the kitchen, and two overlooking Houston Street from Nickie's studio. It was a sultry night, and as more and more of Nickie's generation packed in, an almost visible steam mingled with the smoke and dust tramped up from the floor. Bodies from the neck down tended to disappear, as in a subway crush, and only disconnected heads swirled in Buckthorne's field of vision.

"———'s come from Sarah Lawrence with poetry of social *gro*tesque." The voice was Nickie's.

84

Looking down, Buckthorne saw a pert and childish face near the end of his necktie, and a determined red mouth correcting the introduction. "Social pro*test*. Protest! It may sound old-fashioned but— Nickie said you were a publisher?"

Buckthorne shook his head, blushing.

"*Ad Majorem?* Isn't that your magazine?" the girl persisted.

"In a manner of speaking," he said. Surely she must know —or ought to know—that he had not got out a new issue in seven years.

By the time he had explained this extravagant lapse and she had vanished under the armpits of the larger folk, Nickie had produced others eager to meet the guest of honor.

Nickie introduced him to them all. His introductions ranged from cruel and embarrassing suggestions—"just been fired from a hick university for pedophiliac tendencies," "impresario for young talent," "the thinking cocksman," "gallery-owner," "librettist," "critic of mass-culture," "cunt-hound"—to flattery delivered with an off-key irony—"the man wide-open on the open road," "model for the Saint figure in Kerouac's ————," "TV thinker," "West Pointer," "the Vistular Whistler," "the last mustang," "agitator," "original New Dealer," "corrupter of youth." And these slant, mocking, respectful introductions threaded away into attempts at explanation which, in their turn, drew another sort of wild caricature of the way it had really been in the Buckthorne years. Heady and sour at the same time. He wanted to repudiate all of it; he wanted to embrace it and pack the whole truth on a banner they could glue to the wall.

Nickie introduced him to many, many disconnected heads in the melee. But not to any recognizable as Mrs. Pellew. (In the confusion of tequila and Nickie's double-talk, Buckthorne might have missed a name, but he assured himself he would not have missed her.)

It must have been nearly two in the morning when he

85

drew Vivian to a front window for a breath of Houston Street air and asked her simply, "Won't Mrs. Pellew be coming after all?"

Vivian seemed troubled. "What did Nickie say?"

"I'm not sure. I've asked him from time to time. I have the impression that he's still expecting her."

"Look," Vivian said. She began to tremble. "I like you. Let me tell you. Lois. If Mrs. Pellew doesn't come . . . Lois Capehart. You know you *can* if you—" She stumbled, said, "If you like her." And then she looked so aghast that Buckthorne charitably refused to believe she meant what she seemed to mean.

As if to make up for naughtiness quickly, Vivian led him to another young woman who had just arrived with a baby in her arms and was talking to Elsie Fanchinelli in a corner out of the way. And Buckthorne found himself introduced in yet another way. Mother!

Not only did the young women somehow manage to get the infant into his arms and laugh hilariously while it clawed for his mustache, beard, and glasses. They drew on his seasoned knowledge of formulas, fevers, and exact quotations from Dr. Spock.

He did not mind. This was not his own, wondrous Lance restored to him in a form nine years outgrown. But one baby is all babies; the smell and squirm of each is the smell and squirm of all. For an instant—it was the culminating miracle of the party—he was given back the years. And wept.

Seeing his tears, Vivian Duart glowed at him the way shepherds in devout paintings glow at the Virgin and her swaddled Child. She said, very clearly, "I cannot understand the cynicism of Lois Capehart!"

And yet, only a little while later Vivian was nudging his soaked jacket and whispering, "She's back! Lois is back!"

86

He tried to turn in the direction she nodded and got a neuritic twinge, sharp as the arrows of Apollo in his tired neck. "Come on," Vivian said. "Lois and I will rub it out of you."

The two girls got him down on the bed in the bedroom—where not more than seven or eight drinking members of the party sat or stood in drunken talk and where the Fanchinelli baby wheezed asthmatically between the pillow and the spotted wall. Vivian shucked his jacket off and Lois sank her nails in his neck as soon as they had pushed him flat on his chest.

He said, "Ouch, oh pardon me, but—" and she laughed. She whisked his shirttail up and began to run her nails up and down the creased muscle alongside his spine. "The pain is confined to the upper trapezius," he said. That made her laugh more yet. "How's the party, stallion? You getting any foals?"

He meant to reply, *in the sense that her ironic parody required,* but suddenly she had reached under him, undone his belt, reached farther and given his balls a powerful squeeze.

"You don't need to do that," Vivian said sternly.

"Free circulation," Lois answered her. "Now we can do some good rubbing his back."

"Neck!" Buckthorne protested for the last time. In their competition, the young women were paying no attention to him. One was, in a manner of speaking, trying to protect him from indignities. For which he was grateful. The other was showing off at his expense. Which he didn't really mind.

He thought for a few minutes that he could distinguish between the hands of Vivian and the hands of Lois—the sharp, electric aggression, including a pinky in his ear, and the flat, cool soothing of gentle concern. But it really made no difference. As all babies are one baby for the idealizing parent, all girlish hands kneading him from buttock to crown were the same.

87

And nothing spectacular was going on, after all. None of the others in the stifling room bated their hoots and assertions to watch. Only, when Rodney reared back his head, he saw the small, hardly focused eyes of the Fanchinelli baby staring at him over the pillow it was trying to climb. "Enough!" he said. "The pain is quite gone, thank you."

Vivian left him alone after that. But Lois, after her unexplained absence and return, had attached herself. She seemed to urge him to go on with the story of his life he had begun when she sat beside him at dinner. "I personally dig it very much," she said. "I didn't want to tease you. That stallion-foal stuff seemed too under the spreading chestnut tree, if you follow me. But gee, I don't mean I couldn't go on listening to you."

He smiled his acceptance of her apology. Believed her. Wanted to go on. Wanted, to at least one set of ears in this whirl, to *finish* the accounting. So he could hear it himself, once again, and see where it came out. He opened his mouth for a true confession.

"But it's so noisy here," she said. She lifted her shining mane of hair away from her neck. "It's getting hotter by the minute. I mean, we might as well go outside. I've been walking on the streets and it's a little better down there."

"Yes! Yes. . . . Well, yes. Let's! The only thing is I must find Nickie."

"Hell with'm."

"No. I must find him. I came here explicitly to meet some lady instrumental in his plans. Perhaps he wouldn't want me to leave yet."

Lois stared blankly. "Me! You were supposed to meet me."

She did not offer to explain. He stared at her a moment, then let himself be persuaded that, in some ambiguous, promising sense, it might be true as stated.

7

In the Service

"It took you a long time to come," Lois Capehart said.

"Oh." Buckthorne's squeak was contrite.

"What's the matter? You're not old," she said with a sigh of displeasure, rolling from under his leg and drying herself with Miss Brule's sheet. "You're old." She pinched the skin of his abdomen hard enough to hurt.

She meant to hurt. They had misused each other, and if Buckthorne was satisfied she was not. She had wished to bring him to frenzy. His whole motive had been to arrive at the tranquillity in which subjective and secondary pleasures begin.

If she had been receptive to his story, he would have been content to spend the night in talk and she knew it. Therefore, though it was a damned unfair thing to say to a man who had humped in silence for the last hour, she said now, "I can't stand a man who just wants to talk!"

She had been no less aggressive when they began. Almost before he was well settled between her knees she had cried, "You going to do this again?" She was a girl who could not conceive of happiness or even pleasure in the present. Joy was always in anticipation.

"Maybe."

"Well, I'd like to know. Are we or aren't we?"

He put her knees over his shoulders and said, "If you want to, yes."

"I just want to know if you *can* or not," she said. "Ouch."

"It is with me as was said of de Maupassant. *Quelque chose inconnue dans toute l'histoire de la semence.*"

"Just do it, Buster, and never mind the Berlitz."

Since then his talk—his *communion*—had been directed elsewhere.

Oh, he might have topped her simply in any other bed. Here complexities spun out of complexity. The mere fact of bringing her to Miss Brule's had taken all his nerve, as if it were the crudest sort of transgression to bring a physical female of his own selection into that domesticity he shared in spirit with the older woman.

His breath had come fast on the short stairway mounting from the garbage cans at street level to the door with the brass peephole. *Maybe she's come unexpectedly back from Mexico,* he thought. When he inserted his key, Miss Brule might fly out and set upon them with her broom.

But when he let them into the sweet-smelling gloom among Miss Brule's avocados, the opposite happened. Miss Brule's guardian spirit welcomed them, as though the darkness were her smile of approval. *This was what I intended, Rodney. Be my guest.*

So far so good. "I have a candle somewhere," Buckthorne said as he danced past his girl. He knew that Miss Brule's candle was half gone, but he was willing to use the rest. "And some cold vermouth. The verdure here within is quite at its best by candlelight. And perhaps I can satisfy you that I was not, indeed, lying when I mentioned some of the strange things that seem to have happened to me. You were quite right in objecting to my attempts at professorial wit. The circumstances of Nickie's party inhibited me. But—ho-ho—*here* I shall be able to tell you how it really was." Retold with the justifications that had, in the ancient lost times of thirty years ago woven them into high-hearted life, the facts would lose the garishness of lies. "I'll tell you about—"

To what he supposed might be Miss Brule's amusement, his chortles were cut off by another powerful squeeze on his testicles.

Ah, well then . . . later! He would tell all that afterward. Miss Brule seemed to be admonishing him that he had spoken too quickly. Nevertheless, he was not misled from his true expectations as he undressed Miss Capehart in the streetshine coming through Miss Brule's bamboo shades.

The dim, nymphean form emerging bit by bit from the garments he scattered on chair and floor and avocado branch was his promised Galatea. Breasts like medals, legs like the saplings of a holy grove, belly like the worn stone under a Delphic fountain. Bit by bit he sculpted them out of the dimness, confident that at the last he would give her the powers of hearing and speech.

But when she said, "Never mind de Maupassant, just let me have it, Buckthorne," he distinctly heard Miss Brule whisper, *Never mind. You can tell me.*

By the easiest transition in the world he went back to where he had left off the night he fell asleep with her candle burning beside his bed. She had entered his psyche then like its accustomed mistress. He had sensed her sitting very close by, nodding, not so much in approval as in notation—as if she were adding up the items of his account for him and would presently give him the total. In doing so she would give him the self he had always pursued like a dog chasing its tail. He had told her a great deal of his many wives and mistresses and the passions out of which they had risen into his active life like multiple Venuses out of the foam.

Now, sitting near in the darkness while he served Lois, Miss Brule spoke as if she had been thinking his confession over and had come to a tentative conclusion. And this is what she had to say:

"Rodney, if you look at yourself without that damned modesty that always makes you so arrogant, you will see that you are, truly, the Huckleberry Finn of your time. Where was it that Huckleberry meant to light out for? The *Territories.* And you did too, Rod. It was your wish. You always thought that when your adventures ended in complication and frustration and bewilderment—as adventures must—that you would disown your few belongings and *go.* And where *were* the *Territories* in your time, Huckleberry? The West was closed before you were born. Defunct, as my friend Mr. Cummings said of Mr. Cody.

"Woman. Woman alone was the terra incognita. The dark continent, your Wild West. There has been much talk of 'the sexual frontier' in our time. For most talkers this was a metaphor.

"For you, Rodney, *it was not a metaphor.*"

Thus the veiled lady reassured him.

But Lois Capehart complained, "Do you always mumble to yourself when you do this?"

"Oh, pardon me." He had not realized it was he who had been speaking. He had heard the sound of course, but had chosen to think that the words *originated* with his guardian spirit. Confronting Lois, he might lose this essential faith. So he said, "Roll over."

"All right." She permitted his adjustment, but without enthusiasm. "Now don't you— Just you be careful, now!" she warned him fretfully.

Turning the girl over was like turning a page in his book of memory. It was, in a sense, to expose his album of snapshots to Miss Brule as hers had been left open to him. Tonight he went back to the beginning, to thoughts of his mother.

There was just no doubt (he explained) that Grace Hanover Buckthorne's chief legacy to her son had been the enthusiasm for love. When he was old enough to encounter the poem by Ralph Waldo Emerson that admonished him, "Give all to love, nothing withhold. . . ." he had recognized it as his mother's true and familiar voice.

He was her message to the world. She was his first promise that the Grail had been hidden someplace that women knew.

She was daughter to a prospering doctor in Gettysburg, South Dakota. Dr. Sam Hanover had gone to the House of Representatives late in life, and was thus able to procure the ill-starred appointment to West Point for his only grandson. His daughter had known the great world merely as a projected image, something watched through the mirrors of her poetic, loving sensibility.

She had grown up, according to the tales she told infant Rodney, among adoring, wholesome cousins and uncles, minding the roses that she and her mother made to prevail against the savagery of the prairie sun.

With sprinkling can and bonnet she left the shade to bring forth petunias in beds planted to represent the American flag—and formed her patriotism thus to the notion that the

93

True America was an invisible empire of flowers, red, white, and blue, extending from eternity to eternity. (And this also was part of Rodney's first mystic learning from her.)

She had ridden like a little princess on her uncles' ranches in western Dakota. (Her son would almost believe he *remembered* her girlhood, saw her blond and white-caped on her little bay pony, trotting amid a retinue of cowboys, truer-hearted and more gallant than any Gawains, or Percivals, or Lancelots of that other fable.)

Before her teens Grace Hanover had often gone to Lake Okiboji, in Iowa, where her family spent vacations in the grand hotel with seven pennanted wooden turrets. She remembered with ecstasy how they had ridden the lake steamers *Hiawatha* and *Maid o' Mist*, singing in the summer darkness. On weekends a cornet band played on the boardwalk verandas surrounding the hotel.

Exposed to such sweetness of the old America, she could do no less than respond with poetry and song. By twelve she was remaking all that world for herself and her son-to-come with verse and piano music. She always saw in every situation its potentiality as art: as, in the excesses of a prairie sunset, she saw the possibilities of turning into a waterfowl and flying into it, or, alternatively, burning her father's house down; as, in an evening trip on a lake steamer, she saw the possibility of plunging into the wake, or, alternatively, hijacking the boat and piloting it through the night to China.

Rejecting these possibilities—as she always would through her merry, stealthy life—she nevertheless testified to their reality in compact little fragments of rhyme.

All her family knew that Grace played the piano. She could hardly keep that secret. But her son Rodney was one of the three people who ever got an inkling of the vast, the incredible quantity of poems she made in her thirty-five years. Of them, she published exactly one quatrain in the college literary

94

magazine while she attended Saint Olaf College in Northfield, Minnesota.

When Rodney was old enough to become her intellectual companion and the true love of her life, at the prodigious age of four, she began to read them to him. She never stopped until she died. And at length, when he was still an unsettled prodigy at the age of forty—having attended all the schools and read all the other poems in all the libraries—he had understood his mother's verses to be the polite little notes of regret with which she had replied to all the invitations of the world. Out of all she had seen with her fascinated eye, what had she ever got—or wanted, for that matter—but little Rodney?

She had never stood squarely in the world. She had preferred to hover with her foot at its shady edge. Oh, she had married and borne one child. At twenty-five she accepted a young doctor who expected to take over the Gettysburg practice when her father went to Congress. At least Joel Buckthorne had come to Gettysburg with that understanding. When it seemed that even Gettysburg was too advanced to trust life, limb, or kidney to him (though he had a legitimate diploma from the medical school at Vermilion), he had moved his practice, wife, and child to Thatch, Idaho.

The move to this remote village (camp? settlement? wide place in the cattle trail?) could hardly have been a disappointment to Grace Buckthorne. It was rather as if she had been secretly conspiring for this Westward retreat all her life. It was like her retreat into poetry, as if she refused distinction between The West and the realm of her patriotic imagination.

In Thatch, Idaho, she had her son, her piano, a comfortable little frame house with a flower garden, and a Model T roadster. Her favorite pastime was driving with her son to their hidden places in the mountains while her husband puzzled over the ailing descendants of the pioneers.

95

Under that mountain sky, where eagles hung their dreadful weight like ornaments dangled from infinity, she fattened young Rodney with fried chicken and potato salad. They flung magic stones into the mountain waterfalls. They counted the filaments of shiny spiderwebs. And they—or rather she, it was his mother who originated the tactic—converted everybody and everything below their mountains into poetic equivalents.

Her husband, Rodney's father, became a phantom of healing. Lost weight. Disappeared into the inane like a free balloon. Grandpa Sam—known in reality to his colleagues on Capitol Hill as "Wheat'n'hogs Hanover, the Bull-roarer from the Black Hills"—went out of sight wearing a Roman toga. Schools and trades, cities, farms, and maybe even bodies themselves—everything that existed on the flatland—turned into shadows for the child with his mother on those happy heights of estrangement.

She persuaded him with her poetry. He never, ever, got quite unpersuaded. Its words might be, and were, forgotten. Its feeling was his permanent adjustment to the life that had to be lived down below.

By the time she died in 1924, to the supreme bafflement of her physician husband, Rodney was already able to grasp that this removal was only a logical continuation of what she had always done. She had skipped against the motion of time. Now she veered off from the years altogether, bowing, smiling, and waving her handkerchief like a lady on the tailgate of a buckboard, going farther West. She vanished like the Frontier itself, not changed but intact, immortal, smiling its simpleminded blessing on the corrupt cities and the stinking traffic that moved after it.

And because she had gone intact, his fidelity to her had remained intact. He had been true to her—as now, on top of this rebounding young stranger, he was still true to Mother.

Yet (he confided to the listening presence beside, within, around the squeaking bed) he had struggled all his life for release from this first and ideal love. He had followed the poets who told him to kill the mother as he had followed those who told him to cherish her intact and apart. Poets were so evenly divided in their counsel. . . .

And here, in this educational apartment, where he was trying to become "the right man," he still sought release. With his old love duly recognized, could he not now admit another? To complement the ideal image of the deserting mother, might he not add the quite different image of Teresa Brule?

While his mother had gone on angel wings out of the century, Teresa—here, in the lustful city itself—had met it full on. She had lived a woman's life as woman of the city while his mother had been the true country girl. At last the synthesis and transfer of his loves seemed within grasp. Teresa lingered and beckoned him to follow.

Now, as this conception of the delicate, crucial change swelled in his mind—and with it the frightful anxiety of a baby transferred high in the air from one set of arms to another—as the baby had been handed to him at the Duarts' party—his highly trained fibrovascular system responded to the wild surmise.

"Are you? Are you coming now?" Lois cried eagerly.

If only she had kept out of the conversation he might have made it.

"No," he said sadly.

Forlorn. . . . The girl's anxious cry tolled him back from the mad faith that he was about to show his wings and fly with the nightingale soul of Teresa Brule—off to the land of pyramids and skull-white flowers and shrieking macaws. Instead of flying, he made contact with a distended cervix, blunt as a dog's nose materializing in the dogsbody of lust.

97

"Don't," Lois said. "Do!"

After all, it was in the dogsbody he must live out his days. With Lois. His mother and Miss Brule existed—as the philosopher said—in the realm of philosophic truth, among those *necessities* which are always more shadowy than the transitory substance of our certainties.

Those elder ladies ruled him like number, paradigm, and law. But Lois was here and now—and once again thumping his back with her heels.

Like Faust at the threshold of decision, Juan must choose commitment to the present moment. Must be adequate to it, though his outreaching heart would not yet bid it linger.

Begone, he cried to his shadows, in the synaptic revulsion of ejaculation. And silent as the cry had been, Lois seemed to hear it.

"It took you a long time, but you finally gave in," she said. As if she had broken his stubborn arm in Indian wrestling.

His stubbornness yielded, he went her way instead of the way he had foreseen when he brought her here. They burned the rest of Miss Brule's candle while she talked of her career instead of his troubled past.

He learned that she wanted "eventually to direct."

Under images of her commanding a corner of heavy traffic or whipping a crew of male eunuchs at the oars of a galley, he perceived that she meant she wanted to direct cinematic or television productions. But that was "a way off" though she was at present the "number-two Girl Friday" for A. B. Wherry, whose name Buckthorne certainly should have heard of if he hoped to go anywhere on TV.

"I hadn't counted on that really—"

"Nickie thinks you've got a television future," she said scornfully. She put a forefinger on his lolling head, and in the candlelight, she turned it back and forth as if to study him with a camera's eye.

"My efforts in the medium have been exclusively educational."

"I know," she said. "Culture for cowboys on the local station. I guess that's not what Nickie had in mind for you here."

"He has something *more* in mind for me?"

"Look," she pleaded with sudden earnestness, "don't let him take you in. He's a pure psychopath. I don't know why anyone hangs around him, including me. He'll waste your time listening to his nutty schemes. If you want a TV job, maybe I can arrange it. You do have . . . something. The way you talk is cute." She chuckled uninterpretably. "There's a Long Island macaroni company looking for a type to use as The Gourmet in a series of commercials. I don't think you'd actually have to eat the stuff on camera. I saw a script and you'd be more, like, preparing exotic dishes and ordering vintage wines and larks' tongues. Then you'll beam and roll in your chair when they serve you this macaroni."

"I won't."

"Everybody's got to live. I heard the University kicked you out because you couldn't stay away from *this*." She patted herself illustratively. "And your wife caught you at it with a teen-ager. So that's that."

She could only have heard this from Nickie, Buckthorne realized. "The facts are—" But to mention facts was to open the door to chaos. There were so many facts. They were like the Chinese, militarily ominous in their sheer numbers. He would not stir them up now to answer a frivolous error.

"It was never that I couldn't stay away from it," he said. "Rather, I was like a certain type of drug addict who *doesn't want* to give it up. As for being caught, that is a misleading term. I've never been 'caught' in quite the sense you mean."

"No outraged husbands shooting at you?" She ran her hands over his back and buttocks as if searching for shot beneath the skin.

"Certain husbands have known of my attentions to their wives. But really, Lois, I find that you young people know very little about the mechanism of jealousy."

"Ha! You'll see."

He didn't want to contest the point. He said, "My survival may be due to the fact that there is a very great surplus of unused womanhood in our country."

"You sweet old thing. You mean you've just been *helping out?* You are a monster. And you need love more than anyone I ever knew." She traced his mustache with a fond forefinger, as if the face hair were a child's make-believe that touched her better instincts. "Stick with me, Buckthorne, and I'll help you. I can really get you started in TV. Play along and you won't have to eat macaroni forever."

"I'd like to be helpful to Nickie with his art center."

"Crap! You've been nonprofit long enough. Be practical. I'm not saying that I or even Wherry can make you a Jackie Gleason overnight. But if you want to live and love you've got to make your living. Right?"

"I want very much to live," he said simply. Every time he had said that before, through his long, long life, he had heard the click of a trap. He said it again anyway.

"Well then. Well, *then*—" Victorious in the triumph of her common sense, Lois moved to exploit her victory. With the muttered reassurances of a high school athlete arranging an inebriated cheerleader in the back seat of his father's car, she adjusted Buckthorne to her convenience.

"I'll put you on the little screen," she giggled as she mounted him.

Faithful as the little toy soldier in the poem his mother had once recited to his infant ears (". . . awaiting the sound of a little voice, the touch of a little hand . . . yet staunch and true he stands. . . ."), with no more sensation than a figure of wax, Buckthorne obeyed the certainties of youth . . . while Lois rode.

8

In the Sibyl's Cage,
in a Widening Gyre

Mildred had been his best wife. Her excellence in this role came partly from a generous, well-balanced, and shockproof nature. Partly from her canny determination to be his *last* wife.

As well-married women do, she had muted her sense of her husband's eccentricities without losing her sense of the social norms he violated. She saw him as an exception to nature's rule without suspecting that he was unnatural. Which was her mistake, of course.

She had got him—as she finally admitted to her friend Nixia—by being the handy genital into which he could pour his protest against McCarthy and the execution of the Rosenbergs. Yes and no. Already then, in her girlish astonishment a womanly calculation had been in formation. Secretly she knew she had been no more the seduced than the seducer. She had wanted wonders; she had wanted security. When her womb

102

swelled with their child, she had seen Buckthorne as the potent provider of both.

Better than his other wives she had understood how fiery his periods of meekness were. She had foreseen, better than they, when the crust was likely to break. It was the triumph of her foresight that she had been able to lead him out of his burning, hand-to-mouth existence as a crusading bookstore proprietor in Los Angeles and into the respectability of a professorship at Vistular without a scandalous or disastrous eruption.

What happened—what was about to happen in Los Angeles —was that his impoverished honesties were about to be converted into a travesty of success. At his desk in the squalid, littered back corner of the store—under the Horatian motto that he had inscribed in Roman lettering: SUBLIMI FE-RIAM SIDERA VERTICE—he had been approached by a fellow-classicist who had recently made good.

Eldridge Lowry, who had left his Jaguar parked at the curb with not one but two gorgeously groomed blondined teen-aged vipers to watch over it and wait his return, was now with Antiqua Enterprises, a well-capitalized company ready to advance in all media—movies, television, radio, comic books, and even the literary magazine field. In movies: travelogues of the antique world: columns, pillars, friezes suddenly, delicately animated with real-life California surfers, in various poses. ("Come on over with me now," Lowry invited. "I want you to see the Cretan footage. We got great stuff with this girl and a live bull. It will be bigger than the Mondo series for second-run houses.")

In television: a cartoon strip of the Trojan War *starting with*—how about this angle? Lowry had the credit for suggesting it—starting with Agamemnon putting the knife to Iphigenia instead of the old dull stuff the kids got in school. ("A man trained in the field knows where to *look* for the

103

sexy gore, unlike the *lumpen* at the studio who only know tits and a little Krafft-Ebing," Lowry said.)

For radio and comic books: Cute and catchy for advertising; bloody it up for the kids with twelve hot, sweaty pennies to spend at the newsstand. ("We strike *direct* for the racial memory," Lowry said. "The first time in centuries that's really been done.")

For the literary magazine: Camp. ("We go for the fraternity, sorority market. Get the literary monopoly out of the white hands of apprentice eggheads. Give it to the boys and girls with the golden arms, if you've heard of *that*. Why *shouldn't* Leda and the Swan replace all this juvenile crap about Bunnies? Think of the positions implied—")

All of which explanations might only have amused Buckthorne if they had come from anyone but Lowry. But Lowry had paid his years of loneliness and poverty to the ideal of scholarship, and had a devil's eye for the trends of contemporary culture. He looked around Buckthorne's bookstore and said sadly, "Dear fellow, I know *all* you can say. But won't you see that you'll preach culture for years on your windy street corners and all you'll do is advertise *us* and make *us* seem respectable? Come work with us. Come on over and get yours, old boy. Yours? Let me tell you about those girls in the car, sir. Sometimes they speak as a duet. And last night they chorused, 'Drive us so far out in the desert that no one can hear what you're doing to us.' To tell the truth, I refused, because of a slight bad cold. But soon— Rodney, sir, do you hear me?"

Of course Buckthorne heard. It was as if there had been no Lowry to come and tempt him, but rather a devilish and tempting voice that spoke from himself, a roaring in his ears night and day as he watched his world outrun him. And of course those soulless teen-agers in Lowry's car were figures out of his own Judas dreams. Would he not drive them so far

104

into the California desert that no one could hear . . . and there, in triumphant defiance throw himself on the pyre of their blazing bodies?

Fortunately he discussed Lowry's tempting visit with Mildred. She took his temperature (104°), put him to bed, and gently commanded, "You will take us away. Now."

"Where?" he had asked.

"Oh, Rod. Get a teaching job, at least for protective cover. We can have our own lives quite distinct from that."

"They will shit on me," he said. "I have no proper degree."

"Well," she had said, smiling—bless her heart, "well, why don't you . . . just . . . make up one?"

So he had, and her advice had seemed to work in the years at Vistular, even, as far as she indicated, in the involvements of last year. If it was too much to say that she had respected his rights to fornication with students Maris Mendelsohn and Cynthia Trebogen, she had waited through these affairs with a blend of sheer curiosity and canny expectation which preserved domestic harmony. She knew he loved her and Lance. She knew there was an excess of desire beyond these passions. Was not ungrateful, by and large, to the junior misses who siphoned off the excess in their natural way . . . as long as that led to no immolations in the desert.

She was proud of her composure and her timing—and of her compassion, too—in handling young Miss Trebogen's impossible pregnancy. Which was her mistake, too.

Until he took off in his old Cord roadster, she had not understood how severely Rodney's feelings had been hurt by this intervention. Too late she understood that he would have made the same arrangement, that she had prematurely put her foot exactly where he needed to put his if he was to keep from falling.

So there was guilt on top of her anxiety when he ran off to New York. After she got him on the phone in Miss Brule's

105

apartment, she was trying to atone for this guilt by putting the Duarts in touch with him. And when she got no response to indicate the success or failure of that move, she made another tactical error.

One day among the summer school students on the Vistular campus she spotted the slender hips and large bosom of Cynthia Trebogen. She confronted those brown, tragic eyes once again, and without histrionics—appearing *terribly fair about it,* as Cynthia would say later—simply admitted her husband had gone to New York, giving no indication of when or whether he might return to his family.

"I think it likely he might want to hear from you," she said to Cynthia.

Once again she was loosening the husband-tether, for the classic reasons. And . . . if that goddamn Buckthorne chose or managed to hang himself with all the rope she was giving him, then . . . she would be proud to be the widow of such a man.

Before noon of that same summer Monday, Buckthorne picked up the phone to hear this: "Rod, oh Rod, I messed things up so dreadfully!"

He recognized the propriety—and the threat—of this sentiment as quickly as he recognized the voice. "One could hardly consider you to have been the party at fault, Cynthia." He spoke as a fencer, putting his foil in a defensive position.

Her sobs broke over his guard. "Life does *faut recommencer* and all that," she bubbled. "I've been thinking hard since it all happened. When it was too late I realized I should have had your baby if that's what you wanted me to do."

Something seemed to be sawing a hole in the top of his skull. The morning—as bright in New York as in Vistular, Idaho—was the third following his visit to the Duarts' party. And Lois was barely gone.

106

In fifty-four hours she had purged him like a Turkish bath. She had brought him to the end of his hormonal tether. "Finished him"—to use her remarkably wise observation. She had drained him of dreams and yearnings along with bodily fluids. Like an embalmer preparing a corpse for its voyage through eternity, she had readied him to go home to Vistular and be a decent old man.

"I think you acted . . . courageously," he said into the black instrument that was pecking the side of his head like a raven pipping an egg.

Cynthia took his compliment as encouragement. "If you were here I'd do it all over again, because I understand *why.*"

Oh no, Cynthia, no! The words did not come, but a shameful, ratlike squeak did.

"What, Rod? Part of growing up came from talking to your wife. I just saw her on the campus *now*. But I mean *all* she's said to me. She's one grand gal, and I figured it must have come from what she's learned from you and your example. You've utterly purified her of this *cant* and *hypocrisy* and this social guff that most people live by. As I see it, she's faithful to the real you and not just some breadwinner clotheshorse or status symbol."

The half-naked clotheshorse whinnied ambiguously and looked around Miss Brule's studio for help. He saw the bright avocado leaves on the sculpture stands tremble like girls silently giggling. It was as if Miss Brule were mocking him from beyond for wanting to sneak back to the common and easy life. Then . . . to hell with Miss Brule. His similarities to heroic de Maupassant seemed, this morning, only to include the palpitations and *tremens* that had attended the great writer's demise.

But Cynthia was not through. She wanted him to know she now saw life from more heroic perspectives. She had to tell

107

him how it looked from the eagle's perch to which he had led her.

Once, long ago, he had been fired from a lowly job of teaching at a girls' college on grounds that he had "polluted the minds" of the students. For years he had resented being let go on such a suggestive charge since, for once, he had not laid a single finger on the student body. Now he saw the wisdom of their accusation. If he had just knocked Cynthia up and left her mind alone, he would be spared this continuing entanglement.

"All I'm asking is this," Cynthia concluded. "If I pack my things this very minute and come to New York, will you see me?"

"Would that . . . be wise?"

"I wouldn't ask anything of you except to talk about *important things* with me. Be my teacher, I mean. Oh, I'll get an apartment of my own and look around for a creative job, and if you do know people there—you've told me about some of them . . . this lady editor you used to—"

"Regina Travers," he said. "But I haven't seen her for many years. You must realize—"

"All right," Cynthia said gaily, "don't even introduce me to her. Or anyone. I'll take care of myself."

How could he doubt that she believed what she said? How could he doubt what would happen when she came through that door into this counterfeit jungle of art and avocados? They would begin to talk loftily about truth and error, reality and dream. They would talk of right and wrong . . . and in practically no time they would pass the low wall into the bedroom and be doing one or the other.

For once in his association with this girl, Buckthorne tried a dishonorable trick, reckless of how he would pay for it later. He said, "Cynthia, come! If you get the evening flight you can be here by morning."

108

It had occurred to him that before morning he could be airborne and headed for home.

They would pass each other high in the neutral air, over the Missouri River, perhaps. She would be in New York, where with luck she could find a "creative job." He would be back with his wife and the son who needed him. The vision came like joy. Tomorrow—or the day after—he and Lance would slip away into the mountains for the rest of the summer. They would go into the back country, the country of high passes, with government survival kits. They would follow the timberline trails north to Canada, double back, tack west, bumming their way down the Columbia on lumber barges.

Tomorrow the phone and doorbell might ring repeatedly in this empty apartment. And he would feel a true but diminishing sorrow as he thought of the ringing.

He had loved Cynthia no less—though no more either—than he had loved the other women in his life. He had loved her with an extraordinary intensity in the time of her trouble as poor old Faust had loved Gretchen most in her agony. Then he had loved her practical nobility in accepting an abortion with so little fuss. He had seen therein the dignity of American girlhood doing its best in a confused age, and had paid it the tribute of racking guilt as well as admiration.

All that had been so. Now he was finished.

In this apartment he had stretched out a remarkable fantasy of relationship with a remarkable woman. Fantasy though it had been, had it not also contained nobility?

It had ended in the physical joke of his hours with Lois Capehart. Who had finished him and the fantasy in her own way.

His days in New York were finished. He could go home.

He had his necktie on and his reservations confirmed when

he thought of the plants. He was determined to close the apartment for the rest of the summer rather than risk Miss Brule's possessions with another stranger tenant. But of course the plants could not survive until her return in September.

Perhaps Vivian Duart, if he asked her nicely, would do him the favor of watering them now and again. With the thought came a pleasant image of her among this greenery. He supposed he had liked her—at least second best—among the young people he had in one way or another encountered on this mad trip. He thought of her—and would think of her—as a girl meant for watering can and bonnet. Her clean pink and white complexion, a bit like his mother's he supposed, *fitted* with bucolic things, somehow, more naturally than with the gritty sparkle of the city. Her eyes would glow and her skin flush delicately as she made her way around this studio. He was sure of it.

And, Sure, she said, she could *easy* come in today and other days on her way home from the office, but—

"But, damn it, you can't go away and leave us, Rodney Buckthorne, sir," she cried over the wires. "Nickie will be terribly disappointed when he hears. You were telling me the other night about some of your contacts . . . your friends who've moved here. Collodion?"

"Mike Colloden. He used to tamper with pianos in Kansas City. He's been here for years editing a trade magazine for a record company."

"Adberg Nazeman? The man at the news magazine?"

"When I knew him in Chicago he was trying to reconcile Gandhi and Communism with Abraham Lincoln. Fine fellow. I'm afraid we have little to say to each other anymore. It's painful to try to perpetuate an illusion of closeness."

"You ought to stay long enough to try! They'd want to see you!"

110

All the old bisons who had pawed the uncultured prairie with him. If he had mentioned them the other night to her— evidently he had—he had meant to express the hope that Vivian and Nickie and their friends would not fade as he and his had done.

"I told Nickie I even thought—I couldn't remember—that you said you knew Regina Travers?"

"As a lyric poet. She contributed to my magazine at one time." And he had contributed, in his own way, to her escape from a disastrous marriage to an aluminum-siding salesman in Fresno, California. But no matter now. . . .

"Well, gee then, you *can't* desert us," Vivian pleaded. But when he was adamant she said, "Well, of course I'll water the plants. I've wanted to see your apartment, anyway. I'll come right after work to pick up the key. You'll still be there that long, won't you?"

He regretted that he would not. She could pick up the key at the delicatessen.

He meant to go quickly, without any last sentimental survey of Miss Brule's signs and symbols, photographs, paintings, or books. He would leave, as it were, sprinting.

But, as he moved swiftly to the door for his final exit, he heard something outside on the landing.

He looked cautiously into the brass-rimmed peephole. There, magnified like a sapphire in the forehead of a goddess, he saw a bright blue eye.

He felt that it had been watching him through all his crooked, deceitful preparations for departure. In reality, of course, no one could see in from the outside through the cunning peephole—but, however he might dodge, he must admit that reality had become a relative term in the days and nights he had been in this apartment.

111

In reality the eye belonged to Marsie Cumberland. As a former tenant, she of all people would know that the peephole was a one-way affair. So it had to be taken as part of her odd playfulness that she should startle him thus by pretending to peer in. In any case it was presumptuous of her not to have rung the buzzer before she came right to the landing. It was downright proprietary of her.

"I came back for something," she said to him as he opened the door.

He would believe later, in full submission to the power of his fantasy, that she had not so much come back as been sent. She had been sent by the all-seeing, omniscient mistress of this apartment to intercept his getaway.

As they faced each other across the threshold, he already sensed some powerful trick in her appearance—as if . . . as if Miss Brule had sent her to show a three-dimensional representation of how *she* had looked once, and somewhere else.

The charm of the girl's warm throat and splendid bare shoulders had come to him from afar, like a message from an antique artist, to remind him that *here and now* (any here and any now) took essential meaning from a golden *there* and *then*.

"May I come in?" Marsie Cumberland speaking. Miss Brule asking. So, once, Miss Brule had stood in her blossoming time at the door of some Grand Hotel de Var in the Midi, asking admission of some expatriate hero of the '20's. *Then* on the Mediterranean shore. . . . Behind her the surf and the gold and vast shine of the sea spread eastward toward Crete. Behind her the lineage of goddesses from the dawn country, behind her the rustling of *les cocotiers absents de l'Afrique superbe*. . . . (The sound was only the rustling of avocado plants in the updraft of the stairwell. Buckthorne's ear was exaggerating mightily to hear the mighty truth.)

112

"Yes," he said. "Yes, yes. Come in."

Ambling like a garlanded heifer, Miss Brule's messenger walked past him. He closed the door. Heard the lock snap.

The beauty of women is not in themselves, but in moments. Men are not caught by the charm of flesh, but by surprise.

He had seen Miss Cumberland before, he had imagined her here, but he watched her cross the room with unbelief. He glimpsed a fluttering like doves about her feet. Incredulously he felt the stir of desire that—minutes before—he would have said was gone forever and would have sworn was impossible without at least a period of recuperation. Every superstition of his amorous life was kindled to alertness as she made straight for the bedroom.

She was only partly visible behind the dividing partition as she knelt before the night stand and opened its lower drawer.

He knew that drawer was absolutely empty. Yet, superstitiously, with anxious heart, he watched to see if she might not lift what she sought from its emptiness.

"Oh," she said presently, "it isn't there." She stood up in the bedroom shadows like a column of light. "Well," she laughed, "I guess I did tell you to use anything you found, didn't I?"

He would have been less than Rodney Buckthorne if he had not found this simple speech ambiguously oracular.

"Everything?" His voice croaked like a dazzled schoolboy's. "What . . . what were you looking *for?*"

Marsella shook her locks. The light on them trembled like the flanks of a chestnut mare.

He said, "Perhaps I could help you look if you told me what you were looking for." He tried to move nearer. It was as if his feet were set in blocks of concrete.

She laughed at him, inclining her head toward him as if pointing toward embarrassment. "You look so funny, standing

113

there with your suitcase in your hand. Are you going some-place?"

The lie was ready-made. "Only overnight. Friends on Long Island. . . . The Cape—"

"I thought for a minute you might be moving out."

"No, no, no." He laughed loud. The laughter burned his throat as if he had swallowed flame. *"Won't* you tell me what you were looking for in the drawer? I might have seen it."

Her eyes shone with mirth. They would not meet his. Again she shook her head. "Nothing of value."

"Something of . . . *significance?"*

She would not admit it. Let him worry about significances.

He said, "If I find it, where can I get in touch with you?" Connecticut? Newport? Mount Ida?

Then her eyes were on him, cold and marvelous as a banner of flame streaming through interstellar space to light a new star.

"If you find *what?"* she said.

So. It was a game. She knew as well as he that only the long candle had been left in that drawer when she went away. She was trying to force him to name it. In his naming the candle, she would win.

"Whatever you're looking for," he parried.

"Whoever finds what they're looking for?"

"It's possible," he said.

"You believe in the bluebird?"

How curious and uncertain her tone was! As if she would believe if he would believe. But she would declare nothing until he showed his faith in the miracle.

"Well," she said in a tone of disappointment, "there's something else, too." She went for a moment to the bathroom. Closed the door while he whistled *Madame Butterfly* and studied an avocado leaf. On her way back she knelt again at the empty drawer as if to make very certain the candle had been squandered. Then, reluctantly it seemed, she moved to leave.

"Wait," Buckthorne said. "You told me. . . . The day I rented the apartment—"

"Just last week!"

"Just last week. You said you wanted to find something creative to do."

"Heard of anything?" She smiled, not pausing, but slowing. "Are you interested if I have?"

"What is it?"

The strain in his throat was very painful. It was like the pain he had felt when he looked down from the window of his midtown hotel and tried to force an enumeration of the good things left in his life. His reasons for going on.

"Something very exciting!" he said. "Some young friends of mine—artists, writers, you know!—are raising money to start a new kind of art center. It could be challenging. You might find it so."

"Yes. I might." But she had not yet decided to wait to hear any more.

"As I learn more about it, where can I get in touch with you?" Buckthorne said. He had never tried harder to sound compelling. "These young people have vision! Fire! Your address? Phone number?"

She continued to move away from him like an hallucination fading. At the door she half-halted and said, "I didn't find what I came to look for and you won't tell me if you found it. Maybe I'll come back when I have more time. You've probably rearranged things—"

"Everything is just as it was when I moved in."

But he knew nothing was.

When she was gone he shook his head frantically. Surely she had not told him all she was sent to tell. And had that

115

been his fault? His diffidence that spoiled the visit and kept it from fruition? Why couldn't he, at least, for an experiment, have said: "Yes, I found the candle"?

But had there ever been a candle in the drawer? Hadn't that all been hallucination, too? And if such a thing as that were hallucinated—what made him think he was able or fit to go back to a family and the dull responsibility of a university position? Outside he would just find a man waiting with a net.

Sweating, he walked in to convince himself of the concreteness of the bed in which he had recently slept. He had been lying just so and the trucks had been roaring devilishly across the street that morning he found the candle. He had groped for the drawers like this: One, two, three, bottom drawer.

When he opened it now, he saw it was again not empty. Trembling so his teeth rattled, he reached for what the girl had left. He lifted it, stretched it between the fingers of both hands to the light, gossamer and odorous, the sure testimony that a living and functioning girl had just been here to deliver another clue in the game that was not finished yet.

Game beyond a game. Game in which the other players were always a little ahead of him. Ahead . . . but at least he now caught Miss Brule's message to him loud and clear. As if the transparency in his hands were a letter, he read: *You're not through while you're alive, Buckthorne, old cocksman!*

In a little while—while the hot afternoon sun still struck its violent reflections from the barbershop plate glass and the tenement windows above the truck rental place, and the traffic bellowed like bulls and lions, and the city shuddered on its rock foundations—in a little while sweet Vivian Duart would come to look for the key to this apartment.

She would not find it at the delicatessen as he had promised. So she would come to the apartment to see why he had not gone home yet.

116

Here he would offer her cool wine. As the evening settled, she would go light as a hummingbird from plant to plant around Miss Brule's jungle, lifting her white arms to water the grateful roots.

As he watched her he would speak of his mother—how she had once gratified the roses and petunias of her Idaho garden while little Rodney tagged along with eyes of wonder. Touched by the recreated emotion, perhaps, Vivian would lift her gaze to his through a screen of fern. . . .

And tomorrow Cynthia would come here. Vivian, Cynthia . . . how many more? No matter. The turbulent city around him and the converging aircraft and trains from the corners of the continent would disgorge sweet girls like the multitude of graves that will open for Judgment Day. The unknown girls must be welcomed at Miss Brule's shrine. In her own time, Marsie Cumberland would *return* expecting her welcome.

That was the promise brought to him this day.

Miss Brule's command was: *Take them on as they come. Thy servant, Miss Brule.*

Enchantress! Destiny!

Part Three

9

A Very Short Chapter Adapted from Titian's Painting of Bacchus and Ariadne

Out of the somber verge of the forest comes a troop of sturdy earth people. A chariot drawn by leopards leads the march. Above it, experiencing pure weightlessness, lunging Bacchus reaches a hand of blessing and supplication to the maiden surprised on the beach.

Still entangled with the foliage of the wood, the brown limbs of his followers throb with the rhythm of great natural forces—of seasons, floods, hurricanes, osmotic pressures, and the thrust of root and branch toward the sun. Some wear the skins of animals over their shoulders. One carries a dripping haunch of meat. Another is munching the tip of a cluster of grapes. A magnificent, bareshouldered female tussles with a fat, spotted snake.

Among the lusty mob rides one very different figure mounted on a donkey. He is plump and soft. His body is white as a slug found on a decaying log. His beard is snubbed into the fat of his chest. This is Silenus, patron of intoxication and gastronomic excess, the weakling among the happy creatures emerging from their arboreal darkness. Yet Silenus, too, is divine and shares authority with the electric youth toe-dancing in the chariot.

The eyes of Silenus fly open as his donkey passes the thicket's edge. Has he been stirred from alcoholic reverie by the enticing distress of the mortal girl, as Bacchus has?

The ageless mouth quivers in rapture. The forehead of Silenus wrinkles with anticipatory delight. The point of his tongue darts over his lips.

He has seen a heaping plate of Napa-Barca spaghetti.

. . . And in the dark control room, watching Buckthorne's passion displayed on the four screens above the selection switches, the director says, "Leave it on the black. That's cute. That's cute. Print it."

Beside him the script girl giggles helplessly. She thinks this new series is the real puhzazz. She thinks the young director who strong-armed it through the account exec's hesitations is a wizard who will soon go up from making commercials to big-time stuff with the networks. He's got every film trick you could see in a season at the Museum of Modern Art. Everything he does is a camp. And this series on art and artists he's worked out with the oddball from Idaho would be a landmark for the agency.

But something more than the director's genius has worked to unhinge her giggle box. As she watched the infant, old-man's mouth of Silenus in closeup on one of the selection screens, her brassiere tightened astonishingly, and at the apex of each cup there seemed to be a ticklish, hot needle goading the delicate flesh.

10

Remarkable Happenings

It was a normal day toward the end of June, and Nickie Duart faced it without any special hope. In the morning, after Vivian fixed his breakfast and went to work, he ambled around their apartment paying more attention to a catarrhal condition of his nasal passages than to the status of his schemes. The morning was hot and sultry. The city seemed to express itself to his consciousness solely through the taste of tobacco and street dust at the junction of his oral and nasal cavities.

Last night he and Vivian had gone to the Raysonners' gallery on East 10th Street to celebrate the Raysonners' luck. They had found a backer—envious Nickie was sure it must be Mrs. Pellew—and were hot with plans to move uptown where the money was. So. That was probably all the outlet the woman needed this year for her philanthropic urge.

No word from banker Stepple about the Monarch Hotel. No excuse to call him.

123

And Buckthorne—according to the information his wife had garbled forth last Monday—had turned chicken and gone home to Vistular. For more than a week Vivian had been stopping after work to water the plants in the apartment the yellow bastard had vacated.

The day, therefore, began without promise. Nevertheless, this was the day when the cosmos split a seam and he began to gather up the fallout.

Buckthorne called him first.

"Together we can do it! We must!"

Nickie gathered that the reference must be to establishing the art center in the Monarch Hotel. But it made no sense now. "Encouragement from afar is always useful," he said bitterly.

The old goat was laughing dishonestly. "I infer that you've interpreted my silence as a lack of interest. Not so. I've been occupied. . . . Among other things I've been occupied with a vivid, enthusiastic young person who might have a special contribution to make to the project. Devoted girl with secretarial and organizational skills. Deserves to work for life rather than in the tedium of filing cabinets."

"A payroll we haven't got," Nickie said, with his finger deep in his nose. "Devotion and fifteen cents will get her a glass of beer. When's she arriving?"

"Arriving?" More phony haw-haws. "She's here."

"Here?" Until this instant the catarrhal head had stupidly held the idea that the call was coming from far Idaho. "You mean you're still holed up somewhere in New York?"

"Didn't Vivian tell you? I mean. . . . What has she told you?"

You! You've just told me, Buckthorne! Nickie sneezed so hard that he seemed to hear the ceiling crack above him—the blue shell of the sky cracked!—and he heard it falling like a shrapnel of dusty plaster around him. That walking monkey gland had lured Vivian there to water the plants, and then. . . .

Buckthorne, meantime, was rattling heartily on. "—a young lady I encountered at your party—I believe you know her— Lois Capehart. Miss Capehart was kind enough to give me an introduction to the world of commercial television. Actually, quite absurd. . . . One accepts it *because* of the total absurdity, of course. A series of commercial spots which parody the lives of great artists and paintings. Pygmalion, Goya, Casanova. . . . Quite hilarious, ha. I'm, of course, the buffoon. Very well, I'm assured, if it's for a good cause. And we have a good cause, young man!"

Slowly Nickie asked, "And you never left Miss Brule's?"

Then he hung up without waiting for an answer. He knew it. Of course Vivian—little old innocent Vivian—had been stopping by there, and not to water the avocados.

Water the plants! Why had he not grasped the phony sound of that excuse from the beginning? How could he, Nickie, have ever believed that one?

The worst of all was to realize how easily he had been taken in. Next worst was to realize he was married to an idiot who couldn't cover her trade with a better story than that.

And she hadn't even bothered to square the cover story with Buckthorne. The life Nickie dreamed of was impossible with a wife so inept at deception.

Next worst—and each explanation overlapped the other possibilities—this ridiculous story about watering plants, "actually, quite, quite, quite absurd," might be evidence of their contempt for him. Lying with that old monster, his loved one had said, "He'll accept it because of its absurdity. That Nickie!"

These—the only possible interpretations—made him feel close to fainting. To resist the faintness, he bared his teeth and began to run back and forth the length of the apartment,

125

from the dim bedroom to the hot glare of windows overlooking Houston Street. He paused once at the front window and leaned out to pick off some pedestrians with a high-powered, telescopic rifle. "Aa-aa-aa-aa-aa-aah!" Raining down gunfire on the citizenry, because such play had been consoling to him years ago when he was a timid child.

Again he stopped his galloping to fling himself onto the grimy sheets of their unmade bed. Vivian's smell was there. Her hairpins and the sand from their last outing at Jones Beach still testified to an untrammeled domesticity.

Now finished!

She would sweep in here this evening, smile disdainfully, and say, *But you told me I was to rule Buckthorne by his known weakness.* He had said nothing of the sort, but she would make it stick because now she had the upper hand.

She would realize he needed her more than she needed him. She would make him look for a job. She would wait until he had one and then quit hers. Then he would be finished forever. Someone else would see the potential of the Monarch Hotel and he would read about its conversion in the art pages of *The Times,* on his way to work, on the subway.

He had to stop this onrush of linked fears or he would go crazy. If there was a fix in the house—if he even knew where to get one quickly—that might stop it. But he had kicked even his connections when he began to count on the hotel.

He began to run cold water in the big laundry sink in the kitchen. As it filled he stripped off his yellowing shorts and the socks that kept him comfortable in sleep. When he climbed into the cold water, then, the shock of it began to clear his mind.

The shocking cold spoke to him, reminding him he was not as other men. He was one who made use of bad luck. He was the great Junk Dealer. "Disaster is my business. Call SP 8-1010." He still had his will, his unshakable willpower.

126

With the cold to help, he would master his body's weakness.

And then master the weakness of doubt. All at once his chest seemed to relax. Suddenly he could laugh, not because he had to to keep from shrieking, but because everything had turned out so funny.

When he stood up in the laundry sink, the kitchen floor was seven feet below his eyes. And that is how tall he felt now. He towered over the foolish attempt Vivian and crooked Buckthorne had made to turn the tables on him. He was still their master.

He heard the phone ringing again. He shook the droplets from his body and strode with naked determination to answer it.

If it was Vivian calling—as she frequently called in the morning to see if he was there and presumably confronting his easel—he would toy with her. Intimidate her with hints. Refresh himself with allusions to "watering flowers," "soaking the roots," "raising the drooping leaves . . ."

Just a hint to scare her. Fill it in later. He had something on her now. As the days went by, he would make it stick.

The call was from the banker, Mr. Stepple.

"Mr. Duart. Are you ready to go?"

"Sir?"

"Mr. Duart, do you mean business?"

"You're referring to the . . . hotel? The Monarch Hotel?"

"What else?"

"Well, yes. . . . Of course! I meant to call you. Certainly. Things moving fast. Organizational growth. Growing pains, ha. New corporation head envisaged. Television personality a distinct possibility. Just as Reagan has become the new governor of California . . . . a new age, personalities from the arts moving into managerial, even political, governmental. . . . Rodney Buckthorne, the comic star. Great buffoon—"

"Never heard of'm."

"All very shipshape. Enthusiasm in the foundations. Need stressed by John Canaday. I don't, as yet, have the option money we discussed."

"Of course not."

"But—"

"I have a client likes your idea," Mr. Stepple said. "He might be able to advance your organization the option money."

"Please? Can you explain that a little more?"

There was a sound of impatience from Mr. Stepple. "You *will* understand. Can you meet him in Brooklyn this afternoon?"

"I guess—"

"Mr. Duart!"

"I'll be there."

"Here's the address. Be sure you get it right."

In the shock of happiness, naked and still dripping, Nickie twisted this way and that looking for pencil and paper. Another sort of artist might have had such things handy in his studio. He saw nothing usable. Furthermore he needed a minute to think, to be sure this was not some cloddy friend pulling his leg. "Can I call you back at the bank in just a minute, Mr. Stepple?"

"I am not at the bank," Stepple said. "I am calling from a phone booth."

The name he had taken ought to mean something, Nickie thought. Scrawled in burnt sienna on the back of a canvas it looked very distinguished. V. Diascoli. Retired millionaire? Collector? Tax-dodger? The address was in a part of Brooklyn Nickie had never heard of. He was to call at three.

He was building fantasies around the name when the phone

128

shrilled again. A deadly slow voice identified the speaker as Regina Travers.

"I think we met," she said ominously.

"At a party," he agreed.

No response to his admission. He could sense her slow, misanthropic brooding as she tried to drag words up from a sticky swamp of loathing.

"I . . . remember . . . you."

Was it a warning? Was he being told she had even better ways of dealing with him than by karate? Her communication tonally implied that to the end. But the sense, he would reflect later, composing a sense that was not clear while he listened, was that someone had interceded in favor of his project. Had queried about the possible interest of Mrs. Pellew.

"Are . . . you . . . on . . . to . . . something?" the dread voice demanded.

"Really, I am! Hah. As a matter of fact. Accused myself a thousand times of unfortunate. Presentation. I was to tell the truth. Dreadfully drunk. Contrite. The dreadful self-accusations. Because. A sweetheart of a possibility. Nothing in it for me. For the youth. The young artist. Have I betrayed—"

"You . . . can . . . call . . . her."

"Mrs. Pellew? You've discussed it with her? She's expecting me to phone?"

Again there was the awful, waiting, poising silence, the suspense as if an extinct shape were emerging from the La Brea tar pits and preparing an oracular pronouncement.

"You . . . can . . . call . . . her," Regina Travers said.

In the security of her own apartment (surrounded by golden birds and attended by blackamoor maidens in harem costume, as Nickie imagined her to be) Andrea Pellew was a deliciously different personality than the grumpy woman

129

who had poured a drink on him at a Village party. That night she had seemed—he had the right image for it at last—cased head to toe in chain mail. As if she not only had money but *was* money, so she traveled out among the greedy pigs like a human armored car.

This morning she talked like money lolling at home in its own vault. "Mercy! Fascinating! Thrilling!" she said with languid exuberance. "I do so hope you'll succeed in doing something for the young artist."

"Well, if you will—"

"I'll watch with keen interest!"

Not enough, unless she would express her interest with interest money. But his buck fever counterfeited delicacy and he could not mention the dirty word *money*.

"And I'd be delighted to hear more of your ideas. If you and Mr. Buckthorne can arrange a time—" He heard her mutter a question, give directions. (He saw her plump, jeweled, imperial hand emerge from a cloud of nylon and bleached monkey fur as she commanded a Nubian to bring her calendar of engagements.)

"Buckthorne?" he asked, in pure exploration.

"Aren't you associated with Mr. Buckthorne?" There was a sudden note of panic in the golden voice, a fear of having got everything confused. Hearing the note, Nickie almost dived into the telephone, trying to reach and soothe the bird of his desire before it flew away.

"He's like a father to me."

"I don't know about that."

"I mean he is my close associate. Buckthorne and I. You mean Buckthorne the television personality?"

"I don't know about that. I don't pretend to keep up with art. But I was sure Regina Travers mentioned him as . . . along with you. Yes, she did. Yes, Rodney Buckthorne. Extraordinary name."

130

"Extraordinary man," Nickie promised. "Madame, we shall be there when you can spare a minute."

His overtaxed nerves began a new caper after this conversation. He no longer felt the least chilled. He was burning and his left arm flapped convulsively against his side. He went to sit in the tub of cold water again.

Now his wife's clandestine meetings with Buckthorne showed in a different light. Bless Vivian's cheating little heart. She had put out for Buckthorne, but in return had got him to intercede with his old friend Regina. That was initiative for you, and enterprise beyond anything he had expected from his life's partner. He would have preferred that Lois do the legwork, but, to admit the truth, Lois couldn't be trusted to keep her eye on the ball.

Careful now! If he forgave Vivian completely for doing him one good turn, his advantage would be easy come and easy gone. He mustn't soften.

He mustn't soften even if it had been a misapprehension that had hardened him and shown him the path of conquest. And when he spoke with Buckthorne again, it seemed that any conclusions earlier drawn about Buckthorne and Vivian might have amounted to misapprehension.

Buckthorne agreed to go with him to Mrs. Pellew's—though their date was yet several days off. Then the old boy shifted back to talking about the girl he was trying to find a "creative job" for. Piecing one scrap with another, Nickie inferred that a junior miss named Cynthia had been sharing Miss Brule's pad since last Tuesday.

Which left only one evening when Vivian could have been there alone with the old wizard. Yet she had been late every day last week with the excuse of watering the plants. It seemed disappointingly innocent. But there were the facts.

A more attractive hypothesis replaced the primitive one.

131

His wife, his helpmate, had accomplished her ends with Buckthorne quickly. She might have—she could have!—turned presto to another front, like Napoleon wheeling his battalions away from the channel ports and smiting the foe at Austerlitz and Jena. Clinging to the story that she had been watering the plants all week, she had been giving her boss at the Foundation a little afterhours cheer. That was possible. . . .

For by noon of that lucky day he had reason to believe that anything was possible. He was a gambler touched with luck, knowing any card he turned would be an ace.

And then by four-thirty that afternoon, when he left Diascoli's office in central Brooklyn, he saw what shape his success would take.

Mr. Diascoli was short, intense. He had no neck and no more facial muscles than were required to hold a thick cigar. He didn't look like a collector, an art lover, or philanthropist. He looked like what he was, the hoodlum boss of hoodlums, looking around for a place to get a quick turnover on some cash in hand.

Mr. Diascoli would arrange an option on the Monarch Hotel with Mr. Stepple. In the meantime, while occupancy in the legal sense would still have to be "iron out"—as Diascoli put it—Nickie was to move his operation into a "suite of offices" on the second floor of the hotel. He was to get a telephone and put out a sign advertising . . .

"What you say is the name of your corporation?" Diascoli wanted to know.

"Action Advance," Nickie said. Not bad for the spur of the moment. It had a poetic ring to it.

"Begins with an A," Diascoli said, reflecting on the advantages of a listing in the yellow pages. "Naaaaa. Whazzit mean?"

"Then how about South Village Art Center?" Nickie offered. "That would have the merit of not only associating us with the Village, but would maybe be a valuable new concept for real estate people wishing to develop the area as a whole. Draw in their support."

"You know anything about real estate?"

"No."

"All right. Just don't *worry* about real estate. You fellas incorporated? Worry about getting incorporated. Get you some officers elect. Incorporate limited liability. See? You got any officers? I get you some officers, but you got to be the President, see what I mean?"

"Sir," Nickie said, "we're in the early, organizational, fund-raising stage. We don't have elected officers, but there's a brochure ready for printing and immediate release to possible sponsors. Speaking engagements for Mr. Buckthorne to explain to civic and educational institutions. Our present plans call for a Village-wide fund-raising party in the *hotel itself*. Lavish entertainment. Name bands. Folk-singing. Reporters from *Life* and *Newsweek* and the big dailies. Tableaux of the great old days in the Village. Action happenings. Artists and naked girls cutting up all over the place. Photographs."

Once again he had done well on the inspiration of the moment. Diascoli welcomed the suggestions with dour Sicilian grunts.

"Stepple said you'd make lot of noise. That's good. That's right. Get in the papers."

So it was going to be crooked from the word Go. The hoopla and publicity for an art center were going to cover a real estate manipulation rigged by Stepple and Diascoli.

Only hours ago, Nickie would have refused to let his great idea be exploited this way. His luck was to have been rendered cynical in the nick of time to take advantage of the caper. If he hadn't found out about his wife's infidelity this morning,

133

he would have thrown their proposal in their faces. But as luck would have it, right now he was just the man Stepple and Diascoli needed. A young man who would give them a noisy run for their money as he reached out noisily in another direction for his.

He stopped at a phone booth in Brooklyn before he got on the subway. He wanted to let the little woman share the good news with him.

"It's what I've waited for," he said sincerely.

"Oh, Nickie," Vivian said with a thrilled voice. "Oh, Nickie . . . great! I've been trying to call you this afternoon. I thought you'd want to know that Buckthorne's back—and that will fit right in, won't it? And I won't have to water those darn plants anymore. So I'll be home by the time you are, and we'll have tall, cool drinks to celebrate."

"Buckthorne's never been gone," he said in his new, Diascoli manner.

He threw her the tip out of kindness. He could have waited until they both got home to let her have it, but he sincerely wanted her to have time to iron out the kinks in her story.

He didn't have to believe what she told him. She didn't have to intend that he should. A new phase in their partnership had begun. The new thing was going to work with all the other powers that were working for him now.

11

Confession as Entertainment and Fine Art

"I'm going to tell you the truth," Vivian said in a tone that nicely mixed sorrow and self-importance.

Nickie had bought himself a good cigar. In undressed comfort after the hard work of going to Brooklyn, he sucked on it pleasurably. His brow crinkled until the lines in it were almost as curly as his hair. Without transferring his gaze from the cigar, he gave a small nod to indicate she might proceed to do so.

"It's clear you found out today I'd mixed things up. Hadn't told you everything . . . kept you abreast, about Buckthorne." Vivian was enthusiastically accepting the occasion of his good luck as the right time to confess on favorable terms. The cool drink she held as they sat in the hot sultriness amid the debris of Nickie's easels, canvas stretchers, and paintings was not only in celebration of his election to the Presidency. It was also a toast to her own powers of management.

"Mmmmm," he said. "I'm all ears."

"I don't mean to hedge," she insisted. "I'll admit I gave you the wrong impression about his leaving town."

"You called from the office and told me he was on his way."

"Which he was! That is, he most definitely told me he was. When I agreed to water those poor plants, I certainly did so in good faith."

"But!" Nickie said. *"But!"* Even with the cigar to fix his attention on, he was getting the early twinges of nervousness that had stirred him when he heard Buckthorne's voice and thought it was coming over the long wires from Idaho. "But *still . . . !"*

Vivian waved his emphasis aside good-naturedly. She was enjoying this much too much.

"Get to the point," he growled. "I know he made you, didn't he?"

She smiled and twinkled her eyes above the rim of her glass. Then she sniffed loudly and resumed.

"I went down there that evening and got off the subway in good faith and walked up First Avenue still assuming that I wouldn't find anybody home. And, to tell the truth, I was just a teeny bit thrilled about seeing the apartment. I mean compared to this filthy hole we live in— All right, all right. Anyway, I remember thinking to myself that *after* I took care of the plants, I'd sit down among them and have a quiet cigarette all to myself. Nickie, can you understand that since I have to work all day and there's often one of *your* friends, or more, here in the evening jabbering, or at least you have something on your mind you want to jaw about, that I would welcome a chance just to be by myself?"

"Aaaaaa-ooooh!" he protested.

"I *will* get to the point. *Will* you let me tell it in my own way?"

136

He threw back his arms in a gesture of martyrdom, outrage, despair. "I'll have to, won't I?"

She went on demurely, "But when the key wasn't at the delicatessen as he had told me it would be, I didn't know what to think. I remember looking at a jar of Spanish olives and considering should I bring them home for your dinner."

"But naturally you had to go up to his door and knock to see if anything was wrong."

She nodded. "Well, certainly, after all you'd told me about how he'd come to New York dying and that nonsense."

"You found him still full of vital energy?"

She ignored the hint to speed up. She took another long, Sybaritic drink from her glass. The hue of her eyes seemed to change as brook water changes under the shadows of a cloud. "Now I'm getting to the part that you'll have to *understand*. But it's hard to understand. You will try, please, Nickie?"

"Oh God, yes," he swore sarcastically.

"Well. The minute I opened the apartment door—or rather he opened it and we looked surprised to see each other again after what had been said—and I stepped in, I was aware of this . . . this *presence*. Like a mood. That is, it wasn't him, it was the place, the apartment itself that seemed so familiar to me. And . . . acted on my emotions. How can I describe it? It just came over me, like that."

"Magic," Nickie sniffed.

"Exactly. Or no, *not* exactly. I'm trying my very hardest to tell the exact truth and you keep interrupting me. Will you let me use my own words, please?"

He made a silent sign.

She said, "I'm trying to reconstruct exactly as it was the way this mood came over me, because what happened later was absolutely because of . . . came out of . . . *evolved from*

137

this mood. And then besides you interrupting me it's hard for me to look back and separate what I felt from what he added later by talking about Miss Brule and the apartment.

"You do know he's moved into this apartment owned by a woman who's gone to Mexico. He's looked at her photographs and her books and—I don't know—maybe read her letters. And it's as if he believed she was *there*. That is, he's got this very intense personal relationship with her. That's all he would talk about, but—I mean it isn't all he talked about, even that first night, he talked about me—but when he talked about him and her he was bearing down harder than when he talked about anything else."

"Bearing down!" Nickie exclaimed. Unable to control his impatience anymore he dropped to the floor, rolled on his back, and began threshing around.

"What are you trying to illustrate? I'm trying to make clear to you that this was essentially a psychic thing between us. Or among us. Oh. And the weirdest things he had to say about the apartment of course weren't said that first night, but after Cynthia moved in with him. When I went back there *after* the first night—and as you found out today, I *did* go back to visit with them on those evenings I lied to you about watering the plants, which they were by then watering, of course—the three of us would mostly think and talk about Miss Brule and how she could possibly *actio in distans* this way on Rodney."

"Rodney!"

"Like we were actually conjuring up her presence. Not that we performed any magic rites or anything silly."

"You screwed!"

Even this failed to break the train of her recaptured trance of memory. "As you've insisted to me ever since we were all at Vistular, Rodney can be very . . . almost compulsive. He makes you believe in what he believes in. That's it. That's

138

his secret, I guess. And what you must understand is that something really has happened in that apartment to change him. He doesn't talk like an ordinary man. *Over there* he's not as silly and academic and fish-out-of-water as he was the night at our party when I just felt sorry for him."

"He's flipped."

"Maybe you can call it that. I can't tell from minute to minute what you want the truth about him to be. But what I meant to say is he's like a priest. A priest to Miss Brule. It's not mumbo-jumbo, but he finds a way to link her in with everything he says. 'There are ways of communicating, as Miss Brule knows, which we don't ordinarily take much stock in.' He said that. It's true. You may not see it. Cynthia knows what I'm talking about."

"To the point!"

"Screwing's not the point! But all right. Let me start at the beginning, about how I felt when I first walked in expecting to water the plants and come home. But get me a fresh drink, please. You need another, too."

When he returned from their kitchen with the tall, icy drinks clattering nervously in his hands, Vivian was curled up like a kitten happy in its dreamy recollections. He thought of choking her to make her spit out the facts, the facts, the facts. Only if he throttled her right now, he would never in this world be sure what his motive had been.

She chortled, "Almost the first thing he said to me when I came in was 'I was told to stay.' I didn't understand whether you'd got ahold of him and persuaded him to stay or who had. He explained it was Miss Brule told him to stay and 'see it through.' And of course I didn't know Miss Brule then. So it occurred to me, for a while, that as you said a while ago, he had flipped.

"Afterward, not. Being in the apartment while I heard these

139

admittedly farfetched ideas had something to do with believing them—like being in church with the music and all that has something to do with whether you believe the mumbo-jumbo Jesus stuff. Even you'll admit that. It was like taking off your shoes and going into a shrine."

Nickie pounced like a fox. *"What* was like taking your shoes off?"

"So it's hard to explain, sitting here in another place in broad daylight, just as you wouldn't believe me here if I tried to tell you what I'd thought during a sermon on the Resurrection. But I've done my best to explain. Do you understand?"

It took Nickie a full three minutes to understand that, as far as she was concerned, her confession was fully made. Finished.

He pondered this *fait accompli.* Then he reared forward to his haunches and snarled, "What *happened?"*

"I *told* you!"

"You didn't tell nothing."

"Oh." Her tone was firmly incredulous—as though it just wouldn't occur to her that he would want her to describe the crude and physical part. "Well," she said, "as you know, Cynthia has been there all the time after . . . well, after I spent Monday evening there."

"I mean before Cynthia showed up."

"Don't *shout.* I've *told* you I was there more than an hour Monday evening when I'd thought I'd have to water the plants, because, however you feel about a person, and whether I believe in her the way Buckthorne does or not, I wouldn't want the plants she's raised so carefully to burn up in this heat."

"Sweetheart!" he said with extravagant patience. "I believe you when you say this Cynthia bird arrived on Tuesday. That she is now domiciled with or on our friend. That in her pres-

ence you merely sat around by candlelight and said how Lady
Brule communicates extrasensory messages. *Okay*. But you
start out by saying it is your devout wish to tell me the truth
and you don't even mention the events of Monday evening."

"Oh." Vivian curled even tighter in her chair. She no
longer seemed to be drifting away in a trance. She was wide
awake to the present, rather visibly weighing the alternatives
left open to her for dodging. "You mean, d'he kissme, feel
m'up, 'dress me? That sort of thing?"

"I mean he certainly laid you at least on Monday night and
why'n the hell you been telling me you were watering flowers
these other nights?"

He was foiled by the vehemence of his accusations. "Only
once!" she countered with bright, almost merry triumph at
his mistake. And then, as if she were too charitable and fond
to enjoy a triumph at his expense, she said, "Nickie, you
mustn't feel bad about that! It wasn't like what I suppose you
think. You seem to suspect he's a sort of superman, and I
didn't have that impression at all. To tell the truth, it wasn't
like . . . being with a man. I mean, it was but it wasn't. If
you'd grasped it when I told you how important the mood of
the place was, you'd know it wasn't like being unfaithful to
you. In that sense. It was more like he said . . . doing what
Miss Brule let us do. It was like being hypnotized by her,
and that's all I really can say."

"Buckthorne hypnotized you?"

"No."

"He didn't hypnotize you? You just let him . . . ."

"I said *she* hypnotized me."

Nickie rotated his head slowly as if to purge it of confusion
and keep his impure thoughts straight. "Hypnotized? I'll accept whatever name you want to call it. But honest to God
I get more and more curious about this wizard. Maris
wouldn't tell me. You won't tell me, or you haven't yet. I

141

mean, what's he *got* that can make ordinary insensitive women go around afterward claiming they were hypnotized?"

Now Vivian saw an opportunity for counterattack. "Got? Because you've got a dirty mind, you don't need to think I'm going to sit in my own house—my own living room!—and discuss the size of his dong," she said.

And there the interrogation halted.

For the time it took Nickie to admit to himself that he had been outmaneuvered, he sat humped in rigid silence. His mind whirled like a clumsy dog unable to sink its teeth in a nimble, tantalizing vixen.

And then, in the silence of her victorious frowning, a great hunger seemed to engulf him. It was all around him at first, like sound or scent or light. Gradually it began to settle in his belly.

"Let's go out and get a *good* meal. Drinks. We'll celebrate."

He might have missed a trick just now, but other pleasures beckoned. He would find some friends tonight and electrify them with prophecies of the big money about to roll in.

12

Reality as Fine Art and Entertainment

Truth is a salami we slice according to our taste and appetite. The morsel of it which Vivian slipped her husband was not sliced on the same axis as what she kept for herself.

To begin with, the "mood" to which she had chiefly attributed her lapse from marital fidelity had been by no means so singular and consistent in quality as it appeared in her confessional account of it. There had been a succession of moods, some jarring in contrast, some composed of incongruous ingredients, which finally blurred together in retrospect.

Part of the mood, of course, had been supplied by R. Buckthorne and T. Brule. But even as she had ridden the subway down to the Canal Street stop that first evening Vivian had been making her own moody contribution. She was thinking of Buckthorne and Lois Capehart in an odd mixture of envy, disapproval, and plain curiosity. Willy-nilly she had been competing with Lois for Buckthorne's interest the night of their party. She was just barely conscious of resentment that the rules had permitted Lois to win that competition by default.

Then, when Vivian had actually come into the apartment, the mood—of strangeness, or disorientation—had been mostly created by the deafening roar of diesel engines as the trucks flocked home to the rental garage across the street. The noise made ordinary verbal communication impossible for a while. "It sounds like a mule barn struck by a tornado," she had said, and of course the words hadn't got to Buckthorne's ears. But the sense had. He had smiled so sweetly, so appreciatively, so yearningly in response to her joke that she gave up her bit of resentment against him for having to do with Miss Capehart.

They began to communicate by signs and shrieks. Like two cave people. Pointing. You still here? Shrug. As you see. . . . Water plants? You? Me?

Please, you do it.

The rupture of normal communication in words had made the ritual of watering the plants into something theatrical, make-believe. Their childhood was given back. They were ageless. Grave octogenarians enacting vanished years in the senile uproar of a nursing home. Naughty children dressed in mommadaddy clothes, left alone in the house while studs and jennies bellowed from the barnyard.

Then—still more theatrical—the afternoon light had gone quickly dim as dark clouds moved in over the island from the East River.

In wordless pantomime Rodney offered her wine. She thanked him with a blushing curtsy. They sat down together at the stage-prop café table in the studio among the freshly watered plants, and smelled the rain coming up their street. Then, just as she raised the glass to her lips, just as glass and liquid met the sensory buds of her tongue, there was a god-

144

awful burst of thunder, a white dazzle of lightning, and the swishing roar of rain loud enough to drown the mechanical sound of the trucks.

"Coup de théâtre!" Buckthorne shouted, no doubt already trying to explain to her that Miss Brule was capable of all kinds of such effects here in her enchanted apartment. But Vivian couldn't get what he meant . . . precisely because the thunder and lightning had been so downright theatrically successful. An instant before she had been wondering how long the rain might keep her from starting home. After the stunning noise and flash, she just quit thinking about home. She quit thinking about home the way you do when you're *there*.

Later in the week—and this was a highly special, really inexplicable part of the "mood" in which she had either sinned or not sinned and in any case had done what she had to—she had come to think she always knew what Rodney was going to say before he said it. Right now, while the torrents of rain flowed white as surf down Miss Brule's studio windows, she knew what he was going to do next.

He was going to half-kneel in front of her and unbutton her blouse. She didn't even think of stopping him.

When he unfastened and gently lifted away her brassiere, he stepped back and put his hand on his heart. He said something in Greek.

(On another day—in Cynthia's presence as a matter of fact—she asked him to translate what he had said to and about her. He did, and told her it was a Spartan salute to the girl athletes at the funeral games. "I knew it," she said. And in some sense she had, though she didn't know a word of Greek, not to mention the difficulties of hearing anything while the truck engines were roaring and the rain was so loud.)

And that was all that happened that Monday evening, in spite of what Nickie might think. (In spite of what Nickie might have been cunningly led to think.) The poor, sweet man just stood before her in a pose of adoration, adoring the sight of her breasts. She supposed she did have good breasts. Boys had told her so. But she had never felt anything like the disquieting and finally unbearable pride in them that rose and throbbed in her as Buckthorne fed his eyes on their rose and white.

She could feel something begin to happen the way it never happened with Nickie or the other two boys before marriage, and to keep it from happening she'd *shouted,* "Paint me sometime, huh?" Pretending he was just taking aesthetic pleasure, as an artist would, from looking at her.

Then she'd put on her bra and blouse, and he hadn't prevented her from doing that by even a gesture. As if he was all through, and they both knew it. As if he'd taken her as no one else ever had.

And she supposed he had. Anyhow, when her lunch hour came the next day, she hailed a cab and bullied the driver to hurry all the way down to the crappy block on First Avenue. She meant to explain to old Rodney what she'd meant when she asked him to paint her.

Once—and it was the second most thrilling thing that had happened to her since marriage—Nickie had been fooling around with his paints on a Sunday afternoon. He'd coaxed her into stripping and lying on their dirty floor. Then, with his tickly brush and burny, turpentine-thinned paints, he'd painted her torso into the likeness of a big face. Put eyebrows above her breasts and that sort of thing. When he finished painting—barking laughter all the time—he'd given her a quick "treatment" as he annoyingly called it.

That diversion of a Sunday afternoon had excited her wildly. It also left her feeling degraded and puzzled. While it opened a glimpse of new horizons for their marriage, it didn't seem *the right thing for a husband to do if he respected*

146

his wife. Conversely, it just wasn't right for a responsible wife to suggest the repetition of such a venture to a husband who already showed plenty of signs of mental unbalance.

But in the all-permissive atmosphere of Miss Brule's hideaway—where strange things had already taken place, you bet—why couldn't she suggest lightly that many-talented old Buckthorne paint her like a Greek decorating an urn? Give her the freedom she needed to be herself by transforming her into a *thing,* a nicely decorated thing.

She was thinking about her color scheme as she trotted up the one flight of stairs to the peephole on Rodney's door.

Considering the abandonment of *that* mood, it was a wonder she wasn't crushed to find that Cynthia Trebogen had flown in from Vistular and moved in with Buckthorne since the previous evening. Cynthia, looking dewy-eyed and relaxed as if she'd already been oriented into the rites and mysteries of the apartment.

Vivian rebounded in an exactly opposite fashion. Heartily she chose to be glad that Cynthia's presence saved her from what might have been a first-class disaster. She became, instantly, Cynthia's best friend, and a sort of benevolent counselor to the pair of them.

On her daily visits after that she was positively auntly in her solicitude. She—the older, married woman—offered practical sympathy when Cynthia expressed her intention of "finding something creative to do" in the wonder world of Manhattan. In fact, it was as much for Cynthia's sake as for Nickie's that Vivian began to discuss with Rodney whether there wasn't, after all, some chance that they might make a "going thing" of Nickie's art center—which, should it go, would *need* to hire Cynthia and girls like her.

Vivian lied enough about Nickie's encounter with Regina Travers to persuade Buckthorne that he might—to everyone's

147

advantage—renew the friendship broken off eighteen (!) years ago in Los Angeles. He called the lady one evening while hushed Cynthia and hushed Vivian sat with him among fern and avocado. The expressions on his face assured them he had not met with total rebuff from that dragonish lady.

Between them, too, they quieted Buckthorne's doubts about accepting employment on the television commercials for Napa-Barca spaghetti. One evening when she stopped there after work, Vivian found Cynthia alone, and was told that on this day the absent lover, priest, and father figure had gone to a Long Island studio to commence the filming of the series.

"But he's not out there now," Cynthia said, just a bit tragically.

"No?"

"He phoned that he had to see a Miss Capehart for drinks after work. She's the one who got him the job."

"I know."

"I think . . . she expects something of him," Cynthia said.

Vivian felt like crying, but she said, "I wouldn't worry. I'm sure he doesn't really care a thing about her. I know her, you see, and she's a very cynical person."

"Oh, I'm not worried for *my* sake. I don't intend to stay with him very long. I know he's not for me, and as soon as I get the right kind of job I'll get an apartment of my own. But he was so tired the other morning after he'd stayed with Miss Travers. He felt giddy around the heart, and he's not a boy."

"Mmmmm. Well, can't we— I mean, shouldn't we leave it up to him to decide what he wants to . . . when he wants to—"

"I always do," Cynthia insisted.

They were then, the three of them, practical in their view of the association into which they had fallen. Clearly there were more than practical motives at work in the other world Miss Brule provided for them.

Vivian was in love. Not with Rodney Buckthorne, of course, she told herself. He was just one of the snow-white dwarves who acted out the fantastic fairy tale of the week for her. She could also manage by categorizing him as the amusing old professor fleeing from a stodgy wife and amusing himself with a student girlfriend.

She was in love . . . with a nameless strangeness to which her woman's body and soul responded like smoldering paper in the rushing updraft of a chimney. Rodney had adored her naked breasts, and that wasn't quite *it* . . . wasn't quite the adequate visual equivalent of what she felt had happened to her. She had wanted him to paint her body like a barberpole. And that bit of perversity had been fortunately avoided. She was waiting to be told or shown some sign that would still her restlessness in face of these new feelings.

On Sunday afternoon—when Nickie might have said he'd trot along with her if she had said she was going to Miss Brule's to water plants—she had taken her guitar out, on the excuse that she was going to the Square to sit with the other folk-singers.

"It's going to rain again," Nickie said as she left.

"Then I may not be back for a while," she said.

In just ten minutes, a little short of breath, she presented her flushed face to the peephole in Buckthorne's door. With more time to themselves this afternoon, she felt that the three of them would surely "talk it out."

And so, very shortly after her arrival, she plunged the great question out into the open before Buckthorne and Cynthia. "Isn't it odd that we three, *of all people,* should get along so easily?" This was the first time she had hinted—even so delicately—in Cynthia's presence that something had happened between her and Buckthorne before Cynthia arrived.

149

Cynthia didn't seem to miss the hint. She accommodated it calmly. Rather wonderfully. "That's not strange at all. It's natural."

"Well, it seems—" Vivian said doggedly.

"I know it seems—" Cynthia agreed.

The great voice of summer thunder roared up First Avenue into the stillness. There were no trucks thundering today.

A monstrous glare of lightning (as on the fateful Monday evening before Cynthia came) lit up the apartment and left it dimmer than before. The sound of rain came suggestively into their communication.

From nowhere, Rodney Buckthorne produced a new white candle and lighted it in the middle of the café table over which they leaned.

"My feeling is," Cynthia said, leaning farther toward the light. "My feeling is that Rodney—being associated with him and knowing him as I have—being one who is close to him— he's purified me of this *cant* and this *hypocrisy* and this social *guff* that most people live by. If we three get along well it's because we care for each other as people, not as . . . well, as breadwinners or clotheshorses or somebody who might get us a job. Rodney has taught me to understand that."

Rodney, hearing himself thus characterized, shuffled his feet in the whooshing rain sound. His voice, when he spoke, was again different from any of the voices Vivian had ever heard him use. (Didn't he have a voice of his own at all, she wondered, as everyone else has?) Now the voice he borrowed was quiet, strong, passionate but very, very cool, so she *wanted* to think this was his real voice at last—only with him, how could you be sure?

"No," he said to Cynthia, "I haven't taught you anything, though I believe you have learned from me what you say you have learned.

"There are two of me. There is the *I* who might wish with

150

all my heart to teach what I have learned and what I believe. There is, also, the *I* from whom you learn. . . . You learn what you want to learn, what you already, in some unfocused way, believe. This second *I* is only a point of focus for what is not, properly speaking, mine at all. For the potentialities of your own nature.

"I will not argue, dearest Cynthia, that you could have learned from 'just anyone' the things you suppose you have learned from me. Indeed I have a unique place in the time of your life, and perhaps no other living man could have served you as you learned what you had secretly and subconsciously made up your mind to know.

"Consider the image of me that is about to be released in television commercials—"

"I'm dying to see one," Cynthia said, "aren't you, Vivian?"

She was, but, strangely, she was more eager yet to hear what she knew he had to say next.

"At last it's been proved—to my satisfaction—that there's *something* in the electronic world that atomizes Rodney Buckthorne and recomposes him *for purposes of its own*. We shall see, perhaps, what these extrahuman purposes are. Perhaps not.

"But that is mere illustration. I would insist to you that you are both recomposing me for what you need of me—and that in doing so here you have been willy-nilly involved in a set of influences that neither begins nor stops with me. While you listened to me tell how Miss Brule has worked on my imagination—or how my imagination worked on her; there is no great difference—you have exposed to yourselves certain primal layers of your own personality that would otherwise have remained dormant.

"Is Miss Brule with us now? We may well say she is. And in some ways her presence is more clear to us when the lightning flashes and the thunder rolls than at other times.

151

Because by our wishes and our imagination we *take* the lightning and thunder to be a sign from her.

"It can still be argued, though I don't believe it, that I came to this apartment by accident. I don't yet grasp the purpose of that accident, but I am beginning to believe it was one of that special category of accidents like birth—the recapitulation in my late middle age of the chance convergence of material elements in time which once before made an infant Buckthorne.

"Is that all fancy? Do not underestimate the importance of fancy! I am making here the last bid of my life to grasp what I was put on earth to grasp. By playing imaginatively—metaphorically—with the *ontic* Miss Brule, I have been trying to grasp the greatest of all mysteries, the reification of a spiritual personality. When is it permissible and when is it folly to consider a person a something? How do we separate the dead or the absent from the continuation of their influences? How do we separate their influences from the physical and erotic body?

"You insist, Cynthia, that I have taught you thus and so. How is that different from my saying that Miss Brule has not only taught me things but has made certain actions thereby imperative—or, in simple words, tells me to do things?"

Well, yes. Yes indeed Rodney Buckthorne must have been right when he said the thunder and lightning outside were accidents of nature.

Yes, but. . . . *Right now* they came again; the vast drum of thunder exactly following his question. And as its echoes were washed away in the sound of rain, a splendid, awful, convulsive thrill began in Vivian's womb. (She was sure it was in her womb, though she had never had any sensation which exactly located that organ before, not even menstrual cramps, which seemed like something crosswise in the gut.) The thrill moved outward from her center until, in her ear, it

152

seemed to meet and combine—as a child's lips touch their reflection in a mirror—with the thrill of the voice speaking to her.

The fatherly voice went on: "We—or let me speak for myself—*I* make Miss Brule real in this apartment in order to have some source for what I know—because we have to believe in sources to believe in knowledge, though what we know may be, of course, more important than its source.

"So I have made up—or *reified,* to use that pedantic word —Miss Brule out of the traces of her I found left behind when she left behind the beggarly habiliment of this dwelling. I made her up so I would have a source for the intimation that came to me last winter in Idaho.

"Now I believe—I truly believe, even if it is madness— that *she* came in an ice storm to tell me things are running out faster than any rational measure of the world can show. She told me 'Man is dead' and the period for his resurrection is going fast.

"The great structure of reality is collapsing without Man to hold it up. Against this terrible bleeding of the universe, there is only one course of opposition—the erotic. One takes this course, not in the hope of breeding some new Adam who will survive the holocaust that is upon us—therein I was wrong, dearest Cynthia; therein I betrayed my living son into starless chaos—but because it will perpetuate a little longer the spirit that might again, by Grace, be rekindled: the spirit of Man."

"That's true," Cynthia said.

"Hush," said Vivian.

"That is what Miss Brule continues to suggest to me. I am sorry that I can't interpret it more clearly. Though I have had considerable experience with . . . the flesh . . . I have, none-theless, been essentially a political man. I would like to know, and perhaps I will yet know, if Miss Brule intends her message to be understood in political terms, whether she is trying to warn me against unprecedented upheavals and disasters of war."

"So you could warn them at the United Nations!" Cynthia breathed ecstatically. Vivian pinched her for the interruption.

"I don't know about that," Rodney said. "Yet I have made up my mind to trust her and do what she asks. And to the extent that I have trusted her thus far, she has unfailingly sent the means by which I could understand her better. For instance, though she is not present here to serve me as a woman can, yet she has provided the flesh of woman here to help me toward understanding."

"Yes, yes," Cynthia breathed. Her whisper was hardly audible above the onrush of the rain.

Buckthorne said—or Miss Brule made him say (Vivian was beyond quibbling about that distinction)—"It's always been known to me, though I never dared phrase it so before I came to this apartment, not even to myself, that it is the destiny of erotic man to search for his certainties in that, so to speak, magnetic field of the *cunt*—"

Right with the enunciation of that magical word, the rain stopped.

It didn't stop with the magnificent definiteness of its beginning. It stopped without theatrical effect. It began to dwindle, to leak, to pause, to withdraw. . . .

And in the same queasy, halfhearted way, a meeching sort of Sunday light crept down the Avenue and into the apartment. Vivian pulled her guitar from the floor up into her lap and huddled over the strings, thinking of something sad to play and sing.

The three of them looked at each other with a kind of shame, as if they were all ready to burst into uneasy giggles. As if what they had just known together could not stand the light of day.

154

Yet there was a kind of hungering that still bound them each to each, like the unseemly ligatures that tie Siamese siblings. They still wanted to believe the outrageous words that had been spoken.

The sound of human traffic came from the Avenue. They hated it.

Cynthia said, "Yes, but Rodney, I don't see how talking about wars and men dying helps anything. Maybe we ought to picket."

Vivian said shakily, "I mean, even if everything's going to hell faster than they will admit. We still. . . . There's something that holds us three *up*. Miss Brule or whatyoumaycallit. That's not just a gag, is it?" She struck a sad little discord from her guitar. She snuffed out the candle on the table. The poor thing seemed mocked. She put it out as an act of mercy.

And there they sat. Hangdog. Silent. Beaten. Surrounded by a city that meant to grind them like corn.

Then they said:

"Let's—"

"—all—"

"—three—"

Without further words they rose from their chairs. Like rehearsed performers they went into the stage-set bedroom.

Cynthia stood on one side of the bed and pulled her dress over her head.

Vivian stood on the other side and unzipped her skirt.

Shy Rodney turned his back at the foot of the bed while he dropped his trousers.

Oh my God, Vivian thought, *it's the very middle of the month and my diaphragm's at home on the shelf so Nickie won't get suspicious. But with two of us, it will at least be like Russian roulette.*

Then she thought, *If it happens it will be the words in my ear that did it.*

155

13

The Pronouncement of Dr. Bose

The philosophic man might well be grateful to Miss Brule for providing him with haven, material, and sanction for his alchemic studies. The man of flesh and bone—who had all his life been an admitted hypochondriac, who suffered his attacks of hysteria from scalp to toe—grew daily more terrified of what she now seemed to demand of him. He understood in his bones what had sent de Maupassant to an untimely grave. Flesh and bone of an aging man were not meant to satisfy the requirements of so many devoted girls.

Day by day Miss Brule's commands were wearing him out physically, and when exhaustion came to a peak the woman sent him an awful dream.

It came—airmail from Mexico, so to speak, or maybe on electronic beams from wherever Miss Brule was vacationing this summer—the morning after Cynthia moved out into an

156

apartment of her own. The first night he had slept alone for a long time.

It began with a distorted reenactment of the party at the Duarts'. Instead of being in their railroad flat, he was presiding over a company of young artists and Bohemians in a subterranean nightclub, a sort of cave. Once again they were hanging on his words. *"Unum pro multis dabitur caput,"* he said. They laughed and applauded. They began to light candles from the one that stood painfully in front of him.

Then, outside, in the labyrinthine passage of the tunnel that connected this nightclub with the street, there was a vile disturbance. The muffled sound of shots. The voice of Lois Capehart shrieked, "The husbands have come!"

Her cry, plus his constant *noblesse oblige,* required Rodney, Lord Buckthorne, Protector of Youth and Laudator of Womanhood, to run and meet the threat in the tunnel.

At its remote end he saw *The Devastator.* (The creature's honorific title was known to him without sound or printed caption, in the odd fashion of dreams.) The Devastator was a south-of-the-border figure in burnished silver bas-relief on a black background like that in Miss Brule's jesting "Self-portrait." It was a figure that might have been dug up from a Mexican tomb, with a pre-Columbian skull. Antique, but not in the humanized fashion of Mediterranean antiquity. An utterly American figure of death.

A figure nattily togged out, nevertheless, in a Hollywood version of what the well-armed *vaquero* would wear when bent on vengeance.

The Devastator was understood to be the idol that Miss Brule went looking for when she told her renters she was "vacationing." Her swarthy lovers had helped her find him. Now she was turning him loose in home pastures.

His pistol-packing henchmen crowded the tunnel like train robbers stripping valuables from the passengers who shrieked

157

as they tried to get out. One of the henchmen—a spectacularly short *pistolero,* hardly more than a midget—swirled his holstered guns against Rodney's thighs, looked up into his face, and said, "Is no Juan."

Buckthorne tried to insist he had tried. Recent statistics could be offered.

"You ain't love America," the gunman said.

"Oh, I have!" His voice was thin as an exhausted girl's.

"Wull, you ain't love her enough."

He wanted to hold up his fingers and count off the number of American girls he had made love to right here in this city since he started with Lois Capehart so many beds ago. But he had no fingers and his arms were bound with an odorous, gossamer filament.

He heard his mother's voice, like a night shriek warning him, "Give all to love, Rodney. Give *all* to love." As if beyond the grave she knew what alone would placate the dreadful figure of black and silver.

No wonder he woke in terror, reaching out for Cynthia. Who was gone.

The noise of the trucks had begun. Strangely that pleased him for once. Without that much of the commonplace, his fast-pounding heart would have revved up to an unbearable pace, and he would have had to listen to it.

When he tried to stand beside the bed, the furniture and green plants of the studio spun and melted before his eyes. He could only stay upright by locking his knees, so his walk to the bathroom was the stumbling of a robot. He had said to the girls—oh, grandiose phrase!—that "Man is dead." This was what it would be like to be dead and still committed to walking around like life.

I drank too much last night, he told himself savagely. He had drunk very little. Had gone early to bed after returning

158

from the cab ride that moved Cynthia's suitcase to her new room on Sixteenth Street.

He could not find his penis. The dream and the terror of waking had shriveled it out of sight in his gray hair.

I've got to find a doctor, he yelled soundlessly. *He's got to tell me to give up women.*

So he came to Dr. Bose.

But first he had found the name of a doctor carefully printed in pencil on the wood of the shelf where Miss Brule's telephone sat. He had never noticed it before, and it quieted him somewhat to think that once again Miss Brule was providing him what he needed when he needed it. Dr. Chalmers.

But of course Dr. Chalmers had not arrived at his office at that hour. The instructions of the answering service as to how he could be reached in psychosexual emergency were unintelligible under the bass uproar of trucks starting out from the rental garage. So Buckthorne decided he would walk to that doctor's address on Fifth Avenue—decided he *could* walk that far on his own power.

The long stroll up across Houston Street and over to Washington Square was beneficial to his mental equilibrium. The morning bustle of the city was pushing the bad dream back down into the dark of the unconsciousness where it belonged. He was, he assured himself, still able to solve his problem as he chose. To be sure he had nearly exhausted himself in a binge of sexual overextension. The remedy was simple: Rest. Withdraw from the situation as he had withdrawn himself from Idaho.

A droll self-appraisal had purified his mood as he began to cross Washington Square from the southeast. But there he encountered the signs.

The first was chalked on the sidewalk near the iron-fenced playground:

EAT WHAT YOU KILL.

This was clearly addressed to President Johnson and had to do with the war in Vietnam.

But the second, he could not help thinking, had been chalked there for him:

STOP SPRINTING.

Someone—no more and no less reified than his Miss Brule —was giving him this advice and command.

Yes, he said. *I must and I shall!*

He walked more slowly, therefore, determining to keep himself to himself in spite of *reasons* that Cynthia, Vivian, Lois, Regina, and the others might advance.

And in his leisure he looked up at the great gray arch and saw Washington's advice and command to him:

LET US RAISE A STANDARD.

Yes and no. A man ought to raise a standard, but not all the time. There were moments when he ought to keep the standard in his pants, George. Yet, the authority was impressive.

And then, between good humor, wit, and abject terror, he saw the message scrawled in pink chalk twenty feet above the base of the arch:

YOU ARE BEING SCREWED TO DEATH.

When he lifted his eyes and saw these words, his heart went CUK-UH-cuk-cuk. . . . Cuk-CUK. Very much like the rhythm that rowdy boys beat out on an automobile horn. A jeering rhythm indeed.

He stopped stone still, a smile tugging at his mustache, and bowed to a young mother with a stroller, who seemed to be peering at him worriedly.

Then he started to run.

Then he remembered he mustn't sprint.

He went at a jogtrot up Fifth Avenue until he came to

the stone building where five brass plaques announced the doctors' offices on the interior: Dr. Chalmers, Dr. Stein, Dr. Hasselfand, Dr. Bose, and Dr. Tottel. He went into the lobby and began ringing their bells in rotation.

It happened to be Dr. Bose's receptionist who answered and met him in the carpeted hall. She was a brown-skinned girl in a stunningly white uniform. She did not seem surprised to see him here without an appointment. He seemed to be, if not expected, at least accepted matter-of-factly by the girl and her employer, Dr. Bose.

Dr. Bose was in miniature. When he sat at his desk in the consulting room only his shoulders and head rose above its top. He, like his receptionist, was a dark-skinned child of the Ganges, by the way of a continental medical school. His incredibly white teeth were those of a five-year-old boy addicted to thumb-sucking. His full-size glasses stood up on either side of his nose like embroidery hoops.

About him there was an air of total imposture. He seemed no more, though no less, real than the ominous *vaqueros* of Rodney's dream. Very soon it seemed that his selection by chance was but another in the chain of purposeful coincidences begun with the discovery of the ad for Miss Brule's apartment.

And from the beginning of his examination it was certain that he would offer no genuine alternative to Buckthorne's predicament. He listened to complaints of heart palpitation, sweating, and vertigo as if listening to a prayer in a foreign tongue.

Then he said, "You have been drinking more heavy?"

"Actually not. My quantitative consumption has been rather less than more than I am accustomed to, though perhaps in such matters where the physical metabolism is so mysteriously involved with the psychic exploitation of oxidating processes, one might guess that the body has been

161

drawing more heavily on the volume actually ingested—" He stopped in the face of Dr. Bose's doubtful smile.

"You are a smoker!" Dr. Bose said, with a flashing certainty. Americans who did not drink too much smoked too much.

"Yes, I smoke. Though moderately. Seldom as much as a full pack in a day, with a small cigar—those little ones that are called cigarilloes, I believe—after dinner. But, as I tried to indicate—"

"Do not smoke!" said Dr. Bose.

There was no use going on from there to tell the little man about the girls. Rodney tried anyhow, trying to make clear—without loss of gallantry—how they had come through Miss Brule's in a procession, like generations following each other . . . and Lois begat Vivian, and Vivian begat Cynthia, and Cynthia begat Regina, and . . . every female had brought forth a progeny of reasons for going on to the next. His desire had astonishingly little to do with the matter.

In reaction to the terror of his dream, he found himself pouring out to the little fakir the whole story of how Miss C. had graciously exploited her connections to secure him employment in the making of television commercials. Well, *not* graciously, to be quite candid about the situation, for Miss C. did everything she did for him out of resentment. She got him the job to show him that *though* she resented his lack of enthusiasm in making love to her, she *would* heap yet another obligation on him. As her resentments multiplied, the *least* he was expected to do for her was to visit her regularly in her Bedford Street apartment. On his way home from work at the Long Island television studio—where his efforts seemed appreciated, thank you—he regularly gave Miss C. further cause for resentment, though she would have resented his failures to stop there even more.

162

"Television!" said Dr. Bose in response to this overcomplicated recital.

Buckthorne then told how, dragging home from Miss C.'s, he would find awaiting him Miss T., who felt a straightforward gratitude to him not only for purging her mind of cant, hypocrisy, and social guff, but for sheltering her while she sought her own niche in the city. Miss T.'s gratitude was so expansive that she found assistance in expressing it. First her help came from Mrs. D. Later it came from a collegiate chum, Miss Linda Louise S., en route to Europe for a year of linguistic study on a Fulbright grant.

"Study in Europe!" marveled Dr. Bose.

Buckthorne told how Mrs. D., taking upon herself the ticklish role of go-between in an enterprise set afoot by her husband and supported by Dr. Buckthorne for altruistic reasons, conveyed in person the proposal that the solicitation of funds for the enterprise from a certain Mrs. P. would have to be handled "delicately" and with "personal attention"—and how she had, in the absence of Miss T., rehearsed him in what she meant by those somewhat elusive generalities.

"Funds for culture!" Dr. Bose breathed.

How Miss Regina T. (formerly Mrs. Harold D. of Los Angeles) had put him under obligation, first by supplying an important contact in the enterprise he was undertaking with Mr. D. and second by causing a suitable room to be found near the glamorous confines of Greenwich Village for Miss T. Had compounded the obligation by drawing on his sympathy as a very old acquaintance and publisher of her verse. Had called on him to express pity for the unkindness of the passing years, which had made her a "mean, alcoholic, hateful bitch."

"Alcohol!" Dr. Bose said disapprovingly.

But he had no comment at all to make on the tally of women. If that was a health problem, he had never heard of

163

it. At the end of the count he only repeated his admonition, "Do not smoke!" The wisdom of the East was pronouncing on the flaw at the heart of American life.

"I will prescribe for you," Dr. Bose said. "Something to make it easier for you to discontinue." He stood up, indicating an end of his professional interest. His infant smile was a signal of their inability to communicate.

For a minute Buckthorne felt close to grabbing the midget throat and demanding a strong medical or even surgical remedy for the obvious threat to his health. Perhaps he was close to a weeping fit in which he would demand a psychiatric reference. He could be locked up out of harm's way.

This tiny alien was sending him back out into the city to die. He was not so much counteracting the morning's dream message from Miss Brule as confirming it.

But, as Buckthorne rose angrily from his chair, he saw his reflection in the doctor's glasses. It broadened and heightened until it had gone beyond their rims, like the porridge in the fairy tale, overflowing the possibility of belief.

Then, in exotic tones where traces of Oxford and the Sorbonne, too, mingled with the Oriental, the little man said the one necessary word about Buckthorne's feats.

"Unbelievable!"

Buckthorne's rebellion and fear were gone. Over all the obstacles of communication, it had been understood that he was a hero.

Outside, in the splendid rage of Fifth Avenue sunlight, Buckthorne felt his heart beat like a twelve-pound sledge on a steel anvil. He turned to face uptown, as once Ulysses Grant had turned his shot-thinned army *south* from the Wilderness, while a ragged cheer went up from the ranks. The battle indecisive, the hero chose to call it victory.

The glory of Manhattan's leaves, the glory of towering

buildings and flagged avenues, the glory of men and women moving freely on the *trottoirs* . . . all at once they belonged to the weary conqueror.

All around him passersby were smiling as if in congratulation to him, confirming his role as their scapegoat and the envied hero of their frustrations. The city rushed to meet him like his own image broadening as he approached a mirror. His time at Miss Brule's had been like a night sea voyage which had brought him ashore in his own kingdom.

"I am screwing myself to death," he said in a small wondering voice. That was no longer a horror, but a marvel. Wonderful, wonderful, and yet again wonderful that the Founding Fathers and the Sustaining Sons of the republic had preserved this privilege for him while so much else was lost.

"Sic semper," he said.

14

The Camels Looking for
a Needle's Eye in a Haystack

Nothing upset Andrea Pellew as much as giving money away. The next most distressing thing was being asked to give money. And of course she was always being asked to give. Each morning at eleven, at the desk of her sunny bedroom overlooking 68th Street, she dealt with her correspondence, of which a constant percentage always had to do with the charities and philanthropies in which she and her husband were involved. (And he lived irresponsibly far away most of the time now—in London, Lisbon, Nassau, and sometimes Cairo—leaving her protected only by a few lawyers and friends like Regina Travers from the new solicitations, reports on money being handed over, money already given.)

She did not like to be reminded that they *had* to give money away, though she accepted what her husband and the lawyers told her about it. She would like to keep all their money. What was taken away seemed like a ravishment, as if little by little her garments were being whisked away. Occasionally it

166

occurred to her she would rather be like television—giving away refrigerators, cartons of potato chips, matched luggage plus a trip to Hawaii, or Honda motorbikes. This constant flow of cheap and gaudy goodies was a type of generosity that would have fulfilled her.

And now she was really in a state of extended upset over the daily calls, confusing explanations, and irritating postponements from the young man who wanted money for an art center. She vaguely remembered having met him—hadn't he told her that he *also* had been a champion baton twirler?— told her that before he showed his teeth as if he meant to bite her string of pearls? She remembered most his nasty smell and would certainly have never answered his call if Regina hadn't told her she should.

Then, after she had talked with him on the phone and made an appointment to see him and his associate, he had called back to reschedule that appointment. Then to postpone it once more, for one more day. Then daily to put it off a little more.

First Dr. Buckthorne, the associate, had flown to France for an international symposium. Then he'd been called to Washington, but only for the day. Then something here in town involving the Metropolitan Museum had claimed him for an evening when she'd been led to count on his arrival here.

This morning she had been told by Mr. Duart that—since it was Bastille Day—he feared intercultural commitments at the French embassy might keep Dr. Buckthorne from his long-awaited appointment with her.

She had laughed hollowly. Though Regina had told her Dr. Buckthorne was worth talking to, these hardly credible excuses had worn through her patience. "Perhaps we'd just better forget the whole thing," she said, and hung up before the acrobatic voice scrambled her understanding again.

167

Now, at three-thirty in the afternoon, she was drowsing over a book in her upstairs room, spicing its tediums with occasional glances at the television. She liked to have the set on while she read, because thus she could anchor her consciousness exactly halfway between the page and the screen, like a small white yacht safely placed midway between two reefs.

And she must have dozed for half an hour or so, because she woke to the sound of bowling balls and pins falling. There had been something else on the colored screen under her Signorelli cartoon when last she noticed. The falling pins sounded like the collapse of her world.

But before she could summon alertness to go change stations, something else came on.

A man in the costume of a Spanish grandee stood with his back to the camera before a big canvas on an easel. This was the painter Goya. She vaguely recognized the reclining figure on the canvas, duplicated by a leering tootsie in negligee on the couch beyond it. Goya was painting the Duchess of Alba.

And taking precious little joy in his work, it seemed. For he kept frowning and jabbing at his palette as though someone had mixed peanut butter with his geranium lake and hardly noticing how the tootsie kept wiggling her breasts out from under the cute little vest she wore.

Then—an expression of lusty inspiration crossed the furrowed brow of the artist. Goya saw . . . a heaping plate of Napa-Barca spaghetti.

"There the sonofabitch is," Nickie Duart said to his interviewer, Conway Fingersmith, as the commercial came on through snow and jagged flashes.

The two young men were watching the set Nickie had confiscated in the Monarch Hotel basement and installed in his office on the second floor of that structure.

168

"There he is, but where in the hell is living breathing Buckthorne?"

"Habeas corpus?" said Fingersmith. He had been given to understand by the subject of his interview that Buckthorne's unexplained disappearance—extended for several days now—was the only major obstacle confronting the officers and volunteer workers of the South Village Art Center. He had also heard something of the old boy's eccentricities from his friend Maris Mendelsohn, whose mentor Buckthorne had been in a place called Idaho.

"It's a pretty funny commercial, you know," Fingersmith said. "But would you categorize it *camp?* The seeping down, as it were, of camp from the high to the lowbrow media?"

He was here, interviewing Duart, because he wanted to do a feature on New York camp for the Sunday supplement of his paper in London. Maris had said, "Nickie's got some money from somewhere. That's all it took—all it took him—to bait in the swingers and weirdos from the East Village. They've moved into a fleabag near Chinatown. They've got posters out all over the Village advertising a planned happening in August. Marchers with sandwich boards in the Square. Good Humor men using bull horns. Maybe Nickie's a genius after all. No, I guess what he's doing isn't really *camp,* though having the kind of event he plans in a flophouse still crawling with derelicts maybe *is.* You might go down and have a look, anyway."

Fingersmith had come to the Monarch to find Duart dressed like Douglas MacArthur in suntans, with a corncob pipe, huge and very dark sunglasses, and a floppy general's cap covered with eagles and braid.

"Is your costume campy?"

Nickie said it was the campiest. "I have a commission from the people to reclaim these islands from the perfidious Cong."

"Islands?"

169

"Staten and Manhattan."

The general's garb was a fitting masquerade, Fingersmith reflected. Outside the windows, in doorways up and down the street, the derelicts gathered in sullen clumps to watch the coming and going of the new army, looking for all the world like bombed-out refugees watching the service troops of art take over what had been their domicile. On the marquee a huge canvas sign rippled in the summer wind:

SOUTH VILLAGE ART CENTER
End of the World Takes Place Here Aug. 15

Taken on a tour of the mad old building, Fingersmith had found it a marvel in its own way, quite unlike what he'd seen so far in the New World.

There were remarkably large ballrooms on the first and third floor, used for storage and half-filled with surrealist (and/or campy) junk. Heads of elk, bear, moose, and antelope were stacked up on tables to the ceiling among caryatid columns of scaling plaster. Canopied beds were broken over the dark wood of bars carved in a mixture of Victorian and Egyptian.

"In here," Nickie said, pointing with his swagger stick, "I'll put some of the percussionists and there'll be four projectors—one hidden, one angled up from the floor, and, up there by that moosehead, cages with naked girls letting their hair down to the floor. Stuff like that. Volunteers. Amateurs. You'd be surprised how many high school kids from Brooklyn and The Bronx we signed up one weekend night on Mac-Dougal Street. It's caught on."

There was an outdoor court at the center of the hotel—still cobwebbed with clotheslines from which pathetic underwear and shirts dangled.

"Here," the general said, "I been thinking about bringing

170

in an actual carnival. I'm in touch with an Alabama outfit that ordinarily plays the county fair circuit in the Midwest. Have you ever seen a county fair girl show?"

"Can't say so."

"Neither has anybody else in Manhattan. And of course the fuzz would—*will*—hit it. So we get fuzz in here for free. Only, I've got a plan for when they come busting in they'll see five stuffed police horses with five dummies in uniform slowly being lowered by pulley from the roof. Screams. Confusion. Stardust. You ever hear of Billy Rose?"

"Oh, indeed."

"You know people wouldn't cross the street today to watch Eleanor Holm wrestle an alligator in a goldfish tank. They're sophisticated now. We'll have what they want."

And everywhere, as the two of them walked through the building, there was the silent, resentful murmur and passage of the destitute men who had come to count on a flop here.

"What will you do with them?" Fingersmith wondered.

"Leave them here. We'll still be selling flops the night of the whizbang. Adds a note of social protest. The kids are very socially conscious. They'll like it."

Nickie had put on more than the clothes of the Pacific Hero.

His office—by designation, not by enclosure—was a group of desks in the middle of a long, shallow second-floor room that had been conceived as a Winter Garden when the Monarch was built. At the desks very young girls and long-haired boys painted signs or argued over the wording of the direct-mail ads they would give to Cynthia Trebogen for mimeographing and mailing.

(Each morning now Cynthia bucked the traffic of dispersing derelicts at the front door of the hotel, tidied part of the

171

big room, opened mail—there really was mail coming in by now, the sign of establishment—and prepared coffee before the irregulars started drifting in.)

Near Nickie's personal desk were the desks of Steve Bowden, Liveright Magnus, Sidney Garfield, and Sean Riley. These were the officers, obviously chosen with some care for racial and religious coverage. Steve Bowden had been given, as well, a suite of rooms up on the sixth floor, where he had installed a crazy percussionist named Mina. Before noon each day the whole street could hear Mina pounding her kettles and zooming her tapes (and sawing simultaneously on a bastard cello to which had been fitted the amplifier from an electric guitar).

The colored actor Magnus was much taken by Cynthia and kept quiet near her work area. Riley's friends usually brought pastrami sandwiches in the midafternoon and a great deal of beer for the strategy meetings that followed.

"With all these to help, I can't quite grasp why you need this chap Buckthorne," Fingersmith said.

"Maybe I don't," Nickie said thoughtfully. "Maybe we've got to the point where he needs me worse than I need him. He was in at the beginning. I don't want him shut out of a good thing."

That was his official position on Buckthorne by Bastille Day. Behind the dark glasses, in his private calculation, things looked a little different. There was still a chance—the way things were shaping up—that money, legit money, might be wangled.

In the meantime—while Buckthorne got himself lost—in the room just above the Winter Garden, Nickie's legal partner sat, an expressionless young man named Arentino, supplied as promised by Mr. Diascoli. Arentino was there every day, sitting patiently by the window, presumably watching the comings and goings of the new crowd of juveniles in the

172

street. Occasionally he passed Nickie some money without comment.

So far that money had amounted to exactly seven one-hundred-dollar bills. The rest of the operation was run on noise and promise. Cynthia was taking fifty a week. Typewriter and mimeograph rental, sign material, and paper had swallowed most of the rest of the cash.

Arentino had listened impassively when Nickie and Liveright Magnus proposed a budget for "The End of the World." A crew had to be hired to recondition the bar in the basement. A couple of bands had to be signed up. There was lighting for the court, an advance to the carnival company. Arrangements for the sale of liquor. Big money.

Arentino merely said, "You tell me all your ideas. You tell me what you need."

"Money."

Arentino shook his head. "You tell me what you need. We'll maybe get it for you if it's a good idea."

Without Nickie's touching a dime, crews appeared to work on some of the renovations he and his friends dreamed up. There was hammering and vacuuming in the basement barroom, and a truckload of liquor came from Brooklyn.

There was going to be a big noise here. Someone would get his money's worth. It was still not clear how Nickie would get his.

He might not need Buckthorne, but when Buckthorne went out of sight Nickie fretted. Partly this was superstition. Losing Buckthorne was at least like losing a mascot. And maybe partly it was a feeling that Buckthorne authenticated some of his extravagances, like a mad ancestor invoked in precedent when no other could be found.

And part of it was genuine concern, since when things were going his way Nickie could be disinterestedly concerned for his friends. So he worried his wife and Cynthia and Lois

173

Capehart about Buckthorne's disappearance, but they honestly knew nothing. All the solid news from Miss Capehart was that Buckthorne had fulfilled his contract for eight of the Napa-Barca commercials before he went out of sight. Four were being used in rotation in the metropolitan area. Four others were selling spaghetti on channels west of Chicago. As for Lois, she did not give one whooping damn if there was anything left of the old bastard except these electronic traces deposited in evidence that he had once walked among mortals. "He took his money and went on a binge," she said with a shrug.

No, Nickie reasoned—for how could a man who had clearly been on a binge since he arrived in New York put another binge on top of that one?

But, as the signs multiplied that his own binge of success was going to be a big one, it seemed he ought to postpone the grand opening of the Monarch as art center. And since he had more time, he could afford patience to wait for Buckthorne's return. Arentino was satisfied. Diascoli was reported pleased.

Of this kind of patience Nickie's charity was born, so he thoughtfully answered Fingersmith's questions about the vanished one by saying, "You know, frankly, who he is: Buckthorne's the Paul Bunyan of boo-doors."

"I beg your pardon?"

"He's Tarzan the Tit Man."

"Bit of an athlete in that department, eh?"

"Is is a bird, is it a plane, is it a goat? It's *Superthorne.*"

"Not speaking a bit enviously, old boy?"

"He's Mandrake the Medicine Man, specialist in female complaints."

Fingersmith laughed dutifully. But he had his practical objectives in this conversation. He needed something printable. "Can't you bring him down to earth a bit? What is he really like?"

174

"Buckthorne isn't real. Can't you understand he's pure make-believe? But I'll tell you this, Fingerstiff, if one could harness him, one could abolish the human condition."

All that rankled Nickie's heart was that he went on considering Buckthorne as *his* make-believe, here as in Vistular. The invented creature owed the inventor a practical return, and was hiding out to avoid an honest debt.

In a bar on 47th Street, just west of Broadway, the face of Rodney Buckthorne appeared above Goya's collar on the television screen. He frowned at his palette. And a girl in the fifth booth gasped, "Why, there you are!"

She was a pretty girl of twenty-two, one of the thousands or ten thousands who work in midtown offices and at noon spill out of the tall buildings to make a parade of beauty on Fifth Avenue. She might have been all of them, though her name, Eva Zarzecki, was her own and there was something very special about her complexion. Some tincture of lampblack in her pigmentation resulted in exotic shades of skin, mixing with the natural yellows to make a warm green, with the pinks to make a dull violet. In her face there was something of a jungle bird.

"Of course I'm here," Buckthorne said to her gently, as if she were suffering a mental disturbance. He did not turn to see what she was watching. The sound on the TV was off, as it frequently is in bars, so he did not hear his own voice call for Napa-Barca spaghetti.

Neither did she. Half-drunk by now and utterly lost, Eva was marveling at the double image the stranger offered her. She should have gone back to work hours ago, but when he had met her face to face in the street and said, "Come," she had turned without hesitation to follow him. While they had lunched together in a densely crowded French restaurant and when she had followed him here, it had seemed that a profound change was taking place in her, a dissolution of identity that carried her normal workday responsibilities away with it. Whoever she might be, she was ready for anything, *anything* he might require of her.

At a loss to account for what was happening, she seized on his second appearance on the TV above his shoulder as a metaphor limited enough to deal with. Referring to its surprising appearance before her eyes, she said, "It's like magic. Sort of."

Gravely Buckthorne corrected her.

"It is like being a god."

She laughed loudly but uncertainly. "Oh, you. . . . Oh, *you!*" With eyes suddenly round as watches, she reached across the table of the booth and seized his wrist. "I don't care if you're a Bluebeard or what. Why don't you come to dinner? I mean I share an apartment with this girl down on Third Avenue and we could . . . I'd like to fix you dinner. Wait. It's silly for me to go back to the office now. We could go home now."

Buckthorne looked at his watch. "I have an appointment in a few minutes."

"Later then? I mean maybe Suzanne will go to a movie after dinner, or I can tell her——"

"That won't be necessary," Buckthorne said gently. "I should like to meet Suzanne, too. After my other appointment. Tell me your address. I promise to appear at eight o'clock sharp."

Eva sulked momentarily. "Meet Suzanne? I suppose you'll want to make out with *her* then. It happens."

"Wanting has nothing to do with it," said Rodney Buckthorne. "I shall."

He put the girl in a cab, then hailed one for himself. He

176

gave the address of a small, famous hotel on the East Side.

"Righto!" said the driver.

The mention of the hotel had evidently given him the inspiration for a dialogue. First he threw his right arm over the back of the seat. Then, when they were held up by crosstown traffic, he turned full around and said, "Y'see in the *News* who's in town?"

"I have had little time to read newspapers."

"Estree DeNeuve is who. Know who she is?"

"Oh yes."

The driver wanted to be sure. "Had two babies for this Italian producer? It was in the newspapers? That's her."

"Estree DeNeuve, yes."

"You seen in the papers then she's in town? What is not known by the *News* is where she's staying at. Which is sometimes the prerequisite of we cabbies over the journaless, to know where they're at famous people incognito. You know where she's staying?"

"Yes."

"Well, I will tell you. She's staying at this same hotel where I'm taking you. You might get you a glims of her."

"Yes. Certainly."

"The rumor. She's in New Yorka meet this innational jet set playboy, huh?"

"Quite false," said Rodney.

"Well, *I* wouldn't know about that," the driver said smugly. He turned full round again. "Say, you look kind of familiar y'self. I been turning it over since you hail me. I says, Well, he's not Mr. Clean. I used to see Mr. Clean in his white suit uppin down Seventh Avenue all the time with that little gold ring in his ear he wore in the commercials. But he had a ball head, man it would shine. Here we are. You see that DeNeuve girl, you say you met a fan."

177

"Indeed I will," Rodney said in his courtesy.

In far-off Vistular, Idaho, Mildred Buckthorne was hostess to a den of Cub Scouts that afternoon. She was in the kitchen getting them a pack of ice-cold Cokes from the refrigerator when she heard the little fellows burst into indecent laughter. Returning to the family room she saw all six blue-clad boys clustered in ribald mirth in front of the television set. Lance was laughing as wildly as any of them—at the appearance of his father.

There he was on the screen in a costume that she did not need to be told was the courting garb of the goldsmith Cellini. He had frowned at the cup he was making for the Medicis. He had tossed aside a lady's filmy handkerchief brought by a leering lackey. He walked among maids of the court with ennui befitting the king of a rainy country. And then (this made the Cubs laugh more wickedly than anything preceding it—as it was designed to do, of course), in a straight-on closeup of Cellini Buckthorne's mouth, one saw it quiver, pucker, and draw pitiably open at the mention of Napa-Barca spaghetti. The background music mocked suggestively.

His mouth! His wife saw Buckthorne's mouth quiver in its magnification with the frustration of spiritual hunger, a metaphysical anguish of desire . . . an expression so nakedly and unreservedly expressive of despair in the flesh that no one dared look at it without the defense of laughter. It caught the nerves of risibility like a nigger jigging on the end of the lynch mob's rope, like a napalmed peasant clowning in fire for the troops, like a child's pride broken by a stuck zipper in school.

"Lance!" Mildred screamed. "Boys!"

She jerked the cord from the wall plug and ran sobbing upstairs to her room.

178

She must have cried a long time. When Lance came in to find her there was no sound from downstairs to indicate the other boys were still there.

He put his fine, firm hands under her shoulders and lifted her face a little away from the sopping pillow.

"Don't cry, Mama," he said. "Didn't you see Daddy? He must be all right."

"He's not. Oh Lance, he's not all right if they can do that to him."

"He's in trouble? Then we'll save him."

"How?"

Lance had something of his father's quickness and some of his evasiveness. Unable to answer her blunt question bluntly, he said, "Jim Dandy to the rescue. Go, Jim, go!"

"Ah," she said. "It's too late."

The boy had seen his father mocked with a mockery absolute and ineradicable, not merely mocked by the laughter of Cub Scouts who recognized him but by the very necessities of the medium that superseded their neighborly and personal judgment. Lance had seen his father yield—and voluntarily, you bet—to the wicked giant of commercialism he had stoned from ambush for most of his life.

"He must get paid good for that," Lance said uneasily. "Maybe we'll be rich now."

At best it would have been hard to make a boy of this American generation comprehend such a father. Now surely it was beyond hope to imagine she ever could.

15

Encounters

"Meet me at the Frick. Don't fail me. You are my god." So read the unsigned note in his pocket.

Meet *whom* at the Frick? And when?

To Buckthorne the man-god, such questions of detail were no longer relevant. Upon his entrance into the museum the infatuate woman would, of course, make herself known to him, would supplicate the supernatural power that had invested him in the weeks since he left Dr. Bose's office. And that would be that.

That was the way things had been working out, requiring neither plan nor acquaintance nor foresight on his part, but only compliance. So when he found the scented note in his jacket pocket, he had simply gone to the Frick Museum.

And found himself, for once, unclaimed.

For once he had to wait upon the nameless lady. As his waiting stretched into hours, something (no doubt it was the healing power of art) restored him to his senses.

When he came to himself—and the expression is absolutely correct in this instance; Buckthorne *had not been himself* in these orgiastic weeks—he was looking at Rembrandt's painting of "The Polish Rider."

At that moment of restoration he was hollow-cheeked and gaunt . . . reedy, coughing, and obviously unfit for appearance in any more commercials suggesting he had any interest in food. The fine silk suit he wore was not his own, and he could not remember in what lady's bedroom he had donned it on rising, though a card in the pocket suggested it had recently belonged to a UN diplomat or an acquaintance of that famous man. (To whom, perhaps, the plea for a rendezvous at the Frick had also been addressed. To the man regaining his senses, curiosity about the recent past was too raw a pain to be indulged.) In any case, the suit would not have fitted Buckthorne even if he got back the forty-five pounds recently sweated from his frame.

He found himself leaning on a malacca cane before the painting. A cheap and spotted panama hat rested on his eyebrows and the tips of his ears. Buckthorne's hat size was large. This covering must have belonged to a giant.

He had journeyed far, all right. And it seemed to him now that he had come back to possess his proper self much as that worn, confident figure astride the nag in Rembrandt's painting had spurred momentarily into the light out of infinite darkness.

He had mastered life and death—that horseman who was about to die. His fine red hat became him like the negligence of his cloak and the sheaf of arrows ready on his shoulder. He neither smiled nor frowned, hungered nor thirsted. He was plainly tired from the inconclusive battles fought to get this far. Yet ready for what must come.

I suppose, Rodney Buckthorne thought, with a contented shudder of exhaustion, *that nothing in the world except this particular painting could have restored my sanity*. But, how-

181

ever he had been guided to it, he *had* found it, this image of what he ought to be. He was sane. He was sober.

So there was no need to question the simple reality of the girl standing beside him there on the hardwood floor of the museum—who said, "Didn't you get my message? Where have you been?"

It was Marsie Cumberland. Buckthorne's fingers tweaked the rosy, crumpled bit of paper in his low-slung jacket pocket. Was he after all being claimed by its author?

"As a matter of fact," she said, pouting, "when I saw you hadn't got the note in your mailbox I put another under your door."

"A thousand pardons! I never received them."

"No, you haven't been home for days. I tried calling, night and day, too."

He was delighted, thrilled—and just as mystified. "Whatever for?"

"I wanted to apologize."

In the fitful light of returning sanity he could guess her reference. She wanted to apologize for the vulgarity of the joke by which she had mocked at the supposed frustrations of aged parties like himself and Miss Brule. "For leaving the candle in the drawer?" he asked helpfully.

"Well, that and the . . . other thing," she said, proving that she could still blush in spite of occasional crude impulses. "But the truth is *he* put me up to it both times."

He must, of course, be the young fellow who was with her when the apartment was entrusted to Buckthorne. Odd that she would not now give him a name—odd and dismayingly suggestive of a relationship so close she would not even think of the youth as having a name. *"He* was waiting out in the car when I came back. After he'd haw-hawed so much about planting the candle, he said why didn't I go up and tease you

182

about it. *He's* always thought of nutty things for me to do. That's the dumb truth and I'm sorry. Hey, you didn't tell me you were an actor."

The apology so quickly disposed of, a dumber truth began to claw its way out of her bag. She, like other millions, had seen him disgrace himself on television. Instead of being appalled, her hopes of finding something "creative" had begun to flutter again. She had figured he could help her.

She said, "That day you rented you were too bashful to tell us. Though I admit the next time I came you started to explain something. I didn't realize it was telly."

"It wasn't," he said dolefully. He would like to please her—just to pay back the pleasure her good looks gave him. But for the time being he was too worn out to speak anything better than the simple truth. "I thought you might be interested in an art center project some young people are starting south of the Village."

"Oh! That. Well. But you are an actor, too? When I saw you I thought you were so . . . *talented*. I mean, your mouth is really expressive." She swayed a little toward him to examine the expressive organ. He found hers . . . expressive.

"I know you do other things," she said. "You're a scholar with exclusive tastes, I know. Art and all that. That's why when I couldn't get you at home I've been hanging around the museums where a man like you might be."

He was seared by the thought that while his body and his life were being wasted, she had been uselessly searching for him. "You mean you're here this afternoon to find me?"

She didn't deny it. "Do you think I usually lurk around in museums? Modern Art and Metropolitan?"

"I have set foot in none but this," he lamented.

"Then where on earth *have* you been hiding?"

That he could not have explained to a quicker intelligence

183

than hers. He had, in a manner of speaking, been visiting the Goddess of Liberty, she who presided over this great city. He had been with the women of New York. In a manner of speaking, he had been *broadcast* to the women of the five boroughs, just as his television image had been projected far and wide.

Impossible to count the women he had embraced in this period. The mathematical faculty was simply inapplicable to the acts-beyond-experience accomplished while Buckthorne was not himself. The name of Don Juan—or of Casanova or of Gargantua himself—has no mathematical equivalent, for we understand by these names a confusion of the quantitative with the qualitative that makes enumeration vain.

Suffice it to say that he had charged on New York women from Bose's office like the Light Brigade at Balaclava. Knees to the right of him, knees to the left of him . . . did the British cavalry count the Russian hordes firing into the valley down which they rode?

It must suffice Buckthorne to remember he had been with "many" women. Or to remember that whatever had possessed him—when he was not himself—had possessed more women than an unaided statistician, without mechanical help, afoot and confused by the onrush, could well count when Macy's, Korvette's, and Gimbel's close and the shoppers move down into the subway tunnels heading home.

Would he think that an exaggeration? Indeed, indeed. He had spent a highly exaggerated fortnight with the women of New York.

He had been on the subways like a sultan contenting his harem. On the rocking cars at rush hour he had made his way like a bodiless spirit the length of the train, taking advantage —if that was the right word for it—of the press of bodies against each other to work a will that was not, properly speaking, his own on black and white, Asian and Caucasian,

184

spinster and matron, not to speak of the boisterous high school girls shifting from foot to foot in the aisles with transistor radios clutched to their ears and the grimace of ecstasy on their lips.

He could remember—though not with perfect clarity—the soft-carpeted corridors of great midtown hotels with a multitude of doors opening to the code his knuckles beat on the panels; glimpses of Central Park through (1) venetian blinds, (2) metal bars, (3) lace as fine as bubbles churned in an automatic washer, (4) a rippling fall of red-blond hair let loose to slide over his face like a rosy curtain.

If he strained, he could remember the pants, grunts, roars, moans, encouragements, gurgling laughter, and fierce curses from uncounted throats, a volume of sound like that of the trucks roaring across the street from Miss Brule's.

And a sensation of moisture such as an unborn infant must feel when the first *sentio ergo sum* is uttered in its amniotic universe. . . .

Yet, to all that had happened or might have happened in these many days, he had been present more as witness than as author of the debauch. Indeed his body had been used—his wasted physique was sufficient testimony of that. It had been used like the swan or bull of the myths, by an authority that seemed to have chosen him almost whimsically, launching through his animal loins the seed of a spirit from another realm. Now that he had been used he was cast aside; but in his abandonment was free. He was free as the Polish Rider who had spurred out of the darkness to look squarely at heaven and earth before the brave heels struck again and the beast bore its rider back whence he had come.

Out of the anonymous rout of women who had been served by his body he could recall only two distinct figures. One was a Negro housewife from Jamaica. She had seemed to guess exactly whom she was entertaining while her husband pushed his broom through the deserted halls of Rockefeller Center. She had shown her visitor the apparatus and ritual by which she had conjured him across the seas. She had been in prayer and chanting incantations for weeks since her oldest boy had been sent to the House of Correction. Ananke had come to replace the lost boy. With terror and gratitude she received the answer to her call.

And then in a seedy hotel on 8th Street he had heard himself called to from a doorway, turned to see a tiny figure, barely female, with the gray face of a junkie and the speech of a corrupt eighth-grader.

"I'm hungry," the tiny one said. "I haven't been out for a while."

"I'll bring you fruit and milk from the delicatessen," Buckthorne offered.

"Wait. I'll give you money. I can't go out."

"Pay me when I bring the food."

"No. Wait. I've *got* money. You've got to take it or I know you'll just come back and fuck me, too."

He brought her milk and cookies and oranges. He sat beside her bed grieving like Lear over the body of Cordelia while she gobbled the cookies and sucked at the dripping hull of an orange, intermittently bawling lewd encouragements to him to "get it over."

He kissed her on the mouth with a full, frank kiss of love and went out on the streets again, back to the service for which he had been chosen.

Of so much glory and shame he could only say now to Marsie, "I've been with friends."

Those inadequate words had at least the merit of consistency with the falsehood he had begun to make up the day she caught him trying to leave Miss Brule's.

186

Of course she didn't believe him. "You don't look it. What kind of friends. They did you in. You look like you'd been mugged. You look like you'd fall down right here if somebody took your cane. Hadn't you better go home and sleep?"

He cocked the malacca stick jauntily over his shoulder, looked again for encouragement from the Polish Rider, and said, "Do you suppose I could sleep now, after waiting so earnestly for you to reappear?"

"Waiting? Yeah, sure. You get that outfit at the Salvation Army?" Her bright eyes searched under his hat brim for a sign of candor. She said, "Well, you did promise if you heard of anything interesting for me. . . . Do you think the acting profession's for me?"

And could he perhaps guide her to the right people in the television game? They walked out discussing this impossibility.

They went out onto Fifth Avenue at its finest, into one of those mild and hazy summer days when the graces of New York lie limp and inviting as odalisques in the harem of the richest imaginable sultan. The day opened before their strolling feet like the Red Sea opening in a DeMille movie to let the Chosen People through. Booted chauffeurs stared at them as they glided like figures on a flower-decked float parading southward. Imperial limousines slowed to keep pace with them, dowagers and magnates staring in unbelief at her good looks and his odd clothes.

And before they knew it they had walked all the way to the Battery. Of course they could not keep up a conversation about Miss Cumberland's prospects as television actress for more than a fraction of such distance.

Perhaps because he was so bedraggled, she let all her fear and hostility for the opposite sex lapse and let her exquisite egotism exude like a perfume from her limbs. She was, it turned out happily, much more interested in her sweet and secret self than in what might happen to her, career-wise.

187

"I try crazy ways to express myself. *He's* always been involved in the craziest of them since we were kids together. We burned up a houseboat once. Things like that or putting candles in old maids' drawers. Just crazy, pointless, nasty, and I don't know if they express myself or not.

"Express myself! I'm told all the time to do that and blamed when I actually do. I get it from Mother and teachers at school and everyone: I ought to express myself. That's one reason I got maneuvered into taking Miss Brule's apartment in the first place. You know my mother goes into town in winter and 'studies' with Miss Brule. Either she paints godawful still lifes or worse abstracts. Expressing herself. And why don't I ever do anything but sort of goof around and think about boys and making trouble. I've 'got a good mind.' Well, it happens I haven't.

"But I guess the creative spirit of Miss Brule was supposed to rub off on me if I stayed in her spooky place."

It had, her companion wished to assure her, oh, it had rubbed all over her. But his affirmative was so mumbled that Marsie lost it.

"Pardon? The truth of the matter is that I may not have anything to express. Tell me the truth, what did you think when you found the candle? What did you make of it?"

He smiled enigmatically. If he admitted how very much he had made of it, she would vanish and the city might disappear with her in a puff of incandescence.

He went pedantic again and explained that the poets tell us that such as she not only have *everything* to express but express it by mere existence. Had she not read Valéry's poem *La jeune Parque,* in which the wisest of all moderns had seen the young woman as the sum and source of all expression, the manifestation out of which came all impulse toward art? For, was not art the transfiguration of the erotic, and was not . . . ?

188

You damn well know she had not read Valéry. She planted her big feet in exasperation and said, "Stop that! I don't know what *any* poetry means. I didn't understand what you were driving at that silly day you came to rent the apartment." Her face softened with amusing recollection. "Except that silly comment about your being 'a lover.' Like it was what you did for a living."

"I was nervous, embarrassed, fumbling for words—"

"Well, it hit my funny bone. And you made us nervous, too. You made *him* nervous, or we might never have had the inspiration to put the candle in the drawer. It's a pretty far-out kind of joke and you might not have paid any attention to it at all, except for the kind of . . . *thinker* . . . you seem to be."

The thinker was still at his dirty work, spinning the pieces of the puzzle as she tossed them to him. "And," he guessed, "when you came back later and didn't get a playful response you decided to replace the candle with something more explicit. But you say it was *his* idea. . . . Well then, it was. I thought that it was very womanish."

"Because it's so—" she hit the word frankly, "—perverted? You think women are queerer than men."

"Well—"

"Ah. You know so much about women!"

In the light of his recent experiences, undertaken at so much cost to his health, the scholar faced her challenge. "I happen to know more about the life of modern woman than anyone on earth."

She looked at him with just enough derision to hide her interest in the possibility that he might. Her lips formed an exquisite raspberry. "Then, you wise fellow . . . go ahead, explain me."

"Of course I can't." A fit of coughing so intense it left bloodstains on his handkerchief interrupted his effort to distinguish his (essentially scholarly) knowledge of the female from the irrational, divine metaphor that she wanted and deserved.

"I know," she said. "You think you understand my psychology. You think nobody but a female would think of leaving that candle, because it was a stupid and perverse thing to do. You hate women."

"I don't hate them as you do."

"That could be." Her splendid brow was shadowed by a thought too heavy for her brain. "But I don't hate myself! And I'm all woman! I really am! That's one thing I know, damn it! Do you believe that?"

He did a quick dance step and saluted her with his cane.

"You're livelier than you've got any right to be," she said, smiling. "But tell me this, then. Is it worth it to be all woman? Where will it get me?"

He gave her his best answer. "I'm not sure."

"You'd better be. A man better be sure it's worth while for a woman to be a woman, and when men aren't it's just awful. We're just jokes unless we find the right man. Blllll-aaaaaah! You know something? I've stopped believing there is a right man for me. I don't believe there's a man alive worthy of me. There! See what I am? When I'm not a trembling mass of insecurity I'm totally arrogant. What are you going to do about that?"

"I'm going to believe there's no man worthy of you," Dr. Buckthorne said.

She refused his compliment by observing, "You look like Chaplin in those clothes." The *sequitur* to this was: "I don't know what men and women are supposed to be for . . . to . . . each other. Is it just sex?"

" 'It's that as well, said the stare.' "

She was furious, furious as Diana peeped on by a goddamn

190

mortal with, probably, a camera to snap her in her nakedness. "I *told* you I can't understand if you quote poetry at me."

"I mean, of course it is sex," said the contrite man.

She pursued the admission. "But what is sex? I *know* it's not just going to bed with some boy, because I've done that so much I ought to know."

A wiggling, slithering pain like a long snake ran through Buckthorne's chest when he heard this. With his cane he saluted the anonymous victors, the athletes of reality with whom he could only compete in dreams.

Marsie was aglow with her advantage. "I know it's more than just bouncing some delicious boy."

"It is more."

"How do you get ahold of the more?"

"By—" Dear God, he wanted to be able to tell her. He should have found that out by now, or what a waste his life had been.

But she rolled on like Juggernaut. "You *can't* get ahold of the real thing. So you might as well be religious or something. I used to be religious."

He thought, "Perhaps to be religious about sex—"

"I told you I can't understand you when you quote!"

He was not quoting this time, and she could not stop him. Swinging his illicit panama hat on the end of his stick he said, "To be religious about what's alive in us—about *anything* that isn't dead yet or impossible in our culture, any hunger, any embarrassment, any dirty joke with candles and panties, even to be religious about fear— Isn't that where we might begin to live again? We shouldn't be as afraid as we are. *Really,* we shouldn't be afraid to bow down before what is apparently the silliest in us, to honor ourselves in our grotesque . . . joke with the candle . . . my joke, why condemn it? Why not water the plant and make it grow? I learned from

191

Miss Brule—" He began to cough again. This much talk was
more than his chest would tolerate.

"Why not honor your making a silly ass out of yourself on
television?" she asked brutally. "That's what you were, you
know, and your mouth was just . . . just obscene. Why not
this? Why not that? If a girl just wants to say 'Why not?'
everything is pretty easy. You bet."

And they were still in this rapture of protofornicative talk
when they came to the Battery—to the end of land—and
looked off into the haze brooding above the Atlantic.

They might have gone on talking thus without any conclusion forever and they both knew it.

They would love and doubt each other while the futile
dialogue of words went on. Words were the absence of the
word. The sex-exhausted old man knew that. The hardly tried
girl knew it. There was no more cynicism in his exhaustion
than in her readiness. Neither readiness nor exhaustion
counted, except in the blind falling of atoms from eternity
into eternity. It was not the open sea they confronted. It was
nothingness. They were falling into it, man and girl. And
though they talked with spirit, they knew what was coming.
What luckless night.

So the girl said, all at once, "Do you think I'm beautiful?"

"Oh!"

She preened in his eye. "You said the right thing. Yes or no
aren't enough. Do you know how beautiful?"

He shook his head. "Too beautiful for television."

"Oh, *that*. I've got a flawless skin. You know?"

Out of the nothingness above the Atlantic waste something
stirred, like a movement glimpsed from the corner of an eye.

"I've tried to visualize," he admitted. "All my effort since
I've come under Miss Brule's influence has, I suppose, been
an effort to guess how beautiful you really are."

192

"Forget that old bitch Brule. I hate her!"

The exclamation was so violent that he would have been shocked in any case. To his rubbed-raw sensibility, it came like a burning knife. "But—" And then he almost admitted that he had seen a kinship, close to identity, between her and the older woman.

"Come on," Marsie commanded. "You make me forget television. I'll make you forget Miss Brule. We'll get her out of your mind, once and for all."

The peach-down glow of skin around the moon-crater roughness of her nipples, the dimpling gluteus as she turned, the modeling shadow, as Veronese would paint it, from hip to knee, as delicate as smoke rising from an uncrushed, abandoned cigarette in a closed room. . . .

He had imagined the flawlessness of her beauty as she might stand naked in Miss Brule's apartment. Now he saw nothing that he had not perceived in imagination, nothing he had not foreknown. Even the greatest beauty has no secrets. Its miracle occurs when it offers itself substantially to the appetite it quickens.

She made him sit across the studio from her until even her wristwatch and hairpins were removed, so she could offer herself first to his visual sense alone. And, seeing her thus— really here, really to be his—he confessed what had led him on his wild pilgrimage from woman to woman. It was this: Like a hard drinker who craves the grace and peace of being an outright alcoholic he had thrown himself on the multiplicity of women as if to blur distinctions between one of them and another, once and for all, and to prove to himself that all women were one woman with whom he might couple and have done.

He had served all women because the true Don Juan searches for his veiled lady in each woman, no matter what veil

193

of ugliness or intellectual coarseness she may wear. His hope is to be served at last by finding his own lady without the veil.

Marsella's breasts were no finer, perhaps, than Vivian's, her dimpled navel no more fetching than Lois's, the column of her thighs no more wondrously divisible than the black woman's, who said she had conjured him to her with voodoo spells. But in Marsella all separate marvels were combined and hit his eyes with an overwhelming simultaneity.

"Now," Marsella said. Her movement to the bedroom was made to the accompaniment of tambourines.

Not tambourines. Someone was ringing the buzzer from the street door, one flight down.

"Quick, into bed," she whispered commandingly.

Quick, said the bird. . . .

He tiptoed to lie in her flawless arms while they heard the sound of feet climb to the landing. There was a sharp, repeated knocking on the door.

"Don't answer," Marsella breathed. He shook his head. Of course he had no intention of answering the knock. And yet . . . yet he felt he should.

He felt he might as well. For with the knocking on the door, he knew himself unable to possess what at last was his for the taking.

When the knocking finally stopped, he permitted her not-unpracticed fingers to loosen and strip his shirt away from his bony ribcage. He let go the belt that puckered his trousers around his wasted abdomen. But this was as far as the farce could be extended.

"It's all right," she said. "Don't be afraid of me. I'll help."

She couldn't help him now. His strength had been used up on his way to this moment. The iron paradox of his situation was inflexible. And she said at last, without harshness, but without the grace of kindness either, "I should have let you go on talking. You talk a good game."

194

He could not even weep for lack of strength. He didn't now resent the rude selfishness of her disappointment.

She ran her fine fingertips over the accordion surface of his ribs and said, "I know you're not well. But. Isn't it funny? I'm sure if you'd been healthy when I found you it wouldn't have occurred to me to come here with you."

That was certainly funny, but he couldn't laugh any more than he could cry.

"You might as well turn on the light," she said. For dusk had come and the bedroom particularly was dark, though the glassed paintings in the studio still twinkled with natural light from outside. Avocado leaves near the bamboo-curtained windows still showed a distinct edge.

He did as he was told. In the light she began gathering her clothes. "Don't go yet," he pleaded. "At least don't go again without telling me where I can reach you."

"What for? So you can tell me all about women? So you can introduce me to your TV friends?"

He had no collateral promises to give. "Because I will show you I'm the right man."

At least she didn't scoff at this. She seemed to be weighing it, testing it for its prophetic value.

"Well—" she said.

And he was kneeling to her prayerfully when the rapping on his door began again—this time not only insistent but confident, as if someone had been waiting across the street, watching his windows until a light showed, and now knew beyond doubt that he was inside.

"Rodney!"

"We're here!"

He knew the voices and his face must have shown that he could not refuse them.

"Don't be a fool," Marsella whispered as he lunged to his feet and turned toward the door. "I've got to get out of here."

195

But he was a fool. One foot galloped forward and one foot galloped backward as, somehow, he progressed toward the door. Like the Polish Rider's nag on the way to the glue factory.

He cleared his throat. But before he spoke he opened the brass peephole and looked out.

He saw the blue cap of a Cub Scout and the clean, small fingers raised to its brim in a confident salute.

"Let us in, Daddy," Lance shouted. "We're here to rescue you."

Part Four

16

A Family Scene
at Kennedy International Airport

"Wasn't it neat how we came out exactly even on my allow-
ance for the week?" the boy asked. His parents smiled at his
system of accounting for this economic miracle, because the
hamburger, french fries, apple pie à la mode, and Coca-Cola
he was finishing in the airport cafeteria had been studiously
chosen to use the last penny allotted to him for the period.
The public address system said: "TWA Flight Two Six Four,
leaving for Chicago and Phoenix at one P.M., is now ready
for boarding at Gate L Seven." And the boy slashed hurriedly
at his dessert.

"That's not your flight, honey," his father said to him.
"We've still got a little time together."

"We've still got plenty of time," said the mother, to both of
them.

"I hope you won't think it too eccentric of me if I come

right out and say this has been one of the great weeks of my life," said Mildred Buckthorne—for it was she who was sustaining husband and son through this last hour before their parting.

"It *sure* has for me," Lance said, in a tone that did not too much suggest he was flattering for a purpose. His round, deceptive eyes showed happy reflections of ball games and natural history museums, of puppet theaters and the view from the Empire State Building, of a neat fencing match at the Club des Sports, of the skyline seen from a boat circling Manhattan, and the trees and towers seen from horseback in Central Park.

"You've been *magnificent*," Father Buckthorne assured them both.

He was not yet, on this day in early August, quite restored to the fleshy self they had known at Vistular. He was still twenty-five pounds under the weight he had maintained for many years. But his new clothes had been chosen—by the taste of the three of them, shopping together—for a new man. Mildred had fed him up to meet the smaller waistband. And he understood full well that under her frank evaluation of this week *en famille* in New York lay an innocent pride in having put him in shape again after finding him sick unto death.

She—and Lance, too, for that matter—had enjoyed the touristic domesticity of camping out in Miss Brule's apartment. Once the contretemps of their arrival had been straightened out, it developed that Lance had forethoughtfully brought his Cub Scout sleeping bag with their luggage.

He unrolled it under the ferns and avocados of Miss Brule's studio as if he had known, by George, that he would find a jungle nook in the stone and steel city. He had been allowed to build a tiny fire in the otherwise never-used fireplace of the apartment. And while the little family group sat before the small flames in the dusk, they had sung cowboy songs together. Nothing that had happened could change the reality of what they shared.

Not the least of the magnificence to which the father so gratefully alluded had consisted in Mother's on-the-spot arrangement of a means whereby the nameless girl who had been with Father at their arrival could slip away unobserved.

She had said inspiredly, "Rodney, we haven't brought our luggage from the air terminal. Come out *this minute*—hurry! —and we'll go collect it."

"Hurry *now?* After how long we waited on the sidewalk?" Lance complained. But she had him by the arm, and by the time Father had put on his tie and joined them she had hailed a cab over to the curb of the Avenue. Later they brought the retrieved luggage into an apartment where the bed had been neatly, if hastily, made by the vanished girl.

It was Mother's magnificence to provide the means for acting like a family all week long. Let it be conceded that Mildred wived the impossible man in this department as no other imaginable female could or would have. She knew all she wanted to know, all she needed for her mile-wide sympathy to play over the chaos of his circumstances.

He wanted to make her sure that he recognized all her qualities and effort. But when, as the week of her kindness hastened to its conclusion, he tried to put his gratitude into words, she said, "I know you know I know. That's not much, is it? Not enough."

But that was the only time during her stay that he detected a show of tears in her eyes.

She did not cry—or doubt him—when he named his madness frankly. "I am not technically insane," he said with finicking insistence. "Mine is a condition doctors are specifically trained *not* to recognize, or not to admit in any case,

201

since to admit it as diagnosis would be to abandon the key-stone of their discipline itself. Mine is a condition of health, I do believe, which nevertheless seems inconsistent with healthy behavior."

It was in the nature of her commitment to him not to doubt the excessive refinement of his definitions. But they made more sense to her when he told her how he had lost possession of himself for many days and believed that in this lost time he had fornicated with all the women in New York.

"Well, you damned old fool, I guess you didn't miss it by *much*," she said. "Maybe a few in the far-off Bronx you couldn't find. . . . Those accidentally stuck in elevators—"

"But there are millions of women in New York," he protested, as if she and not he had been the victim of delusion.

Magnificently she joked, "I have great faith in your powers, Father."

Her joke was intended to cover, as best it could, the fact that he had not and apparently could not make love to her in these days of convalescence. She was offering him a way to laugh off this deficiency with a joking pretense of happier times ahead. But he refused the lighthearted evasion. He terrified her by explaining:

"I *say* that while I was possessed I traversed this city erotically from the spinster studies of Washington Heights to the executive couches of Wall Street, the boudoirs of Sutton Place and the lofts of Canal Street, through lesbian clubs and YWCA's, with ladies' bowling teams and goddesses of the mass media. So it *seems* to me.

"But then again it seems to me I spent my entire time of hallucination in one of those theaters on 42nd Street. You know they have movies running round the clock. And while I was there I fell asleep like Rip van Winkle; and once when I roused a little I found that my foot was dangling over the

202

railing that separates one section of the balcony from the next. Someone was licking the sole of my shoe. I remember a pair of eyes searching up for mine through the darkness. They were expressing love—"

"No!"

"Love," he said steadfastly; and again the wife denied it, because if he were right then the last walls of her hope went down into the dust.

She set limits to her understanding, though not in her eager response to his Miss Brule. She looked at the photograph albums with him and saw with his eyes the unique person he had inferred from these clues. She stood in front of the black "Self-portrait" and squinted at the glass to catch the image reflected and yet modified by the colorless impasto beneath. In doing so she felt . . . *something* happen; as once, long ago, when she was a little girl she had gone to visit a Mormon uncle on his farm in the Utah desert and the old man, who witched water professionally, had linked arms with her while each held one prong of a forked peach stick, and she had felt the incredible tug of water beneath the sand as they walked together toward it.

Something . . . and what she felt was, she admitted, quite inexplicable except by the extravagant metaphor her husband had made of his absent landlady. If Mildred missed the caress of flesh (and naturally she did; she damn well did, with a fearful jealousy that had to be mastered almost hour by hour) yet her husband's creative aberration made up partly for what she missed. She had married him . . . well, because from the beginning she had guessed he might fly to an extreme (of crime, insanity, or sheer creation) no one else was capable of.

Now she could say, "Miss Brule is your great invention."

Flattered as he was, Buckthorne could not help quibbling over the definition. But when he shook his head his wife amended, "I don't mean she's a machine. You're right. Edison made inventions." That contemptible tinkerer in his New Jersey factory, turning out gadgets for the market. . . .

"I meant that Miss Brule is not a poetic creation," Buckthorne specified.

"She's more than that!" the good wife enthused. "You've invented something alive. Something that could—you know—I think sometimes she could walk right into the room with us."

So far so good. The deluded man and his misled wife were in high sympathy. It could not hold to the end. They might walk on clouds together. When you walk on clouds there is always the danger of slipping off the edge and falling.

"I think she did!" Rodney said with a terrifying gleam in his eyes. "I think that's just what she did. In spite of Miss Cumberland's denial of any kinship with Miss Brule, I am convinced that *they are one and the same person—*"

He broke off then, in contrition realizing the implied accusation: At the instant I might have embraced her, you and the kid knocked at the door. So, unworldly, absurd, and perverse as the accusation might be, it stood between them like a blade. It was nothing . . . it was only words . . . it was the cryptic code sign explaining his impotence with his lawful wife . . . it was the estranging sea itself.

He was saving himself from her to serve the phantom he had invented.

Therefore Mildred—though she neither wanted nor hoped to maneuver him to the nut ward for shock treatments—insisted that he go with her to the able Dr. Chalmers. Dr. Chalmers filled him with vitamins and tonics, cured his cough, recommended not only diets but, in his urbane fashion, fine medium-price restaurants where a family visiting New York

204

from the West could enjoy a varied cuisine and simultaneously put some meat on Father's bones.

And they were parting now at the airport on the assurance that Mildred had won. The reference to Miss Cumberland's double nature—double aspect; what was the right term?— had been the flicker of a retreating nightmare. It was perfectly understood by the family unit—even Lance had been involved in this part of their armistice discussions—that father was to remain in New York until after Labor Day.

Remaining, he was to decide their future. "I won't have anything to do with the decision," Mildred said with gallantry and gaiety. "You are the Herr Papa. Where you take us, Lance and I follow. *Capisce?*"

Only, it was well understood, she devoutly hoped that he would decide *not* to return to Vistular. "We could get along another year there, of course. We can do anything. But we'd be less comfortable. *Even* less comfortable *now* than we have been among those, them pricks."

"There's been talk?" Buckthorne asked with a kind of innocence that made his wife gulp a little.

"There's been *incomprehension.* Oh come on, you joker. When was there not talk about the queer Buckthornes? They'd have smoked us out sooner or later. And you must understand there's been a real summer shower of tee-hees about your appearance on this TV commercial. 'Unseemly,' 'unacademic,' 'not in keeping with faculty decorum.' I think every man, woman, and child in Vistular has seen your passion for spaghetti. And for some it's a kind of revenge to see you— well, humiliated—after what they took to be your superciliousness when you had your own program there. See?"

"Those who are sure of my humiliation will perhaps even be anxious for my return."

"Yes," she said. "And we can live through that, too. We can live through anything, us family. But still—" Still she hoped he would decide, and find a way, to bring her and Lance soon to New York. Or take them to the Mediterranean lands.

And how to finance their emigration? Let it be understood he was *not,* under any conditions, to make any more television commercials. The money from his recent efforts of course had been expended "when he was wandering around with amnesia."

Perhaps, after all, the best hope for getting started away from Vistular lay in this art center promotion that Nickie Duart was pushing: Mildred had been taken to see the activities at the Monarch Hotel, and, while she couldn't believe her eyes, she could almost persuade herself that any enterprise with so much momentum must be going someplace.

At the Monarch these days everyone was swarming over everyone. There were mean-eyed bands of high-schoolers swarming the street with the derelicts and pouring like ants in and out of the door. Crews of carpenters were raising dust in the first-floor ballroom where unskilled labor was reshuffling the junk that had accumulated over all the years of the hotel's history.

Young Duart, in his MacArthur costume, seemed to be well in charge of the activity. He had been overwhelmingly flattering to Buckthorne when that fugitive showed up with wife and child. The day they visited he was particularly elated because of a tie-in his project had made with a Philadelphia disc jockey. Already the DJ was plugging "The End of the World" on his programs heard by the young throughout megalopolis. If the money could be guaranteed, the Philadelphian would bring his show to New York for that wild night. In this hope, they were postponing the event until after Labor Day. "Time, time is on our side," was the Duart-MacArthur slogan. "The more time we can buy, the more money we've

206

got to buy it with. This thing may be as big in art history as the Armory Show in 1913."

"It seems . . . frightening, but there it is," Mildred said. "It's frightening to see what can rise up out of a manhole and call itself art, but apparently they're taking your young friends seriously." For evidence of this she had *The Times,* and she read:

> Duart, who now balks at being called a "painter," says he tries to create environments where "the relationship of visual images can be determined by the viewer acting in collision with the prearranged situation."
> His innocence allows him to accept his eccentric ideas as perfectly normal and to pursue paths that others would condemn in advance as ridiculous; yet precisely in his willingness to take such risks lies his success. He has an intense curiosity about many areas of life, a keen intelligence, a strong memory, and an unusually tenacious capacity for concentration. He feels immensely contented with the life he has begun to live this summer. His plans for "The End of the World"—as he calls the festival, rally, or "happening" to be staged in the old Monarch Hotel—are not the end of his plans as creative entrepreneur. . . .

When she had read this, husband and wife sat in marveling silence for a while. Then both together murmured, "It will sell."

"It will sell," Mildred said, "and if you went along with the operation, is there or isn't there a chance that you could redeem it?"

"There might be a chance."

"In some ways it's so much like what you tried to do most of your life with your art galleries and little magazines and bookstores."

207

"It is. Nickie continues to make that point."

"Then——" There was ambiguous hope in her voice. It was clear to both of them that she did not care if the whole island sank into the Hudson River, if Nickie fleeced a whole generation, if art itself were consumed in some ultimate bonfire to gratify the teen-agers rallying down from MacDougal Street toward the apotheosis at the Monarch Hotel—she didn't care as long as this dear, impossible human she had married could find in the process some way to stabilize the plummeting course of his life.

Buckthorne said, "We'll see where it ends. In any case I've promised young Nickie and myself to stay through his opening after Labor Day. I will urge the merits of the project on Mrs. Pellew. After this story in *The Times* perhaps that will not be difficult. I have promised to go into consultation with some Foundation people, looking toward a longer-range program than Nickie can support on his present resources. I have committed myself."

"Whatever you do——" Mildred began.

Her husband finished fondly, "——is all right. Yes, I have to believe that you mean that."

They parted on that promise.

And on the unspoken understanding that while he waited a while longer in New York he would probably make further attempts to "see" Miss Cumberland. Oh—after so many and so much—what difference did it make if he screwed another college girl? As long as he didn't think he was putting the wood to a witch with two aspects. . . .

Beneath the swept-back wings Manhattan faded. One minute it seemed as if the arrogant towers ruled the visible earth. When Lance Buckthorne looked again they were minute and almost out of sight in the haze. Down there he had gone to a great ball game with his father. It was cool to watch the

208

little white figures like dolls moving on a hidden track dash here and there on the green field under the amplified light of the sky. But he had been utterly bewildered in guessing why his father had brought him to such a spectacle when, somehow, as he flew east with Mother, he had expected something else.

Then there was the day in the Museum of Natural History when Mother had been shopping and would meet them later. Lance and his father had come into the room—the hall, really—where the great, weightless whale hung suspended, painted in the colors of life.

The size of the whale had impressed him most, though he knew from both reading and daydreaming that a whale is supposed to be big. This one was *bigger*. And its eyes were tiny. One little eye looked out from one side of a head bigger than a car. You had to walk a long, circular way to come around the head to just the other eye. He had been on one side, looking at one eye. His father was over there on the other side of that huge, incomprehensible body where the other eye was. And you wondered if the whale might really see both of them? You wondered what *both* meant in such a case. Did the whale see him who was young with one eye and his father who was old with the other? Or did it see just one?

Manhattan and the Hudson Valley were vanished out of sight behind the plane. A mile beneath them innumerable small clouds scattered above their shadows on the green mountains of Pennsylvania. Up to the north—could he really see it or only think he saw it because he knew from the maps it must be there?—was the blue darkening that might be one of the Lakes. It was not a big country anymore, his teacher had said in school, because, look how quickly you can fly across it now. But, for an instant, with nothing to last as evidence that he had really seen, he knew how great and far this continent spread.

He said, "Mother, why are you crying? You and Daddy agreed about everything. I thought you did."

She said they had. Of course they had. They really had. But she went on crying all the way to Chicago.

17

The End of the World: Part I

There were police in the street on their stately horses . . . and it was a Success.

Very far back in the unconscious of Barston Karmite pranced the horse. Long before *The Times* had come to represent authority to him, the horse had done so. He had been born a farm boy in a Border State, and from childhood on had breathed easier when there was a horse in sight—at the plow or on the track or behind white board fences, the whereabouts of the horse did not matter; for it was in Karmite's nature to believe that wherever the horse showed itself, power and money could not be far off.

Therefore when he saw the horses of the mounted police directing the traffic and the crowd in front of the Monarch Hotel, Karmite was relieved to think he had not erred in lending Foundation Presence to the opening of young Duart's "End of the World."

After the story in *The Times* he had (1) promised Vivian Duart he would attend, and (2) established a separate file drawer in his Foundation office for the dossiers of the young artists Mrs. Duart said were associating themselves with the project. There were good names. Some of them had been runners-up for Edison grants of recent years; and there were three Recipients. Yet he had been cautious and might have been indisposed this evening, or in Washington, if his wife Lollie had not so much wanted to come.

Now, as he helped her from the cab and they made their way into the crowd at the entrance of the Monarch, they heard (over the whistle and thump of the New Music from a loudspeaker in a second-floor window) a rising shout from the end of the block.

"There's Jackie. Jackie. Jackie."

Karmite smiled with the confidence of a man with inside information. He had had his staff check and they had confirmed that Mrs. Kennedy would *not* attend this opening. But the cry established the mood of the occasion.

"Where?" said Andrea Pellew. "Do you see her? I've been received by the Queen Mother, but never . . . I can't see her, can you?"

Regina Travers shook her head. Once. Decisively. She did not move her lips to reply. In spite of a fifth of bourbon consumed during the afternoon, she was absolutely terrified by the crowd, the noise, the searchlights, the nightmare faces of derelicts, like masks at a Halloween party, appearing here and there among the better-fed. As usual, her chief concern was with Andrea Pellew's safety, and she did not know how she could guarantee that in such a mob.

At Mrs. Pellew's other elbow Dr. Rodney Buckthorne murmured, "If she is here, be assured, dear lady, that she will want to meet you."

From a window of the office on the second floor Vivian Duart heard the cry of "Jackie!" and watched her boss bring his wife under the marquee of the hotel. What she felt was pure Idaho shame, shame as fresh and sturdy as a mountain flower growing by a mountain stream.

I'm the only one that knows, she thought. *Nickie's so confused by his own lies, he simply doesn't know anymore. Buckthorne won't talk sense to me since his wife was here.*

So she was the only one who knew how empty the center of this noisy show really was. She knew why Barston Karmite had decided to come. He came because she had made clever use of the Foundation files. She had gathered from one file the names of young avant-garde artists who had been well recommended to the Foundation when the last grants were given. When Karmite heard these names from her fresh, enthusiastic lips—one or two at a time over the weeks—he had simply called for the same dossiers she had consulted to get the names. She had seen his growing confidence as he combined these together in a new drawer labeled "South Village Art Center."

Since Nickie caught her in the lie about Buckthorne, she had also brought home a considerable amount of Foundation stationery. Cynthia Trebogen (who would *never know* what she was really doing at any given moment of her life, Vivian thought) had typed a great many letters on Foundation letterhead. And signed them A. North Whitehead, per C.T. (the signature Nickie's inspiration). Discreet letters of inquiry to art departments of Eastern colleges. Was there, on the staff, a critic or art historian prepared to evaluate (in strictest confidence, for Foundation eyes alone) the contribution of the

213

Nickie Duart circle? Stamped envelope provided for return to PO Box 1083. Letters expressing Continued Foundation Interest to the young men and women who had *almost made it* the last time Foundation cash was spread around.

The smell of honey.

And when Vivian had tried to discuss with Buckthorne her guilty part in spreading the smell to people who (theoretically) deserved better, he answered her with irrelevancies.

" 'A. North Whitehead.' Very clever touch. The avaricious academic will in most cases reason that a relative or namesake of the philosopher has become a Foundation consultant. It's really not forgery, my dear Vivian."

Whether that particular trick was or was not forgery, she no longer cared. She knew that of all the promises made to bring this crowd here tonight, not one of them was honest.

As late as this afternoon she had heard Nickie assure Maris Mendelsohn (his friend! his dirty co-conspirator!) that yes there *would be* a county fair girl show imported from Alabama featured tonight. Fingersmith was ready to cable his story to the London paper, and Maris was just calling to check for accuracy. But Vivian knew that Arentino had vetoed the girl show weeks before. Cost too much. Makea trouble the poh-lice.

What skin shows there were, as part of this circus, were strictly unpaid volunteers. And they had been lied to, without exception. Like that really beautiful girl who came in saying she was interested in doing *what she could*—which evidently wasn't anything involving brush, chisel, typewriter, or drums —had been promised there would be other Go-Go girls in cages around hers. But there was only one cage. . . .

Oh sure, there was a dance band complete with famous disc jockey to entertain the teen-agers in the ground-floor ballroom. But art? Of the considerable number of practitioners

214

baited in by the smell of honey, the kooks and noisemakers had been carefully screened from the parade. They were assigned rooms for tonight's brawl, while the others drifted bemusedly away, presumably to await further notification from the Edison Foundation.

"In our time, perhaps no enterprise can succeed without achieving visibility," Buckthorne had advised her with phony profundity.

Make a noise. It was what that thug Arentino kept saying, and if she heard it again she would go for his face with her nails. But Buckthorne . . . ? His wife had put a kink in him.

There was plenty of noise. Every floor had its complement of tape recorders (playing doctored tapes, making new ones out of the old ones), drums, dangling pipes, bedsprings wired to amplify their squeals. In the corridors and on the stairways art noise mingled hellishly with the band music from downstairs. Stick your head through an open window and you merely got the noise of arriving traffic and pedestrians, plus police whistles, added to the rest.

Noise, noise, noise. A universe of noise. At its still center there was a white mountain flower of shame, stepped on by a dirty boot.

NICKIE D.: The pig still game to go through with it?

LOIS C.: You couldn't keep her from it.

NICKIE D.: Does she know yet she'll be the only one?

LOIS C.: You wasted your time conning that girl. You didn't have to, is what I'm trying to say. She is going to do it, regardless.

NICKIE D.: Arentino says no total exposure. No naked quiff.

LOIS C.: So let Arentino keep clothes on her.

215

Lollie Karmite said, "I'm glad I didn't dress either up or down."

For the crowd that jostled them and carried them as they moved into the lobby of the hotel was a heterogeneous mass migration from a weekend night in Greenwich Village. There were files and packs of high-schoolers. Tight jeans. Boots. Lettered jackets. Funny hair. There were young faculty-type visitors from the commuting cities, with wives and girlfriends too highbrow or too jaded for even the off-Broadway theater.

There were cocktail dresses. Business suits. Some tuxedos, perhaps rented. Here and there an expensive camera, ready for action, hung from the tweedy shoulder of an art historian about to catch up with the future. There were—not a few; there was not a "few" of anybody in the tide of people— women in evening dresses and glittering capes. A number of light fur pieces, in case it grew chilly before the evening broke up.

And on the street as well as in the lobby there were derelicts and hungover sailors, waiting for a flop on their last night ashore. These damn well still lived in the Monarch Hotel and were entitled to their rights. A queue of them was lined up across the lobby, in front of the desk, trying to register for the night with money they had panhandled in recent hours.

One of these, a huge and hulking Scandinavian, suddenly confronted the Karmites and said, "Gimme money! Gimme money!"

Karmite was unprepared for this passionate and direct request. It was with panic and embarrassment—and an unfamiliar sense of his own humanity—that he began to dig in his pocket.

"Don't give him a thing!" Lollie Karmite ordered. To the towering blond giant she screeched, "Why should we? Why?"

216

The giant wobbled a moment. His bleary, red eyes blinked down at them. Then he had his reason clear.

" 'Cause I'm a Puerto Rican," he said. "Victim of police brutality. You people like that."

For this display of creative imagination the Edison Foundation donated twenty-five cents to his cause.

"But it is art." The girl insisted. The crowd in the room swore to it.

"Is not nice. Is not art," Arentino said.

Stairways mounted on either side of the lobby. Between them was a chipped and broken marble balustrade over which hung a few Vietcong flags. Pistol shots rang out above the heads of the crowd on that balcony. Douglas MacArthur was waving the Stars and Stripes and firing into the air with a .45. On either side of him appeared bearded young gents in the fatigue uniforms of Castro bodyguards.

Nickie Duart yelled, "We are introducing our very special guests at this opening—" The Castro guards shoved people back from the balustrade to clear a little space. As room was made for them, a terrified middle-aged woman and a gray-haired gentleman with glasses, mustache, and beard were eased forward like stuffed animals on a cart.

"—Madame Andrea Pellew and Meshoor Rodney A. Buckthorne. With Madame's permission, I declare The End of the World to be at hand."

Behind the guests of honor Regina Travers scowled and shook her head.

"I don't see anything," Andrea Pellew said.

She could not have meant this literally. For instance, since she didn't travel by subway, she hadn't seen so many people pressing close around her since she was a poor Southern baton twirler and once, after a football game where she twirled at halftime, had tried to fight her way down through a departing crowd to the dressing room where her boyfriend had been carried with a broken leg.

She meant, of course, that she hadn't yet seen any Art hanging on the walls where even a well-coached patron would expect to look for it. There seemed to be a lot of old bedsprings—some festooned with toilet paper; some pasted over with cutout figures from an enormous comic book—and rubber tires hung oddly where one would expect to see paintings.

Dr. Buckthorne had made her understand, before they came, that she must expect something *akin* to surrealism and dada. Good. Thirty years ago in Paris those varieties of art had been once and for all explained to her by a man who rather strikingly resembled her present escort. She expected the new thing to be old stuff to her because of her opportunities to be on the inside.

So she had ridden tranquilly down through a lovely September night expecting to find pictures of ladies with mustaches painted on them. She might have to sit through a badly made silent movie where they sliced up eyeballs with a razor. She could take that and appreciate it as well as anyone.

But the only paintings of any sort she had seen thus far were some big old landscapes, brown with varnish and badly cracked. They looked to her like the clearance sale of an auction gallery. But in front of them a crowd jammed the corridor, pointing and teeheeing, and cocking heads as in a museum. An Ivy League instructor was backing into the crowd to snap flash pictures of the pitiful canvases, so she asked point-blank if *they* were the art on display at this opening.

Dr. Buckthorne coughed and blushed. "My dear Mrs. Pellew, the art is not to be looked for in the canvases *per se.* It is in the *collision,* so to speak, of the hypersophisticated

218

modern taste with not only these representations of an abdicated fashion, but with other sensibilities colliding in a *prearranged sequence* with the same anachronism."

"Oh, that's nice," she said. "You mean to say this is all planned?"

Behind her, she heard Regina Travers growl deep in her throat.

"There are . . . other displays upstairs," Dr. Buckthorne said painfully. "The whole building is, so to speak, the entity or entelechy of which—"

She trusted Dr. Buckthorne and his nice explanations. But when she took his advice and looked down the corridor at the faces in front of the poor old paintings she thought: *They all know more about what's going on and why it was allowed to happen than me.* She wished she could sign a large check and go home. Even the fifteen-year-old girls with legs slender and frightening as jackknife blades, the nasty, hooting boys who swaggered in bunches like oversized hairy caterpillars. They knew and she didn't.

"It's really a stunning blow at convention, isn't it?" she asked bravely.

Rodney Buckthorne assured her there was "no going back after this."

Vivian Duart said to herself:

> Must a little weep, Love,
> (Foolish me!)
> And then fall asleep, Love,
> Loved by thee.

It was part of a poem she had learned a long time ago and

219

treasured because it stood for the way a girl ought to feel about her husband after they had quarreled, as, she always knew, married people sometimes did.

Two men who looked exactly like Arentino and were perhaps his brothers came to reinforce him. They began to drive the onlookers out of the room.

"Throw that lion down the airshaff," Arentino said to his brothers. "The girl opens her mouth again, break her arm."

After the pistol shots and the introduction of his guests of honor, Nickie went back to his command post, consisting of the desks in the library room at the front of the hotel. From here, through the open windows, he could keep track of what was going on in the street out front. By telephone he could stay informed as to what was happening in the various "activated" parts of the whole hotel. The door was barred and furniture piled against it to keep the crowd on the mezzanine from pushing in to disturb him and his lieutenants as they coordinated what they had created. Cynthia Trebogen, Lois Capehart, Sid Garfield, and Steve Bowden were with him as the returns came in. So was his wife, who was not being much help. She was very whitefaced and tired tonight, and he thought he knew why.

Now Vivian put down a phone and said, "That was Liveright. He's up in the Village. In some teen-age bar on MacDougal Street. He says the word's getting up there that we've got a rumble on. Fast as they come in they head down our way. He says count if more cops come down too."

Nickie clapped his hands. Cynthia started to look pleased, but glanced at Vivian and folded her hands, looking puzzled instead. Then she followed Nickie to the windows to see what the latest chorus of police whistles signified.

"The weather even is against us," Vivian said shrilly. "I

220

wish it would thunder and rain. Oh God, if it would only suddenly pour!"

"Cut it out," Nickie said fiercely. He went to her and put his arm around her. He patted her belly forgivingly. She shook his arm away. "Come on, sweetie," he purred. "Come on. This is the way we planned it. A place on the Riviera. . . . Helicopters to Paris. 'End of the World' in London, Paris, Rome—"

"I think it's fine weather," Lois Capehart said. "Why the hysterics now, Vivvy?"

"Nice weather for gangsters!" Vivian flared.

Nickie jumped away and looked to see if Arentino had come back down. (Arentino and the men who looked like him kept in circulation. They were in charge of the bar in the basement, the dancing on the first floor, and the desk where the poor were renting their flops—the only three places in the hotel where real money was being handled. They only dropped in here occasionally to smile and show they were pleased with the turnout. But when they came they came unobtrusively.)

"Let Arentino hear you talking like that and you'll find yourself in the East River," Nickie said to his wife.

"I'm sure I may!" She meant that was the pass he had brought her to.

"Sweetheart," he coaxed. "You've worked too hard. We've all worn ourselves out. But now it's happening. It's falling around us like snow! 'The End of the World' is not the end of the world. Let that be our slogan, love!"

"Piss on you," Vivian said evenly. "I'm going home."

"To Idaho?" He was daring her to say it.

"Home," she repeated wearily. She might have been willing to say something more, but just then the phone rang. Nickie grabbed it to answer and said, Yeah, yeah, sure—if there was that kind of trouble he'd be right up. Vivian went out while he was talking.

Before Nickie went troubleshooting he instructed Cynthia and Lois, "If Canaday or the museum people come, tell them I'm right back. The people from *Look* and *Life?* You got their names, Cynthia. For Christ's sake *memorize* them. They must have their photographers here by now. Funny they haven't looked me up."

To Sid Garfield he called, "I couldn't make out what's with it in the street. The siren. Traffic tie-up or what?"

Garfield, who had overheard the quarreling and liked Vivian much more than he liked Nickie, said, "Why not rain? What's wrong with a little rain out there? Serious people come here and find you haven't got anything but a bunch of wired-up bedsprings and a teen-age dance, and where are we? Up shit creek, Doug."

"I've got something else," Nickie said. "Come on, Sid. I'll spring it at the right time. When I've got all the photographers here. Trust me. What was the siren?"

"Siren? Some of your teen-agers poured gasoline on a bum and lit him."

"You're kidding!" Lois Capehart said with glowing eyes.

"That's right. I am kidding. I couldn't see if it was a fight or what. There's too damn many people down there and too many cops to see what's going on."

Mrs. Pellew, from where she stood, couldn't see over the shoulders of the people in front of her. So she couldn't make out what the girl in abbreviated lion-tamer's costume was doing. Dr. Buckthorne wouldn't explain, except to say that the girl was "articulating the space around a big, stuffed lion, that is to say, *not* a lion, but a toy of extraordinary size and life-likeness, though it appeared to be very old and motheaten. It

222

still bore—or had been adorned with—a sales tag from F. A. O. Schwarz."

She could, however, make out that the three gentlemen of Italian extraction were trying to clear out the room. One of them had begun quietly repeating, "Is not art. Not nice what she is doing. Not art." Then he began to say it louder. The crowd was muttering and pushing out of the room. Nobody seemed to want to resist the Italian gentlemen.

But then, just as she and Dr. Buckthorne and dear Regina were about to be shoved into the corridor with the others, she heard a blood-chilling growl.

Regina stepped in front of her to protect her. She saw something like a long, slender pouch dangling and swinging from Regina's hand. And whatever it was it made the Italian gentlemen stop.

"Lady, you put that thing away. Somebody get hurt," one of them said to Regina.

Regina growled again and the Italian person seemed to reflect that *he* might be the one who got hurt. So he said, "All right. We discuss it like ladies and gentlemen. But is not art, that's all I'm saying. You tell her, Buckthorne."

"I'm not prepared to make an evaluation of such delicacy," Buckthorne said, sweating. "Shouldn't you call Mr. Duart? I don't wish to take sides—"

So one of the Italian people had apparently called Mr. Duart to settle the question.

Mrs. Pellew heartily wished to go home after that. It would be cozier and no doubt more educational to sit in the comfort of her flat and have Dr. Buckthorne elucidate the art they had been experiencing rather than wade through any more of it.

The gallant gentleman acquiesced. He gave her elbow an affirmative squeeze to tell her he understood her feelings exactly. But perhaps—since it was Mr. Duart's express wish—they might stop off for just one moment more at the third-floor ballroom.

She was going to murmur that of course they would do whatever he wished, when she saw him reel back—they were descending a stairway at the time, a very ragged old stairway, and she thought he might have caught his heel on a splinter of wood—and turn absolutely white.

He gasped, "You are—" He was staring at a very handsome young fellow in evening clothes, who had been climbing as they descended.

The handsome young chap laughed and said, "I'm Amory Blaine. We met, you know, sir, when you came to rent Miss Brule's apartment from Miss Cumberland. I've followed your career. That is, Miss Cumberland and I sincerely enjoy watching you on the television. I hope you're enjoying the apartment, old fellow."

Dr. Buckthorne started twice to reply. At last he said in his most formal tones, "And is Miss Cumberland here with you this evening? I haven't seen her in quite some time."

Amory Blaine winked good-naturedly. "Not since the time when you had your . . . ah . . . *problem* with her, eh?"

Dr. Buckthorne wobbled as though he might faint. He said, very low, "Be that as it may, I hope to speak to her if she is here this evening."

Amory Blaine laughed as if this was the funniest thing he had heard or seen all evening.

"Is she here, old sport? Oh, very much *so,* old top. I believe she even has a small spot in the show. I'll tell her you're looking for her, old sport. She and I talk about you quite often.

224

Don't feel you're of no more interest to her. Oh no, you mustn't feel that."

After this encounter Dr. Buckthorne looked so ill that Mrs. Pellew suggested he might indeed require medical attention. Or, at the very least, a drink before they went on home?

But no. He just would not be persuaded to go before he showed her a few more features of the new art. He was insisting on his health and liveliness when he guided her into the ballroom on the third floor.

Left to herself, Mrs. Pellew would have sworn that this huge, lofty room, at least, was not intended to be part of the art show at all. It still looked exactly like the storeroom of a hotel that had suffered many years of bad luck.

Heads of elk, bear, moose, and antelope were stacked on tables and in piles twelve feet high. Detached plaster caryatids rose into the upper gloom. There were beds of all description and broken pianos stacked helter-skelter over the floor, and enough rusting stacks of bedsprings to explain where the hangings in the rest of the hotel had come from. And it seemed to Mrs. Pellew that this room, also, was teeming with people only because there were so many crowded into the building at this hour that they had been squeezed up here.

She heard an Oxonian voice nearby shrill, "Veddy good. Oh, veddy fine. My dear, do you see that *canopied* bed *atop* the armoire? Isn't it—I ask you, isn't it?—the most devastating satire on the sexual habits of the bourgeois family? You see how that bed is *straining,* don't you, dear fellow—"

Only a couple of unshaded bulbs lit the entire space, and Mrs. Pellew could not make out that the beds were moving at all. "Is this art, too?" she asked her guide.

He took a gallant breath. "What we see in this room, as it

225

is, might be called an example of the art of *reduction of intent.*
I am in a somewhat privileged position because I have been
told by the creator, Mr. Duart himself, what he *first* conceived to be the proper expressive contents of this room.
Later, as I can explain, he conceived a reason why each of
his intended contents should *not* be installed. What we see now
is, as it were, an art of erasure. Of subtractions. Mr. Duart
once intended to put, over there, a group of percussionists."
  "Drummers?"
  "They pound on various things. There were also to be several movie projectors, projecting images from films of the
'20's on flat and irregular surfaces. Also psychedelic film crea-
tions. There were to be—"
  He had been ready to explain that there were supposed to
be cages with naked girls suspended from the ceiling when—
all at once—to the accompaniment of a deafening screech and
glissando of a tape being zoomed on a tape recorder—red,
white, and blue spotlights played simultaneously on a cage
made of bedsprings wired together. It was being lowered
through a trapdoor in the ceiling.
  There was a stark naked girl in the cage.
  It was Marsella Cumberland.
  And right behind them Mrs. Pellew heard the voice of
handsome Amory Blaine saying, "I told you, old sport, that
you were likely to see her here."
  Dr. Buckthorne wheeled on the laughing young man.
  Who said, "Marsie *loves* to strip. As you know. Because of
her flawless perfection, old sport."
  Dr. Buckthorne grabbed Blaine's lapels and began shaking
him, though he could not quell the hearty mirth issuing from
the handsome mouth.
  Dr. Buckthorne said, "My God. It isn't safe for her to appear like that in a crowd . . . a mob like this."

226

"Rather *not!*" Amory Blaine laughed. "Because of her flawless perfection she can't abide being safe, old sport."

At this instant—though he was certainly obliged to see her safely out of this madness and home—Dr. Buckthorne deserted Mrs. Pellew and ran looking for a ladder or a stairway from which he could rescue his darling.

18

The End of the World: Part II

Guiding spirit Nickie Duart was explaining to the reporter: "We refuse to draw a line between life and art. Every person here tonight should see himself as part and *not* part of a creation he is making and being *made* by. Its the ultimate of democracy."

"Yes," said the reporter, "but how come there's so many bedsprings and old rubber tires stuck around in the corridors and hanging from the ceiling? Everywhere I turn I bump into this junk. Does it express something about our culture?"

Nickie blinked at him. "Bedsprings? Tires? It's because tires and bedsprings are so cheap and easy to come by. Don't you see?"

The reporter sat waiting, as if he were interviewing a political candidate who had just bragged about robbing an orphanage. There must be a point still coming. But Nickie stopped right there and grinned uninterpretably.

Lois Capehart sprang to his assistance. *"Cheap* is another word for free, as in freedom," she said. "Gee, even those of us who work right with Mr. Duart have to sit down and figure out what he means by his statements sometimes."

"I'll bet you do," the reporter said.

"And, as you will notice, not all the bedsprings and rubber tires employed are just hanging around. They're being employed in a cheap, ignorant way—*cheap ignorant* are other words for free dumb," Nickie said, giving in helplessly to the momentum of his hysteria. He roared and gasped with laughter, holding his sides.

"I had noticed that," said the reporter.

"Because we can laugh at ourselves doesn't mean we're not serious," said Lois. "Snap out of it, Nickie, and tell the man what it all means."

"N-n-n-n-nothing," Nickie said. "He can see that for himself. It needs explaining? It's pure release. Who cares what it means as long as it's such a bang?"

"You are a new breed," said the reporter.

At the rear of the second floor there was a labyrinthine corridor, reached by an alley entrance and leading to a suite of rooms that in another era had been the private apartment of the hotel manager. In the largest room of this apartment members of the new breed were contentedly playing *Oedipus.*

A figure wearing a surplus decontamination outfit sat on a pile or throne of bedsprings, holding a split rubber tire on his lap. A figure draped in tablecloths and sporting an extra papier-mâché leg emergent from his side ran across a carpet of bedsprings to the throne and knelt. A tape recorder played a long-drawn-out hiss of puncture. Someone set off a stink bomb. The lights in the room changed from amber to unshaded white.

A chorus of bedsprings, upright on edge, chanted, "Do you remember when taffeta went snap! crackle! and pop!?"

A female figure with a single papier-mâché tit stuck on her back waddled in astraddle a truck tire. "When Manawassa stoops to fabric and finds too late that men display, with Worsted-Tex she wraps it up—Jump! Reach! Stretch! Pull!— and sends it back to Ell Bee Jay."

Other figures begin to pour colored paint on piles of bedsprings and on the floor.

"Don't peep, Tom!"

"Oh, oh, Tom!"

"Are you 'all mouth and no eyes'?"

"What is the greatest asset both parents can have in seeing a son through a normal and happy adolescence?"

"Eat what you kill."

"Don't sprint."

"Fatal Ananke rules the common herd."

"Gina, don't light that goddamn cigarette in here! The paint's inflammable and so's the goddamn building. We'll die like rats you drop your cigarette and start a fire."

There were twenty-seven people in this room and only one of them could be said to constitute "the audience." After watching for something like half an hour he announced, in a loud, calm voice, "All right, kids, I'll tell you what. If you can wrap it up I'll buy it."

Elsewhere bedsprings that filled the floor of a corridor from wall to wall had been rigged for sound. Passerby were invited to jump in a creative way on the springs. A tape record-

ing of the sounds thus produced was played back while someone else took a turn at jumping creatively, and another recorder combined the sounds. This implementation went on
until a hauntingly continuous pseudo-melody of great volume
was achieved.

A perfect version of the tapes was being packed in an
envelope and addressed to the Museum of Modern Art when
Rodney Buckthorne scampered through that corridor, looking
for an attic above the third-floor ballroom. The frantic shake
of his head was taken as refusal of an invitation to initiate
a new tape.

Earlier in the evening bedsprings had been made to express
something about our culture in the room where the lesbian in
lion-tamer's costume had been performing abominations with
the toy lion. Bedsprings had served there for a stage. Now
they, with the lion underneath them, lay at the bottom of an
airshaft. The girl in the lion-tamer's costume was wandering
the upper corridors with bruises on her right cheek, the shaft
of a broken whip still clutched in her hand. When Buckthorne grabbed her and breathlessly pleaded for guidance
she stabbed him in the pit of the stomach with her whip shaft
and left him writhing on the floor.

As she walked away, she menaced him again with the
stump. But he understood her to be pointing. He waddled on
his knees to the service door she indicated, thrust it open, and
saw the winch that had lowered Marsie through the floor.

And now toward midnight—while hundreds of people
milled in the street outside and other hundreds were in the
building and the noise inside and outside was at its peak—a
gang of hungover sailors from a steamer of Panamanian regis-
try surprised Regina Travers at an unlucky turn of the corridor.

231

She was, as a matter of fact, trying to follow or find Rodney Buckthorne, since she had promised Mrs. Pellew she would. As a matter of fact the sailors intended to rape her, and with this intention dragged her into a room they had rented for the night. She broke one arm and four heads with her black-jack and came out of the room smiling for the first time all evening.

Beside the trapdoor in the ceiling of the ballroom, Buckthorne knelt. He steadied his trembling body with one hand on the rope that went down from the winch. At the other end of the rope the improvised cage of bedsprings still waved above the swelling, chanting crowd. Within the Sibyl's cage Marsella Cumberland preened and posed, minus even her wristwatch and hairpins. Buckthorne felt the lively vibration of the rope in his hand as he leaned perilously down to watch what was happening.

The cage in the red, white, and blue spotlights was too high to be reached by anyone on the floor below. But around the edges of the cage a watcher from above saw what looked like a perimeter of small flames, like those that might surround a settler's tiny cabin in the midst of a burning prairie.

These waving flames were the hands that strained above the faces of the crowd.

"Winch her up about two feet or they'll pull the bottom out of the cage."

I should have commanded that, Buckthorne scolded himself. But the order had come from one of the husky college boys he had found when he entered the service door.

In spite of the chug-a-lugging of his heart, Buckthorne found breath to cry, "Bring her all the way up, friends. The comedy is over!"

The boys at the handles of the winch might or might not

have heard him. Though they were tolerating his presence at their operation they were paying no attention to him at all.

At their own pleasure they made exactly three turns of the old-fashioned winch and then locked it in position. They bent down beside Rodney to watch. Like him they saw the crowd below growing denser and darker beneath the flicker of reaching hands.

Rodney felt the rope jerk and they saw the bottom of the cage ripped away by the crowd. Some tall man or jumper had got a grip on it, had ridden off the floor when the winch was turned. Others had tried to climb his stretched body, and the weight was too much.

As the bottom went out of the cage, they heard rise up to them a girlish scream of either laughter or fear or both, sweeter and more piercing than the noise of the crowd.

But the sides of the cage remained intactly wired, and Marsie now clung to them with bare fingers and toes. She was writhing more. She was either having the time of her life or was scared out of her wits.

"Quick, quick," Buckthorne pleaded with the deaf young winchmen. In the corner of his eye he saw the flash of corridor lights as someone else entered the stifling little room through the service door. "They'll be climbing on each other's shoulders next. The cage won't hold if they get their hands on it. Get her up!"

The newcomer spoke. "Cut the damn rope and let them have her. She asked for it. We gave her a costume to wear."

It was Lois Capehart—of whom Vivian Duart had once declared that she was very cynical. "Hi, Rodney. That yet another of your girlfriends in the cage?"

"I have nothing to do with her being here." Of course he had not sent her directly to Nickie. He had been unhappily unable to find her at all in these weeks since she slipped away from Miss Brule's apartment, leaving the bed carefully made behind her.

"Men," he said desperately, "would you stand back from that winch? I must get her up. My daughter, you know. College drop-out. Most unseemly. A great worry to her mother."

The young winchers looked at him without either belief or disbelief now, only a healthy amusement at his agitation and its cause. They might have let him take over from them and try his strength on the winch handles, but Lois put her hand on his chest and shoved him away from them. "I came to see this," she said. "Damn little else to see here."

"The girl is innocent!" Rodney said.

Lois laughed. "Get with it, old man. I told you your corn won't grow in our town. Tootsie babe down there wants kicks. Don't you know that yet? She's waiting for the right man with guts enough to cut the rope, and you're the sonofabitch to do it. Somebody got a knife for the old fraud?"

He tried to protest, but as in the overpowering dream of impotence he had experienced at Miss Brule's he could not escape Lois's charges.

"I loved her," he offered.

"He loves his daughter," one of the winchmen said lightly.

There, too, was a confusion that might be fully explained if there were time for explanation. But for the complexities that had governed his conduct through life, no time remained.

Lois was ahead of him in explanation. "Girls come to New York looking for 'something creative to do.' This old hypocrite works them up by talking about art. Then he lets them go their merry way when he's through. You know how that is."

The young men were nodding as if they knew exactly what their contemporary meant. And it seemed that they understood more than she told them. They might know how many histories of ruined American women were packed into the

234

formula she had just given. They knew about all Buckthorne's wives—depended on, abandoned. About the girlish confidences he had inspired and never repaid. It was a formula— Rodney Buckthorne was the formula—that explained why the girls of this republic came to cynicism. It was not a cynicism forced on them by the nature of the world, but by him, the gray seducer.

Again now the sound from the ballroom came up through the trapdoor like a blast of heat from the pit. Now the crowd was making room beneath the bedspring cage to which Marsie clung. The hands like flames no longer circled the cage shape where the defenseless body jittered and clung.

The handsome young fellow who called himself Amory Blaine was organizing them. Under his direction they were pulling junk furniture and moose heads together to make a pile they could climb to get the girl.

"Pull, you men!" Rodney begged.

"Cut the rope," said Lois. "If none of you nice boys has a knife I'll find someone who has." She bounded through the service door into the corridor.

Then Buckthorne was in space. The rope burned his hands. He was in silence. He had been seen by the crowd below.

Recognized, too. Some TV watcher saluted him for his bold leap with a sibilant cry, "There comes Spaghetti!"

Marsie saw him now. Her blue eyes were fixed on him in a stare that might have been awe as he descended toward her.

"I love you. Never anyone but you," he called with headlong gaiety.

The crowd—Nickie's crowd—laughed mightily at this and sang, *"Love!"* It was all part of the entertainment. It was part of the new art.

Now he realized that Marsie's heavenward gaze was directed to something above him as he slid closer to her cage. A quick, last glance toward the trapdoor caught a flicker, showed him Lois's knife on the rope.

"Don't tell us kids we don't know about jealousy," Lois yelled.

Then down came Buckthorne, rope, cage, Marsie, and all.

19

Waiting for Marsie

Thank God for the natural cycle of seasons, thank God for the alternations that replace night with day, the heat of summer with the sobriety of autumn. Thank God for the natural conservativism of civilized society. Thank God for the police!

They had charged—New York's Finest—into the snarling, shouting pack on the ballroom floor and saved Dr. Buckthorne and Miss Cumberland from either violation or dismemberment or perhaps both. The flying wedge of blue power had swooped into the crowd in the nick of time—while the cage was still falling through the air after Lois cut the rope! —and Miss Cumberland had been carried out wrapped in a tablecloth. Dr. Buckthorne was set on his unsteady feet and walked out within a *cuadrilla* of uniformed men.

Naturally—and thank God, also, for such procedures and routines—Miss Cumberland had been hauled away in a

237

paddywagon, with one more shrieking siren added to the din in New York that night.

Dr. Buckthorne, of course, had not been detained. How could police mentality begin to comprehend his responsibility for the absurd and immoral crash of a naked girl into a mixed crowd of art lovers? So Dr. Buckthorne rushed home without attempting to ascertain the whereabouts of Mrs. Pellew.

There in Miss Brule's apartment he lighted no light, nor did he undress. At the little café table in the studio he sat hour after hour waiting. He had declared himself as he slid down the rope in his futile and unnecessary attempt to save Marsie. With exactly as much hope as the situation warranted—and that was obviously very little—he was waiting to hear if she had heard and believed his cry from the rope. Only you, Marsie, ever, forever.

The others . . . ? As Flaubert had labored to teach him, "The rest were only mattresses for the one I sought." *All* the others? His wife, too? Mildred, that stainless woman who would always forgive him his folly and wickedness? It had to be said. His wife was only a mattress. There was the truth, and for whatever comfort it gave him he waited with it.

Just before dawn the phone rang.

"They're letting me out on bail," Marsie said. "My mother's here at the station—somewhere around here—and they're remanding me in her custody. What's remanding? I just called to tell you I saw you up there. You were the best of all. You were trying to beat the others to me."

"Yes."

"When I saw you sliding down I knew the next time wouldn't be . . . like last time—"

"It won't," he promised.

She hesitated a little, and he wondered if she might not be calling from a phone unsheltered from the casual curiosity of

238

police and nightbirds loitering in the police station. Then she said, "And my question was answered. You're the only one who could understand that."

"Question?"

"About me. What I am. Hanging in that cage after the bottom dropped out, I felt like *myself*. I knew the reason for being what I am. You told me once, funny man, that you knew more about women than anyone on earth. You still think so?"

"I think so."

"You better, 'cause I need help or I'll forget what I knew. You saw what was happening?"

"I saw it all."

"I've got to believe you, don't I? 'Cause maybe no one else would ever see. Hey, Buckthorne. Wait for me."

"I shall."

"Wait for me tomorrow. Today I mean. Don't go anywhere! I'll come to you as soon as I can sneak away from the old lady."

He went back to his seat at the table and waited there while the light came up from over the Atlantic and drew an edge on the avocado leaves and etched bright lines between the shreds of bamboo woven into curtains for the windows. He waited for the roar of trucks to begin in the Avenue; then remembered that he would not hear it this morning because it was Sunday. He rather missed the sound. It was at least neutral, and it might have drowned the echoes of last night's hellish babel still ringing in his ears.

At eleven o'clock Vivian Duart called.

"I didn't see you climb down the rope, but I heard about it. You were the star of the show after all."

He breathed in fear, as if he were hearing the announcement of another cycle of humiliation beginning for himself and those he worried about. But she had something else important on her mind and quickly told him, "I'm leaving Nickie, you'll be pleased to hear. We finally had our showdown. He never laid a finger on me, Dad! Goddamn, though, it was a mess, and I might have really damaged him if the police hadn't come for him too. About an hour ago. Poor bastard's in deep with them. Creditors. Gangsters hunting him—"

"I wouldn't take it as too final," Buckthorne urged. "Don't you feel that even if he's been arrested he will—"

"—make a good thing out of that too? Oh, he will. You bet he will. Nothing could have made him happier. When they took him away he was saying that he was going to enroll in law school now and prepare himself to lead the fight against censorship. But I'm off his sled for good. Rodney, I told you I was leaving him. And quick. Can I come see you? Now?"

"I'm afraid—"

"Anytime today?"

"Not today."

"Please? There's one little item I need to discuss with you before I go back to my daddy in Idaho. Please?"

"No," he answered steadfastly. He had promised to keep true vigil here.

She showed a rich anger (which he appreciated as the poet Keats had told him to). "I don't want you to do anything. I really only want to be held a little and kissed on the forehead. Don't you know women only want that sometimes, you, you *professional*—"

"Of course I know."

"Then—"

"No."

"Rodney Doctor Buckthorne, this is no way to give you the news, but the fact is I'm pregnant."

"I'm very happy for you."

"Don't you understand? I mean you made me pregnant, not Nickie. I mean it happened because I believed your *words*. I mean I still believe them, but what's the word for this physical thing that's happened because of them? What does it mean?" She seemed to be crying, then, but controlled her voice and said harshly, "You bastard, couldn't you have let me come and see your face at least when I told you?"

He coughed lightly, touched the drooping tip of his mustache, and said, "You must have the courage to think it means nothing at all."

"Oh!" she said furiously. "Oh, thanks a lot!"

"I'm delighted to think the child may grow up in Idaho. It's a wonderful state for children."

"Oh!—"

Beast, liar, fraud, and cheat to the end. Buckthorne waited as a truly commissioned knight should when he has made a promise to his lady.

As the afternoon passed, his stomach growled with its own innocent hunger. He quieted it by thinking of all the plates of Napa-Barca spaghetti it would be spared. His only motion was to finger, from time to time, the threads that dangled from his jacket. In the melee on the ballroom floor someone had ripped his buttons off.

From where he sat, so nearly motionless, husbanding his strength for a final trial and proof when the girl showed herself once more to his eyes and offered herself to the hunger of his soul, he could concentrate on Miss Brule's self-portrait. But the angle was wrong. The glass threw no reflection of himself back at all. Instead of a human form the light on the

241

glass made an abstract shape such as nature makes only in the most primitive of organized forms—an amoeba, a nebula of whirling particles far out in space.

At four o'clock—or thereabouts—his wristwatch had stopped at two-fifteen, whether last night or this afternoon he did not know—a lewd memory from last night's carnival flashed through his mind. The lesbian on the howling springs, writhing and creeping around the hindquarters of the stuffed toy lion. As the fiery vision flickered in his brain, he knew that his girl would not find him wanting in prowess when she came.

And just then he heard a car stop in the street below his windows. With a shudder and a burning through his chest, he flung his body across the room to a point from which he could look down.

In the back seat of the cab he saw a flurry of black skirts. Then a woman's figure, veiled in black, stepped onto the curb. When she straightened up, she rose taller and taller until she seemed three times the height of the cab. And he knew her.

He was beaten again. Marsie *would* come. But the real Miss Brule had returned from her Mexican vacation an hour or a day too soon.

She had come back in an aura of those far places and extravagances that one imagines south of the border. As Buckthorne went out to the landing to greet her decently and introduce himself at last, it seemed to him he heard from the street below the brave cornets that blow for the hero at bull-fights. Hearing the music, imagining the music, he straightened himself like a Don, and pressed one arm across his chest in a gesture of classic pride and eternal devotion.

She had entered the building now. She did not look up

242

toward the Castilian figure as she climbed the stairs with a firm, almost masculine, tread. But he, looking down, saw her skirts and cloak rise on the stairs like a puff of dark smoke, expanding and obliterating all that was behind and below her progress.

Then she was on the landing with him. Nine steps away. She paused as if she had recognized him without a formality of introduction. She threw back her veil.

Singing, they rushed to embrace.

ABOUT THE AUTHOR

R. V. CASSILL is "an embittered, middle-aged man who has been romancing the arts for thirty-odd years. He was once a painter; during the Second World War a soldier; after that a teacher, novelist, lecturer, critic, family man and grim optimist." He has taught at the University of Iowa and at Purdue (as Writer in Residence) and is currently a member of the English Department at Brown. He has been published in many literary quarterlies and major magazines, has won an Atlantic "First" and an O. Henry Prize, and has received a Rockefeller Grant. His many published books include the widely praised novels *Clem Anderson, The President* and *Pretty Leslie.*